MW01274756

Not Just One Reviews

Five Stars! "...unique and absolutely engrossing...a thriller with the right slow burn."

"...each new development has me amazed and eager to find out what happens next."
Reader's Favourite Book Reviews by Lit Amri

"...the combination of humor and intrigue was such a delight..."
Terry Houlden

"...action packed suspense with hilarity...a whirlwind of heart-warming scenarios and a single Mom's fears."
Carlie Kearns

"Hard not to read in one setting. Riveting and comical. Laughed so hard my coffee sprayed. Refreshing sense of humour. Looking forward to the next mystery!"

J. Hyde

"It's a toss-up who is more loveable – the hyper eight-year-old Warren or Mini the psychic friend who sucks at deciphering both the English language and her messages from gay spirit guide Sebastian."
Toni McKilligan, Director and Head Librarian Houston, B.C.

Not Just One

Also by DebiLyn Smith

Running From Cancer: a tilted memoir

Not Just One
Running from Mystery

DebiLyn Smith

QUEEN BEE
BOOKS

Copyright © 2013 by Queen Bee Books. All rights reserved

ISBN 978-0-9919093-3-9

Queen Bee Books
3001 Gushwa Rd.
Houston, B.C. V0J 1Z1
Canada

Cover design by Danijela Mijailović
Interior Design and Typesetting by Erika Q. Stokes
Edited by Christine LePorte

This is a work of fiction. Names, characters, places and inci-
dents are products of the author's imagination and are used
fictitiously and are not to be construed as real. Any resemblance to actual events, locales, organizations or persons, living or dead, is merely coincidental.

For Karly and Lorne

Kelly and Lindsay

The REAL Characters in My Life

From the outside, the place looks like your typical sleepy, rural town.

It's the perfect setting for things that want to go unnoticed.

CHAPTER ONE

The knot of panic choking her transferred from the phone to my ear. I refused to give in to it.

"In fifteen minutes, it will be forty-eight hours. Judy still hasn't called you or shown up?"

Janice asked this because her daughter, my babysitter, was missing.

"No, but she'll come. Judy will be home any second." This was the third call I'd played defense for.

Miss MIA's name was Judy Charlie, the cute Wet'suwet'en girl with high cheekbones and gleaming sable hair who phoned five years ago about the desperate ad I had posted at the high school:

> *"Wanted Immediately. Mother's Helper after*
> *school weekdays. Must be reliable and good with*
> *kids. Knowledge of how to lasso and rope small*
> *speeding objects an asset."*

I was serious.

My two children used to make a run for it every call to the

bath tub. Presently, aged nine and eight, they still became blurs, only now at the drop of a chore list.

"I am finding this so hard to believe," Janice told me. "Judy was smart enough to make the Grade Eleven Honour Roll last year, but for some reason, she's not able to pick up her phone and tell me where she is. Wasn't she supposed to see you on Sunday about the next week's schedule?"

"Yes, but she didn't show." My tolerance was thinning as well. It's one thing to be in love with a different hockey player every month, but when it affected everyone else . . . something had to change.

As if I needed more stress.

My name is Kathy Sands and I am a 37-year-old hamster on a wheel. I keep running and running but the scenery (and my weight) never changes. My attitude is "Screw Women's Lib!" I'm so busy I would welcome being someone's pet and having an owner. At least I'd get fed and my cage would get cleaned. And the occasional scratch behind the ears wouldn't hurt either.

I was in perpetual overdrive and now Judy had fallen off the face of the earth without a clue. Well, there *were* clues. Teenaged trouble-maker clues, although no one wanted to rat on where she'd taken off to and with whom.

Without Judy, the juggling of a single mother without special powers became impossible. She used her car to take Wendy and Warren to the birthday parties, the BBQ fundraisers, the sport games and wherever else they needed to go.

"I'm getting fat from all these goody bags and leftover hot dogs they make me eat," she complained.

I said a thankful prayer that it was on her butt and not mine. Women her age passed the ketchup bottle and lost five pounds. If Judy ever hit the 100-pound mark, I'd eat the next dozen hot dogs. I felt safe with that bet.

As helpful as Judy was, I often sensed I was raising three

children. I really loved her, but Judy could be a typical teen-ager: moody, knew everything and was constantly distracted by the latest piece of downloadable plastic.

She had also started hanging with an older crowd. Janice said Judy came home hours past her curfew two weekends ago barely able to weave her way to her bedroom. Last Tuesday Judy forgot to pick Wendy up after Brownies ended, having lost track of time while at the park with kids my son said were "spiked." Warren had been impressed with all the studs and facial piercing.

"Can I wear a nail in my head, Mom?"

"Really, Janice, I'm sure she's out running with the big dogs."

"Well, I talked to her about that and she said she could handle it. I don't like how she's handling it. Time seems to get away on her so easily."

I admit I was on edge about what could have happened, but I was also pissed off. I'd need help with my kids until Judy decided to come back. I mean, if she was in trouble, which I highly doubted, that was one thing. Eighteen young girls *had* gone missing along this stretch of highway in the past 40 years, but they were engaged in what the police called "high-risk activity," by soliciting strangers, hitchhiking or walking alone in a secluded area. None of that applied to Judy. She was a sensible person, even if she let the wild out a few times.

In all likelihood Judy was gallivanting care-free with a group of drop-outs whose idea of getting ahead meant scoring a regular welfare cheque that got completely blown on beer and rent for a flop house used to seduce young girls (yes, I knew that for a fact about one of the fellows). Of course, I said nothing of this to her mother.

"Another day and she will be here full of bad excuses," I told Janice, truly believing myself.

"It's too hard to wait and do nothing," she said. I listened as she blew her nose. "We're starting our own door-to-door and ground searches today. Can you help?"

"Oh . . ." I tried not to sound as surprised as I was. "Already? Don't you think we should give her another few hours, until dinner maybe?"

"The printing store is already running off the 'missing' posters with her picture. I could use help putting them up around town. Maybe when you get off work tonight?"

I assured her I would be there. Any stereo or satellite installs I might get that day would have to take a backseat . . . for the first time in the Halston Electronics World's history, I added to myself.

Judy and I would be having a very serious talk when she returned, which I knew would be any minute now. Each time the phone rang, I jumped, thinking it would be her. Where could she have gone? Why hadn't she used her cell phone to call one of us?

"My neighbor figures she ran off to Vancouver and it was all I could do not to kick him. He seemed convinced. What do you think, Kathy?"

"I don't think it for a second. Judy is very close to you and treats my kids like family. She taught them to make fancy radish flowers with a paring knife, something I probably wouldn't have let them hold until they were twenty." I knew I was babbling, but I couldn't stop. "Now they're into planning creative cupcake baking for charity. Sounds messy. I can hardly wait."

I heard an unbelieving chuckle through the receiver at my ear. Or a gurgle? Hard to tell.

I added, "Judy would never abandon the people she loves. Not without saying good-bye."

Another strangled sound. I bet Janice hadn't slept since Judy went missing.

"I have total faith she'll be home soon. Either way, I'll come over tonight."

I said this and thought this because I couldn't bear to acknowledge any other possibility. Like what if Judy *had* been nabbed by someone? Locals still buzzed about the television documentary on the disturbing disappearances along our quiet 720 kilometers of highway between Prince Grange and Prince Ruden. Young girls, aged fifteen to early twenties, were vanishing, including one since the show aired. Their bodies, if found, were never more than a few towns away from where they were last seen, buried in shallow graves or abandoned like trash on a side road. It was tragic. It was horrific. And our community stood directly in the middle of it.

I pacified myself with the fact that Judy didn't hitchhike. She had a car. It was an old junker, amazingly worse than what I drove, but it got around. Judy was fine. She had merely given in to the prince that swept her off her feet. She would return with rosy cheeks and a foolish grin that made us all remember our first love. After saying "awww," I planned to give her a blast about responsibilities and commitments. Make her feel as fabulous as the rest of us living in fear for her.

Right, I was such a hard-ass. The truth was when I saw Judy's smiling face again I would feel as sheepish as the rest for doubting her ability to look after herself.

"Try to hang in there," I told Janice as we disconnected.

Enough of that. Judy was fine! I did a mental gear shift to the checklist at hand. The school lunches were packed, Wendy was gobbling down her toast and Warren had yet to be seen.

"Warren," I hollered down the hallway, "three minutes!" I caught sight of my son's bare bum streaking from his bedroom to the bathroom across from it.

My heart sank. They would never make the bus.

"Two!"

Wendy appeared beside me, lunch sack in hand, peanut butter ringing her lips.

I grabbed Warren's lunch and toast from the counter, swiped a paper towel off the holder and headed to the front door, wiping Wendy's face as we walked. "Do you have the cookies we made for the bake sale today?"

I received a brown-haired affirmative. I gave her a quick squeeze.

"And you remember that you have to go to the office after school and see what arrangements I've made for you, okay?"

"But I'm going to Erica's birthday party after school." I got a look of sheer indignation.

"Oh, right. I forgot. I'll work that out. Remind your brother for me."

"Where *is* Judy, Mom?"

"Judy is busy with some other things right now. But don't you worry. Maybe I can get Mini to pick you up from Erica's when the party is over. Would that be okay?"

"Do you think Kenneth will have any pie?"

I smiled. Felicitie "Mini" Merkley was my best friend. She was also French Canadian, but I didn't hold that against her. (That's a joke.) Since birth, she'd been called Mini after the French word *minuscule,* for tiny, another joke as she weighed in at a whopping 14 pounds. Today she was five foot five, said she was "over 200 pounds on a good day; over 300 on a bad one," and was married to Kenneth, a self-trained French chef who worked at the local sawmill.

"Sorry to burst your bubble, honey, but if Mini does have any time, today, she will be coming over to our house. You won't be going there. I might be late getting in tonight, so I want you to be where your beds are, alright?"

I got "the face." It was amazing how much we looked alike. Same rebellious brindled hair, wide green eyes above a

Milky Way of freckles and plump rounded cheeks. Wendy looked much cuter without the autobahn of deep lines around her mouth and eyes, though.

I checked my watch. Egad.

"Warren. Now!" We were out the door and as I turned to close it, my son flew by, thankfully with clothes on, snatching his lunch bag and breakfast from my outstretched hand as he passed.

He skidded to a stop and turned to look aghast at me.

"Hey. There's nothing on my toast."

"You snooze, you lose," I told him. It was the same thing I'd said Friday and the day before that. You would think he'd learn to get up when he was told? You would *think*. Sigh.

I blew a kiss at the back of his sandy hair as he readily tore off the front lawn to meet up with friends headed to the bus stop.

"Bye," I called to them with a wave. Another day they were going to make it and I wouldn't have to drive them, making *me* late for work. Whew.

I went back inside to clean the usual frenzied aftermath in the kitchen, fold clothes from the dryer, put another load in the washer and then get myself ready for work. My thoughts drifted back to Judy.

Going that long without phoning her mother *was* out of character for her, although between peer pressure and raging hormones, anything was possible. I remembered what my raging hormones had led me to. I seemed to recall my mother's hair prematurely turning full-on grey the year I turned eighteen.

No wonder Janice had been starting to fear the worst.

I was starting to fear asking my friends for yet another favor.

It was a huge problem because I worked 8 to 12 hours a

day, Monday through Friday and some Saturdays, managing a retail electronics store. After I closed the shop, I was often found in a customer's home setting up their new stereo system. Like on Friday night with Jeremy Staple's big purchase.

"You want this delivered to where?"

"Apartment 420 in Mt. Tsalit apartments. Fourth floor. Halfway down the hall. Here's the key."

"What exactly does that mean, 'here's the key'? You're going to be there to help me cart all this up those four flights of stairs, aren't you?"

"You said delivery was included."

"I said delivery. Nothing was mentioned about my signing up to have a single-handed coronary in your stairwell. THAT costs extra."

He looked me up and down. Okay, I looked pretty healthy for what I ate. The key still dangled between us.

I tried another tactic. "Look, you're twenty years old with big muscles. I'm almost forty with two kids and muscles that sag in places you don't want to know about." I applied my best smile.

It took fifty minutes for me to jostle and curse seven hefty stereo boxes up those stairs. My face resembled a purple balloon about to blow. It was a day to wonder about my sensibilities. Why did I always believe people would do the right thing? And where had the respect gone for one's elders? For women? Young men seemed to think the word "chivalry" had something to do with scotch.

I was also expected to swing from balconies or ladders to install new satellite systems, usually still clad in my dressy work clothes.

"Just a little further over, dearie. No, no, bend over just a little more."

"Mr. Harvey! Is that a video camera down there in your hand? Shame on you!"

And shame on me for being such a doormat. I should have ka-powed that old man right in the kisser. But no, word would spread, sales would drop, my commission would shrivel and there went the "spare money" for eating meat four times a week.

We lived in the small northern Canadian town of Halston. Yes, like in Texas. Only besides having no oil wells, we had no shoe store, no movie theater and only one gas station. We *did*, however, have a shopping mall and that was where you'd find me. At the Halston Electronics Warehouse, HEW for short. Contrary to belief, I didn't own it. I just spent the majority of my life there so I could afford to live. I know, totally lame. But it was good money for someone with only a high school diploma and a life major in Gullibility.

Despite its lack of amenities, Halston seemed to be a better place than most to raise a family. It was friendly, quiet and relatively safe. You rubbed elbows at the supermarket with the teachers, your doctor and your bank manager. You were not afraid of anyone but the dentist, and it wasn't his fault you had soft teeth. It was a very close-knit community.

Being the High Kahuna at HEW also meant I might get home hours after dinner, often barely in time to kiss my kids goodnight. That's a lot of time to ask a friend to take over as mother for me, especially at the last minute.

And it wasn't simply babysitting favors. I was sure my neighbors cringed when they saw my number on their caller ID. "What does she need now?" This month alone I had to get help removing a gigantic tree that had tried to flatten our roof and a salamander my son had sucked up into our vacuum cleaner.

I bit my thumb nail. Judy's sunny face floated across my brain. Where could she be?

The kids and I usually had tae kwon do class that evening. We got to fake kick and punch at each other and learn how to defend ourselves at the same time. I bet Freud would have had a field day with the whole scenario, but it worked for us. That night, I thought looking for Judy was more important, if she wasn't already back by then. Which of course she would be.

Maybe Judy had a stomach flu or food poisoning? I knew how I'd felt the few times I had my head stuck in a toilet bowl. I was too busy making deals with the Big Guy above if he'd let me live to have bothered phoning anyone.

I was glad they were ruling out the fact that Judy wasn't merely lost in the forest. If there was one thing we had a lot of, it was vast stretches of wild bush. Judy wouldn't last long in the outdoors without shelter – not in this weather.

Halston had been locked in the icy fist of winter for the past five months. Spring had only started to pry the fingers loose. The scraping sound of people shoveling fresh snow from their driveways had passed. The thawing lawns were covered less in snow and more in salted gravel sprayed up onto them by snowplows in earlier months. But it was still too cold to walk long distances. There were no subways or transit buses and most of Wendy and Warren's friends lived on acreages scattered miles from the suburbs throughout the vast valley. My kids didn't have bikes so without Judy it would be difficult for them to get around. The one taxi in town was hard to track down when we needed it the most. Like on Friday night:

"Hi, Vespio. It's Kathy Sands. The kids need to go from our house to the McCormacks' on Buck Flats Road at four o'clock. Can you do it?"

"Aw, Kathy. I got a card game with Howie and the guys at the Legion hall at that hour. It's a tournament."

"You're a taxi service, Vespio. We need you."

"But that's way out of town. It'll take me a half hour to get there. Then I gotta get back."

"Twenty bucks, right?"

"Aw, crap. How did you know I needed twenty bucks?"

I bet he couldn't even *spell* chivalry.

The RCMP had come by to ask all sorts of questions regarding Judy, but I didn't think I was much help. Judy was a girl who usually arrived on time, despite rain, snow or menstrual cramps. I also told them about her new shady friends but they were already aware.

Delores at the Dollar Store said her daughter saw Judy at a midnight bonfire party on Friday. Judy had a part-time job Friday night from 5 until 7 and a 10 a.m. Saturday shift at the deli right beside the HEW. When I was there, it was usually Judy that ran me over a salad when I couldn't leave the store.

But I didn't work last Saturday, and neither, it turned out, did Judy.

CHAPTER TWO

A crisp wind whipped around me as I locked the front door to my home. I eyeballed the towering pine trees that swayed drunkenly around my property. The roof already leaked thanks to the downed tree. Another one could spell disaster.

I tried to cheer myself up. The power often went out on days like this. That could mean a day off from the store and another turn at being a fun, inventive mom. The gale forces picked up and I made it to work after swerving my car to avoid an airborne garbage can lid and driving over a fallen highway construction sign in the middle of the road. Even if the power didn't go out, I considered this a lucky day because my tires were thinner than cheap toilet paper and they hadn't blown.

I parked my courageous chariot at the shopping center's east-side entrance, waving at my friend Neil as he headed into his workplace across the street. I put a lot of effort into my wave. He didn't seem to notice.

Once inside the mall, I finger combed my helter-skeltered hairdo, passing papered picture windows with "space for rent" signs taped to them. Halston was bookended by towns that continued to grow with box stores. It was a constant battle to keep our shoppers and our shops.

I made my way to the middle of the building's "L" shape and unlocked the glass door to the Halston Electronics Warehouse.

The phone was ringing.

I threw my purse and carry-all bag to the floor and put my heels into high gear. Four rings, five. I attempted to vault the service desk, feeling the hemline of my skirt catch on something, throwing me off kilter. I managed to land on my feet, but my weight still traveled forward. Thinking it might be Neil, I scooped up the phone with my right hand as my left fell with full momentum onto the sharp six-inch tack we push receipts onto. I held back the scream, sucked in a breath and said . . .

"Good morning, Halston Electronics Warehouse, Kathy squealing . . .

I mean speaking."

My eyes took in the blood seeping from my pierced palm before looking at the wall clock that confirmed it was still ten minutes before we opened. I pulled my hand up off the tack. It stuck for a second before sliding out. It had almost gone right through my palm and out the other side! The tears swelled before everything blurred.

"I just want to warn you," said the soft voice of my girl-friend Mini, "Sebastian show me something 'orrible. I think you are going to get 'urt pretty bad at work today. There's going to be blood, that I do know."

"You're a bit late," I told her before hanging up.

Mini and Kenneth Merkley were the first people I met after moving to Halston. They lived in a farm house on acreage bordering the campground I called home for years. It was the smell of fresh baguettes coming from their oven that drove me to Mini's door. A simple knock and we had been swapping recipes and popping corks together ever since.

You should also know my best friend Mini had an annoying ability to foresee things. She had help from someone in her head named Sebastian. He was a spirit guide, she told me, like this was something normal. Mini experienced "visions" and then had to decipher what they meant. When Sebastian didn't have his panties in a knot he often saw things dead on. That didn't necessarily mean Mini would figure it out, though, which drove Sebastian insane. He had been a master charades player when he lived.

Today Sebastian and Mini had won the game show. Vision correct, just late. Lucky me.

I ran to the staff washroom at the rear of the store to wrap my pounding palm in four feet of toilet paper. The emergency kit hung on a bare nail stuck in the middle of the wall and I pulled it open. A bottle of pain relief tabs and an airplane bottle of Maple's Irish Cream fell out. I flipped off the tablet lid with my teeth and shook two into my mouth, followed by a shot of my favourite potion. I looked dubiously at the bandages, which seemed ridiculously small for something that hurt so much, before I opened and applied three of them. They had pictures of little rainbows on them, which made me feel a *little* better. I wrapped more toilet tissue around my hand and went to get the coffee started. The half-bottle of Maple's came with me.

Starting my day with booze on my breath. The rumour mill would be delighted.

The phone jingled again just as the smell of java wafted to me from the back of the store.

I picked up on the third ring, having my own premonition that it was Mini calling back.

"I couldn't wait for you to call me," she said. "You sounded upset. 'As something 'appened already?"

I looked at the spot bleeding through the layers of bandage and tissue. "Well, Mini, let's just say the drought is over. I was getting nailed when you called, although I was in here by myself."

There wasn't even a pause. "*Merde!* Sebastian didn't show me the vision until after I agree to turn on *Days of Our Lives* for him. *Mon Dieu*, I like Oprah. Sebastian love the men with the bubbles under their skin."

I propped the receiver between my ear and shoulder and unlocked the cash register drawer. "I think you mean muscles."

"*Oui*, muskels. Anyway Sebastian show me more things to tell you before you 'ung up. 'E show me a little bed with a frilly, pink cover. Under the bed were the dusty rabbits . . . "

"Dust bunnies," I corrected.

"Bunties, *oui*, and then I 'eard a phone brrring. It come from under that bed."

My heart started to race. "Do you think it was Judy's phone you were seeing? Have you called her mother?"

"*Certainment*. And Janice say she 'ad already look under dere, and I say look again. And she pull the bed out from the wall and found the phone 'ung up on a strip of molding so it 'ad not 'it the floor."

I was in shock for a second as to what that meant. Judy was out there somewhere without a phone. It was probably why she hadn't called. But everyone she knew had a phone. Why hadn't she used someone else's to call? I chewed my bottom lip. Unless there was another reason why she couldn't call?

My worry tightened a full notch. If she *was* in trouble somewhere, maybe she wasn't able to phone.

"Did you call the police and tell them this?"

"*Non*, Janice was going to do that. But I 'ave other news for you. News you would love. I think you are finally going to find out where Monsieur Billy 'as been 'iding. Oh, and one more thing. You need to watch out for a snake. Of that, I am *tres certain!*"

"A snake? Jesus, I *hate* snakes. Sebastian does know we're in Halston, B.C., not Texas, right?"

"All I know is what 'e shows me. And it was a big snake, Kathy."

"So he doesn't know where Judy is? Or if she's . . . *okay?*" The last word squeaked out.

"I 'ave tried to see it, but Sebastian keep sending me weird things. Blurry green colour. I feel sick whenever 'e make me see it."

This was so frustrating. And speaking of something else frustrating, "Do you see any cheques showing up in my mailbox?" Like today, I thought, already worried about Warren's dentist appointment the next day.

"*Non,*" Mini told me, "nothing about money. But 'ave you 'eard about that newspaper role you went in about?"

"You mean the job, and no, not yet," I said. "Mini, I have a customer. I need to call you back, okay? And thanks for the tips."

We hung up as I glanced over at the dark-haired stranger walking up to where I stood behind the cash counter. Halston was a small community and we could spot someone from out of town in a flash – especially someone that did justice to the name *Levi's* like that. Judging by the smooth ripple of bulk beneath the tanned skin on his arms, I would have said this stranger worked with his hands. A labourer? A millworker? A masseuse? One could only hope for the latter. I might have been broke, but I could put together a garage sale in one big hurry if I had to go for a professional rub-down! What did we *really* need our couch for?

We both grinned at each other.

"Hi, can I help you?" I started, my mind totally in the gutter.

His voice was deep and resonating, with a slightly Eastern accent.

"Yeh, hi. I want to look at your iPods." This was what he said. But from the look in his eyes and that big grin I had a feeling he wanted to look at more than my iPods.

Or so I hoped. I was the last person to know what a man was thinking.

"Sure. I'll just grab the keys for the cabin." Jesus! My face turned the color of a ripe strawberry. "I mean the cabinet." I slipped the keys into my skirt pocket.

His smile widened, now flashing even white teeth against the warm color of his fascinating face. He had a strong, short nose with long, chiseled cheeks and full, dark lashes which drew me deep into a pair of engrossing grey eyes.

I heard a noise to my right and watched two young teenage boys dressed in baggy pants and old army jackets tiptoe into the store. They quickly slipped from my sight behind a wall of boom boxes.

"Was there any particular use you need the iPod for?" I asked, starting out from behind the desk. I walked toward the iPod display, looking for where the two teens had wandered off to. My good hand held onto my pulsing palm, and I could feel the wet of fresh blood on the saturated toilet paper.

"I want to use one while riding a motorbike," said the Levi Man from behind me.

A motorbike. Mmm. I loved a hot man on a motorbike. Even better, I loved holding tight to a hot man on a motorbike.

I stepped another five feet down the aisle and glimpsed the boys' heads bent over the CD racks. Their backs were to me, and their arms touched so that they formed a solid wall; their hands were blocked from my sight. I casually approached them.

"You gentlemen looking for something in particular?" I asked.

They did not turn to acknowledge me. The taller of the two mumbled, "No," while they kept their stance, tight as a drum. I moved to their side to better see what their hands were up to. I didn't see anything unusual. They really did seem to be merely looking. I felt bad for doubting them and walked away, concentrating on my other customer.

The phone rang again.

I pointed to the locked case of portables and iPods, telling the Levi Man I would be with him in a minute.

I picked up the phone to hear my daughter Wendy in tears. "Mom, I just barfed! In class," she moaned. "In front of everyone. And it's still on my shirt!"

I moved my head around but couldn't see the two teens at the CDs from my desk. Nuts! You could sure tell it was a Monday.

"Oh, Wendy. I'm so sorry to hear that. Are you okay now?" All I heard back was my daughter crying and it didn't sound like it was going to end any time soon. There was a history of theatrics in my family. It wasn't something you could outrun. I'd tried. Of course, if I ate a few less chocolates . . .

"I'll call Mini and see if she can come and pick you up. Is that okay, honey bear?"

The two young guys entered my sight once more as they headed out the door, their feet moving them quickly into the mall's hallway. They never looked up at me once.

"Wendy, I have a situation here and I really do have to go. But will you be okay?"

She sniffled and her little voice wrenched my heart with an, "MmmHmm."

"Mini's on her way, kiddo. You just hang in there. I'll call her as soon as we hang up."

Nothing was worse than hearing one of my kids cry and not being able to comfort them. But there was no one else to call to cover for me. Making an independent chain like the Electronics World work in a small town took time and commitment. We couldn't hang a "Back in a Flash" sign on the door every time we needed to zip off and do something. According to head office policy, it was an offence punishable by dismissal. I couldn't risk it. This job stood between us and living in the tent town with the rummies.

I had an employee to spell me off on the six-day week we were open, but Lana was on a spa trip with her mother. Lana did not like to work, freely admitting she came when I called merely to "see everyone." Not a lot got accomplished but she looked fabulous behind the counter. Lana had body curves that should have been outlawed. She'd caused more than one motor vehicle accident just crossing the street. In my defence, finding casual staff at minimum wage was next to impossible around here. Not with two mills and a molybdenum mine. Anyone with half a brain could be making triple the minimum wage.

I rest my case.

With a heavy heart, I hung up on my daughter and quickly dialed. Thankfully, Mini answered. She had the morning off and could rescue Wendy and when Warren got home from school, stay with them both until dinner time. "I might 'ave to leave a bit before you get there," she said. "But I'll tell your neighbor Sharon if I do, and the kids can call 'er if they need someone."

It would have to work. We hung up for the third time that day. Thank goodness for friends.

I noticed droplets of blood on the counter top of the desk and looked down to see spots had dripped from my hand onto the crotch area of my light grey skirt. Ugh. How long would this day be?

Freed from the desk, I hurried over to the CD case. Sure enough, eight blank spaces gaped where CDs were supposed to be. Another store policy was to keep the stand full at all times, so you could see at a quick glance if any had been stolen. The suits at HEW's head office were too cheap to put in alarmed security bars at the exit. That would have been too easy and practical.

I walked over to where I'd left Mr. Levi. He was missing as well. I looked in the accessory aisle for more empty spaces or boxes. I knew he was too good to be true. What did he steal? IPod speakers, headphones, cell phone case?

Nothing seemed to be missing in that section. But why had he left the store so quickly?

The phone's ringer sounded again. I ran over to it.

"Halston Electronics Warehouse. Kathy speaking."

"Want to go for a run tomorrow morning?" charged the voice of my sister Ann.

"Sure, I could do that, but I have a favour to ask first, well, actually two favours aged nine and eight, sweet Auntie Ann."

"Love to, but can't. I'm working all week on an extremely classified project. I'm afraid I'd have to keep Wendy and Warren locked in seclusion again. They hated it last time. Still no sign of Judy?"

"No. Not even a clue of where she's at. But thanks anyway, it was a long shot."

A shard of hesitation at my sister's end. "Of course, if you're desperate . . ."

She let that dangle like a worm on a hook and I wasn't going to bite. It was an age-old sibling thing, only this time *she* was sitting on top of *me* demanding, "Say uncle. Say you're desperate and you need my help. Say it!"

I would rather be boiled whole in oil.

I would never admit to being desperate. Because I wasn't.

My sister and I worked out together two days a week. Not because I was sports oriented – my heart was more egg-roll oriented. All the ParticipACTION stuff started when Ann moved to town last year. I only went because I was trying to at least keep up with her. My younger sister could do everything better than me. So I wanted to be there to take in the moment if she tripped. Of course I would pick her back up, but not before rubbing it in a bit first.

What? It's what sisters do!

To tell the truth, I wasn't really sure what Ann did; something about being an information specialist for the government. Ann said if she told me the details of her job she would then have to kill me. I was pretty sure she was serious.

But apart from that, we were very close now that we were older.

"Come by in the morning," I told her. "I'll be ready."

With my back to the door, the sudden sound of voices behind made me flinch. I hung up the phone and whirled around to witness the two teenagers being led back into the store by my handsome Levi customer and my handsome friend Neil.

Neil Thomas was the freckled, autumn-haired cutie I waved to earlier that morning. Single technically, but still in the "splitting the sheets" stage of his divorce. Neil worked at the District of Halston office but I knew him mostly from his being the mall Santa Claus for our past three Christmas promotions.

Since his break-up Neil had taken to the gym like a duck to water and was the number one topic of the month with all my girlfriends. He sure couldn't play Santa Claus anymore, but everyone was still hot to sit on his lap.

I used to have a husband. Right up until I discovered why he was over-tipping Linda, our first babysitter. The over-developed eighteen-going-on-twenty-five gal was trying to work her way out of her parents' trailer on her knees. I should have known. The girl's nickname had been "Hitch," from the joke about chrome coming off a trailer hitch.

His thing with Linda didn't last as long it took me to file for divorce. We're talking hours here.

In the seven years following, Billy had moved on. Literally. Although the kids got lots of phone calls, we hadn't seen him in person for a good eight months.

If I only knew exactly where he was, I could have directed my curses a little more effectively.

It was Neil who talked first. "Hey, Kath . . . missing anything?"

I moved my hand to cover the stain on the front of my skirt and nodded. "Eight CDs seem to have sprouted legs and walked out of the building."

Neil pushed the teenager he was holding toward me. "I can maybe help you with that. I watched these guys from the courthouse, hauling CDs out of different pockets as they walked past. Then I saw this fellow here," and he jerked his thumb at Mr. Levi, "come charging after them. The kids saw him too and bolted so I figured something was up. We managed to stop them another half block down the street."

Neither man looked like he'd broken a sweat.

One of the teenagers began pulling CDs out of his pocket. The other flamed me a death glare.

"Want me to call the police?" Neil asked.

"Sure, thanks. I'm supposed to let them handle this," I said, watching as Neil reached across the desk for the phone.

The death glare was followed by a raised middle finger. How sweet. I was getting a salute.

Every store in Halston had a zero-tolerance policy for shoplifting. The kids knew it too. I would tell the attending officer that the one fellow seemed eager to comply. The other guy I worried about.

"Wow," I said to my two knights. "I can't begin to thank you enough. Neil." I nodded toward him. "And Mr. . . . ?"

My customer blazed a hundred-watt smile at me then stepped forward with his hand extended. "Riley," he said. "Riley Wells, at your service."

My breath caught in my throat as I noticed the length of his fingers. I blushed.

I couldn't shake his hand without exposing the red spot on my skirt so I just grinned at him. Then I remembered my manners.

"Riley, this is my friend Neil Thomas." The two men shook hands, as Neil waited for someone on the other end of the phone to answer. He looked Riley over very carefully.

"New in town?" he asked.

But Riley never answered, lifting my wounded hand up with his own.

"What's this?" he asked. "You're bleeding!"

The tissue wrap was mostly disintegrated and the tiny rainbow bandages were no longer stuck to my flesh. He pulled the debris away and a fresh trickle of blood ran from the little hole in my palm.

He whistled softly. "Ouchey, Mama."

"Yes," I said. "And it's on my skirt, too." My face flushed red again.

Neil began talking to someone over at the RCMP station. Everything seemed under control for the moment.

"I better rinse this," I whispered to no one as I took back my hand and headed to the bathroom. "I'll just be a minute," I called over my shoulder before realizing Riley was right behind me. He crowded into the miniature bathroom with me until all I could smell was the fresh outdoors mixed with a slight dose of weaken-your-knees sweat oozing from him. My legs swayed a little unsteadily. This was bad. It had been too long since being this close to a man. I was out of practice with the power the opposite sex had over my body fluids. I was a tiny boat on a turbulent sea.

He took my hand once again and ran cold water over it. He patted it dry with the nearby hand towel and helped put more bandages on it. He was just so close to me in there.

Jesus, was I panting? Was that me?

Riley balled up some paper towel, wet it under the tap and began dabbing at the stain in my nether region.

"I'll get that," I snapped, grabbing the towelette from his hand.

Without giving myself a chance to think, I whacked my injured hand on the hard porcelain sink. Instant pain shot up my arm, but at least I had quit tingling in all the wrong places.

"You should keep your hand up," he motioned, pointing at the ceiling.

"After I fix my skirt," I managed between clenched teeth and a throbbing hand. I started to rub at the stain. "Where are you from?" A diversion to get my mind onto something other than worrying about the colour of my underwear.

"From Ontario. I'm driving truck for a rock crushing outfit that's just moved into town."

"Well, nice to meet you, Riley. I'm Kathy. Kathy Sands and I . . ."

"Sands?" asked Riley. "As in Billy Sands?"

My head skyrocketed straight up, almost smashing into Riley's chin as he bent over me. "Have you seen him? Was he in town?"

Had Mini been right again?

Riley studied me with those deep eyes, taking a minute to answer. "Are you his beautiful sister . . . or his beautiful wife?"

I groaned. "His EX-wife and I have a framed certificate to prove it. But I need to talk to him about some things and he hasn't been around for quite a while."

"I see," said Riley. He pulled my drooping hand back up into the air above my head. "So you want to shoot him or something like that?" His smile was huge.

"No," I lied. "It's just a matter over the kids."

"Kids? You have kids?" The grin looked frozen. Or was I imagining things?

"Two. A girl named Wendy and a boy, Warren. They're great kids."

I heard shouting in the store.

"Excuse me," I said, pushing my way past Riley. It was getting too hot in that bathroom anyway.

Neil had one of the teenagers pinned against the door. "They're a little anxious for their fun police car ride," he said as I approached. Neil glared at the space behind me so I figured Riley was standing there.

"Riley was just helping with my hand," I said, holding it up to show the freshly bandaged palm. "I had an accident this morning." I felt new flames seep into my cheeks and wondered why I was acting like a 14-year-old.

"Really," said Neil, looking at the Levi Man with a strange expression on his face. I watched him check out Riley's biceps and muscled legs. Neil's usual smile turned down to a frown.

Being all about business, I never skipped a beat. "Now about that iPod." I pulled the cabinet keys from my pocket.

Riley turned up the lamps on his eyes. Or was I imagining things again? "Only if you first promise you'll have a drink with me tonight."

Neil let go of the teenager and stood there staring at Riley and me. His mouth opened like he was going to say something, but he never did.

I sauntered back to the iPod cabinet and Riley followed. He reached for my hand and pulled it back into the air. "I, Kathy Sands, do solemnly swear to meet Riley Wells at the Happy Mac Pub at seven o'clock tonight."

I couldn't help but smile. But wait, tonight I was going to help with the search for Judy. With Wendy sick, Warren might opt to stay home, especially if I managed to get the Menzi twins to babysit again. That boy was gaga over the twins. They liked to put his hair in curlers and dress him in tights "like Superman," Warren would holler, before leaping from couch to chair and back. (I was only slightly worried this would grow into a weird fetish for him. Although they charged big prices, the Menzi girls had first-aid training and tonight that would be important, nylon prancing or not.)

"I can't make it until later. Like about ten?" Okay, call me crazy. I didn't know this man from a hole in the ground. He could be a lunatic or a criminal. I felt my face flush hot again. He might try to make me do things I didn't want to do, like take off all my clothes and play doctor.

I reasoned with my mind. It was one harmless little drink, and if Riley knew Billy, then maybe he knew where the deadbeat was hanging his hat these days. And maybe he even knew something about that snake Mini and Sebastian were worried about.

At least that's what I told myself with my sensible voice. The other voice in my head was already trying to remember how the game of doctor went.

CHAPTER THREE

I locked the door to HEW, wincing as I had to use both hands to pull as I turned the key. I had phoned home earlier and got Warren. Wendy was still sleeping off whatever bug she'd picked up and Mini had gone.

I thought for a minute to treat us to a pizza night, but realized I couldn't afford it. Not that *and* get the twins in tonight. Besides, Wendy would miss out with a sick tummy. Pizza was one of her favorites and I wouldn't do that to her.

I hit the auto-start button on my car key's remote as I meandered down the mall to the outside doors. I might drive a 1993 Sunbird litter box but at least it was cheap on gas, always started when asked, and came with a funky sticker on the back that said, "If you drive like hell, you're bound to get there." I named it Patches because it had a quilted paint job with duct tape and bondo-filler.

The calendar declared it was time for spring in Halston, but until that snow came down the mountains in the form of melted run-off, the winds would drive that cold right through the valley. We wore heavy sweaters until June, and then put them back on in September. I told myself if I continued to stay here, I would eventually find thick black fur growing on my chest. The Law of Adaptation, or Metamorphosis or whatever.

I wedged into my toasty warm car and headed to the 7-Heaven, a 24-hour convenience store in the middle of Halston on Highway 26. It was nicknamed the Sev by everyone; yes, we were big on monikers. I grabbed four litres of milk, two loaves of bread and two tins of mushroom soup. Warren was a garburator when it came to food. He was going to be seven feet tall if I didn't start binding him head-to-toe with duct tape!

While I was in the line to pay, I noticed Judy's best friend, Rebecca Plait. Rebecca was sometimes at the house with Judy when I got home. I asked her if there had been any news.

Rebecca pushed back the wispy hair from her face and gave me a funny look. "There was a witness that saw her on Saturday."

I brightened up. That was good news, right? Then why did Rebecca look so sour?

"Brad Shaw saw Judy at the Sev around eight in the morning. She babysat for the Tilertons Friday night until midnight and then went to the bonfire party at the microwave tower. She was on her way home to change for her shift at the deli."

"And . . ." I was getting nervous from the way her eyes kept boring into mine.

"And then your ex, Billy, saw her and picked her up. They drove off together. Looks like they were headed to her house up the Buck Flats Road."

I just stood there. Billy? He wasn't even in town. Never mind here on Saturday. That was two days ago and there had been no calls to the kids. No appearance. This couldn't be right.

"Did Brad say what Billy was driving? Did he get a license plate number?"

"He just said it was a white pickup. The big kind with a backseat and no tailgate."

"An extended cab?"

"Yeh, that's it." Rebecca paid for her slushy and then turned abruptly to leave the store.

I ran after her. "Wait. Rebecca. Where was Judy's car?"

She spun and I got a look that told me I was so-out-of-the-loop, with exaggerated eye rolling and pinched lips. "She left it at the party. There wasn't anyone sober enough to drive it."

She hesitated, then, "Your husband better not be doing what they say he's doing. Judy isn't that kind of a girl."

"He's not my husband anymore," I declared to her back as she marched from the store.

She didn't even say good-bye.

The whole thing rattled me. My cheeks heated up and I wasn't sure why. I hadn't done anything wrong and I was sure Billy hadn't either. He wouldn't mess with a teenager again. Other than to give her a ride home. He'd been down that road before and only barely managed to escape being ripped apart by Linda's father. Not to mention Judy was nothing like Linda.

At least I was pretty sure she wasn't. I frowned, remembering I used to think Linda was a sweet girl, too.

I got back into my Bondo-heap and chugged up the hill, turning right onto Hagman Crescent. I slowed down so an older couple could cross the street. They were customers of mine, having bought a DVD player before Christmas. I had spent five minutes in their home hooking it up and three hours giving them basic lessons on the remote control.

They had no sooner stepped safely across the road before

my Sunbird lurched twice, backfired loud enough to wake up the mill shift workers in the townhouses behind me, and then died.

Aaarrrggghhh! What next? Armageddon?

I turned the key in the ignition but nothing happened. Not even a sound. Totally dead. "What a piece of . . . fudge," I said, reminding myself at the last minute of the Swear Jar that sat on top of our fridge.

The Swear Jar was my children's bright idea to help me curb my excessive "potty mouth" habit. It also gave them an "entertainment" fund. They used the money I put in to rent games and movies when my pay cheque was tapped out, which was always. I wasn't sure the concept was still effective because Warren and his little arcade nerd-friends had taken to trying to make me swear. Last week they used the "company only" fluffy white bathroom towels to clean their muddy boots. Yes, he was grounded from television for a week, but not before sucking 10 bucks out of my purse for the jar.

I realized I was not going to get any closer to home just sitting there. With a loud sigh, I scrambled out, grabbed my cloth carry-all and purse and stomped down the dark sidewalk toward my house. As I turned onto Jewel Street I saw a large muddy pickup truck I did not recognize parked in our driveway. With Mini gone, the kids were home by themselves. I broke into a cold sweat followed by a run.

I made the front yard in record time and raced up the steps, throwing open the screen and wood doors. I took giant sprints down the short entranceway and stopped abruptly like I'd hit a wall.

Billy was sitting at my kitchen table. He had my phone at his ear, a toothpick jutting from his lips and Warren wrapped around his neck like a scarf. Wendy had yet to see me and lay on the couch trying to hide the fact she was sucking her thumb. Wendy's version of a security blanket was a

purple satin pillow with a pocket stitched on the back to put
her pajamas in, which she was using to cover the arm that led
to her mouth. When stressed, she stroked the satin on the
pillow, which she was doing right now. Her fine brown hair
was messed up and her face looked puffy with sleep.

"Guess I'll let you go, Mom," Billy crooned into the
phone. "The warden just walked in, but she says hi." He
winked at me with one blue eye and then replaced the phone
on its stand.

"You used my phone to call your mother?" I hissed. Bill's
mother lived in Florida. My ex-husband was famous for ringing up horrendous long-distance charges at all his friends'
houses. And he never paid anyone for the calls. I thought I
couldn't afford pizza. I wondered if it was too late to return
the bread and soup!

"She sends her love," he said, like we were still married,
not water under the bridge. "Are you making supper?" He
asked this while opening my fridge, bending down and peering in with Warren still hanging on.

I walked over, concentrating on calmly closing the fridge
door. I slowly removed Warren, who bounded from me and
scurried to his bedroom, screaming, "Mom, look what Dad
bought me!" as he went. Billy stood there grinning, twirling
the toothpick in his mouth.

Warren returned seconds later with a drum and some
drumsticks. "He bought me a real drum set. It's *way* cool!"
He demonstrated by bashing the drum repeatedly with one
of the sticks.

Something behind my left eye tightened and I felt a
pound at my temples. I noticed for the first time a new Barbie camper van parked under the table. It was the size of a
bread box.

"Billy," I said, "we need to talk." I pointed toward my
bedroom down the hallway, the only place we could have

some privacy from the two little sets of eyes and ears. "Mom and Dad will be out in just a minute," I warned them as I shut the door behind us.

Billy was on me in a flash. "Why didn't we think of this when we were together?" he asked, his hands under my shirt already. "Just tell them we need a minute?"

I shoved him away. "Get your paws off me," I huffed. "This is serious, Bill. We need to straighten out some things."

He flopped himself onto my bed and eyed me up and down like he was very hungry and I was a big, juicy steak. "You sound a little sexually frustrated," he said. "I could help you with that." He threw his toothpick to the carpet and then wiggled his tongue back and forth like a snake.

A snake! I quickly looked around me. Was *that* the snake, or had Bill maybe brought a snake here, into my house? Would he do that to try and scare me, so he could be a big hero and have to save me and then I would come back to him? Was that the plan? Or maybe it was a poisonous snake? Maybe I had to die so he could take the kids? We had a joint custody agreement – Billy's idea – and it wasn't working out. He insisted on taking the kids for a few months each year, giving me "fair" access and no payments during that time. It gave him a big break from paying $500 a month child support to someone who "spent it all on her wardrobe and hair anyway."

The problem was Bill never said when he was taking them or leaving them. Poor Wendy and Warren continually had their lives disrupted at the drop of a toothpick. Billy ignored their medications, a regular bath or bedtime and let them run wilder than monkeys in a jungle. They looked startled when I said they couldn't eat their spaghetti with their fingers anymore.

"But Dad says it's okay. And he also says you're a bad mom!" Unquote.

I narrowed my eyes at the man on my bed.

"Did you bring a snake here?" I asked.

His face scrunched into a puzzled look. "A what?"

"You heard me." My hands went to my hips. I glanced again around the room. "Trying to get rid of me isn't going to work, you know. And no matter what you do or say, I am not going back with you." I pulled up the bed skirt and looked at all the mini tumbleweeds peering back at me.

He laughed – a big laugh that came from his stomach. "Now why would I want to get rid of you, Kathy? I just want to snuggle your brains out, that's all, baby doll."

"Well, the snuggles and snakes stop here, Bill."

I had no idea what that meant, but I said it with conviction!

"And speaking of snuggles, what were you doing with Judy Charlie in your truck on Saturday morning?" I asked.

Bill gave me another "she's in outer space" look. "What are you talking about?"

"Judy. Our babysitter. Someone saw you pick her up at the 7-Heaven."

"I wasn't at the Sev on Saturday morning. I worked the night shift so I was probably sleeping on Saturday morning."

"Probably?" I eyed him suspiciously, remembering what a liar this man was. "*Why* is the babysitter sitting naked at my feet?" he'd said to me. "Linda is looking for her hair clip and got too hot. My pants are down because I got hot, too. I'm surprised you have to ask."

I let that thought go.

"Did you know Judy was missing?" When he said no, I filled him in on the details.

Billy didn't seem concerned. He flipped a "that's too bad" at me and then stretched out, laying his head down onto his hands like he was going to have a nap. Right there on my bed!

"So you had nothing to do with Judy on Saturday. That was someone else?"

"Yeh, wasn't me. End of story," he mumbled into the bed spread.

It sounded relatively convincing, but I wasn't finished with him yet. "Okay, now I want to know about the support payments you haven't sent for eight months. We have a signed agreement, Billy. I'm behind on all my bills and Warren has a dental check-up tomorrow. I don't know how I'm going to pay for it."

"So don't take him."

My eyes grew wide. "His teeth look like a broken-down fence and some are sprouting in the middle of his mouth."

Billy reached one arm around to his back pocket, keeping his eyes on me. "Here," he said, removing a fat wallet. "Here's a hundred dollars. Go get yourself a nail job." He took a toothpick from another part of his wallet and stuck it in his mouth.

Steam shot out of my ears. "A nail job! A NAIL JOB! Is that what you think this is about, you self-righteous idiot? Billy, this is about hockey camp and skating lessons. It's about our mortgage payment, and medical and school clothes and school outings and books and, and PIZZA," I screamed.

Someone tapped on the door. "Mom," asked Warren. "You okay?"

"We'll just be another minute, honey. Could you open those two cans of mushroom soup I put on the table, please? Thanks." I glared at my ex-husband, wondering why I didn't annually celebrate our divorce. The occasion was right up there with birthdays and Christmas.

"Billy, we need money until I can get some of these bills paid up. I've applied for a second job so that I won't have to beg from you anymore, but right now, I need it. You're behind four thousand dollars. A hundred dollars is not going to help much, especially when our car just broke down."

He sat up on the bed, twirling the loose toothpick – a habit he'd had since before I met him. "Now why didn't you say so before this," he said, like he'd had a real phone number or an address all this time. As if! Billy had been on the Credit Bureau's top 10 delinquent list for years.

He opened the wallet again and peeled off ten more one hundred dollar bills. "This will have to do for today, but I'll write you some post-dated cheques before I leave. Let's just settle this at three thousand flat. That's more than enough for the past few months. What do you buy these kids anyways? Gold bars?"

I ignored that, feeling a glimmer of hope. He was working. He was going to pay us what he owed. Well, most of what he owed.

He continued without waiting for a reply. "You can cash those cheques on the first and the fifteenth of every month. Guaranteed, like clockwork."

"Thank you" was all I could think of to say. I sighed heavily. There was $1100 sitting in my hand. I had won a lottery.

"Want a bowl of soup?" I asked, suddenly feeling gracious. "It's what there is for dinner."

"With all the money I give you," Bill quipped.

I struggled not to hit him. He might have taken the $1100 back!

Warren didn't want to go canvassing, even though it was to look for Judy, because his dad "was staying home." I reminded Warren that his dad was NOT home, that he did NOT live at this address and we did NOT live together anymore.

Billy offered to watch the kids until 11 and offered me the use of his truck, so, although it felt weird, I headed out.

The command centre for the diligent "search-angels," as they were dubbed by Janice, was at the Charlies' house. The place smelled cinnamony – a comforting smell I used to assume was Judy's perfume. I figured out why when I saw a mountainous stack of cinnamon rolls adorning a Styrofoam cup–littered table. Take-out Chinese food cartons overflowed from the garbage can, an empty pizza box sat stuffed behind it and the place reeked of coffee, both stale and fresh. Food for busy people. Everyone was active, phones planted on ears, maps laid out, groups being instructed. I was quickly welcomed by Janice, handed a cinnamon bun and shuffled toward the door with a stack of glossy papers, a box of tacks and my girlfriend/neighbor Sharon. We were off to paper the town with pictures of Judy and posters which asked for any information on her whereabouts.

We talked as we worked, Sharon explaining she had checked on the kids when the strange vehicle had pulled into my driveway. Billy and the kids had told her it was alright. Had she done the right thing?

I put her at ease and went on to talk about Judy and my suspicions that were starting to crumble. Sharon doubled as sympathetic friend and the mayor of Halston. This meant she was privy to more information than I might garner on the missing women situation. Girls *had* gone missing over the past 40 years, she said, but it wasn't until the past 8 that the number of murders had intensified and the media attention began. In this area, that included the disappearance of a 16-year-old found strangled and sexually assaulted near the Tessak airport, a 15-year-old between Spencer and Halston, another shortly after dumped in the bush near Banner Lake. Haunting highway billboards depicting the victims urged young girls not to hitchhike. But the disappearances continued.

Now Judy was missing. A huge chill crawled up my spine and I repeated to myself, "Judy *will* come home . . ." but I wasn't so sure anymore. A sheepish panic threatened to rise.

Sharon mentioned a special RCMP task force currently looking into the cases. They refused to comment if the deaths were committed by various men, or if the murders were similar enough to suspect a serial killer.

With the last poster tacked into place, Sharon and I hugged, our hearts heavy, and we headed off our separate ways.

I couldn't shake the weird feeling of using my ex-husband's truck to meet a man at a bar while my ex-husband sat at my house watching our kids. Did it get any stranger than that? But Billy always had a way of overriding the small stuff. He would probably invite himself for drinks if he figured my date would pay.

It hit me for the first time that I *was* headed to something like an actual date. I hadn't had many of those in the last while. Okay, I hadn't had any in the past five years.

I parked Bill's truck in the large parking lot of Happy Mac's pub. There were half a dozen vehicles, none that I recognized. I felt relief for one second before hopping out of the vehicle and noticing the colour beneath the mud on the truck side panels. With everything going on I hadn't noticed before. It was a white pickup.

The same colour truck Judy supposedly got into at the Sev. Was this the same vehicle? Had Billy lied? And if so, why?

I gave myself a minute to think it over but came up with nothing. I flattened down my messy hair and pulled open the double-wide doors to the bar. As usual, all eyes swiveled toward whoever walked in, so I waved at old Mr. Wringer who looked up from the jukebox selection and at the Sheppard family clustered around two tables that had been pulled together. Judging by all the balloons, they were celebrating someone's birthday. Two young women dressed in very tight shirts and jeans two sizes too small leaned across the sole pool table. They looked disappointed when it was only me that strolled in.

At the far back in the shadowy last booth Riley sat with a ball cap pulled down over his face. He appeared to be hiding (possibly from the two pool cougars on the prowl). He was wise; no man was safe in this place after dark, or at least after some of these women's first shots of tequila.

I slid into the booth facing him and felt the electricity as he pulled my wrapped hand into his own. The dark navy Taiga sweater he wore accented those smoky eyes, making them even more exotic. Sigh.

"How does it go?" he asked, removing his cap.

I smiled at his choice of words. "I wish it would just go away," I said, thinking of Billy back at my house. I hoped he really would leave at 11 like he said.

"I'm pleased that you met me." Riley adorned that rich smile I was growing very fond of.

"I can't stay long," I told him as he ordered two beers from the waitress. "Just enough for a quickie."

Riley's eyes widened along with his grin.

I turned purple. "That's not quite what I meant to say," I stammered. Or was it?

"A quickie. Would that be enough time for me to steal your heart?" he said, squeezing my hand but not hard enough to hurt.

My cheeks burned. He laughed.

"I meant a quick drink. And thanks again," I said without stopping, "for bringing those kids and CDs back. I'm far too trusting with them, I guess."

"It was no problem, although it turned out the officer that arrived was on foot, so I helped walk them over to the station. The kids never did get their squad car ride to brag to their friends about. They were disappointed, probably because they were so high. Most kids would have been quaking in their boots. Turns out they were going to resell the CDs because they have a new drug habit they're trying to feed."

"A what! A drug habit? Here in Halston? But they were just young boys!"

"They were thirteen, and the officer said it's become a huge problem at the high school. Seems a new kingpin has moved into town. He's formed a ring of sellers who recruit more salesmen, and in a town this size, they sell to younger and younger kids to make the quotas to support their own junk habits."

"Junk?"

"Heroin, coke, crack. It's all here in Halston. As available as milk."

I was floored. Who knew? I made a mental note to talk to the kids about drugs again. The kids. That reminded me.

"I saw Billy tonight," I told Riley, who immediately pulled his body forward so that our faces were almost touching. I could smell his breath – earthy and fresh. My head whirled a bit. "He was at my house when I got home from work."

"What did he want?"

The pub's owner herself, Tori Popitch, swooped down, dropping off two frosted mugs and two bottles of Kokanee beer. We both sat back abruptly like we had been caught doing something inappropriate.

She gave Riley the once-over, twice, before whisking away again. The two cougars from the pool table swarmed on her like black flies on a first-year tree planter from the city. They ogled us, before pressing foreheads and whispering.

I poured one of the beers sideways into a mug. "Billy said

he just wanted to see the kids. He hasn't been around for quite a while." Yes, I thought to myself, but he'd been in town on Saturday and hadn't come around. What was up with that?

I took a few big gulps of my beer. "So how do you know Billy? From this crushing outfit?"

"Yup, we met when I signed on in Prince Grange. We crushed there for a week, and then ended up here a few days ago. It looks like we have a big contract with the District of Halston."

Riley leaned forward again. "So how did you two meet?"

"Who, Bill and I?"

Riley nodded.

I squirmed a bit, wondering where to start, vaguely thinking it odd that he wanted to talk about me and my ex. "After graduating from high school I loaded up my duct-taped Toyota and moved from New Brunswick to British Columbia. It was the mountains that drew me. I was so naïve that I paid someone to teach me to become a door-to-door vacuum cleaner salesperson and yes, the man hoovered up all my money, then vanished. He even took the demo vacuum with him. I was virtually left 'holding the bag.'"

Riley laughed at me.

I ignored him. I was telling the painful truth here. "Broke to the point of vagrancy, I got a job at the first restaurant I ate in. After finishing a hamburger and chocolate shake, I explained that I couldn't pay and worked for free for two hours that first day. They let me keep the tips . . . and the job."

"Quite the tactic," Riley commented.

"I waitressed at the Village Inn for a year before running in-to a salesman of another sort. Unfortunately, this one I married and followed north to Halston. It took every dime we had to buy an old van and rattle the twelve hours north, only to find nothing new. Whatever Billy had been looking for wasn't here. He *did* find a lousy apartment and a lousier job. I've been here ever since. So how well do *you* know my ex?"

Riley merely smirked. "Well enough. So why Halston?"

I straightened, my voice carrying an edge I couldn't curb. "Who knows why Halston? Bill Sands rarely told me the truth about anything. He's a spellbinder: one you believe even if you know better. If pressed between a rock and a hard place, Billy would forge signatures, steal gas from ride-a-mowers and charm more than casseroles off of his friends' wives. Give that man an inch and he'll steamroll you."

Riley laughed again, a warm, friendly sound. His eyes softened. "And you gave him the boot?"

"No. I left him with everything. I wanted a clean break from anything Free Billy was involved in. And speaking of things he's involved in, did Billy ever mention anything about a snake to you?"

Riley leaned back into the couch cushions behind him. "What kind of snake?"

"I don't know what kind. I was warned about a snake that might come into my life in the next while."

Riley threw his head back and barked out a single loud "ha." Then he turned serious. "There are many different kinds of snakes," he said with a wink before taking a long swig of beer.

Back came the blush to my cheeks. Oh, I think I got it. Riley was implying he had a scary trouser snake; I'd never thought of that. *Watch out for the snake.* What a joke. I couldn't help but feel relief before wondering just how big that snake was that I needed to be warned. A dirty little smile spread across my face. Sebastian was most likely jealous, thus the warning. Freaking me out for no reason! If Sebastian had been real and not just a part of Mini's imagination, I would have kicked him.

We talked for almost an hour, Riley telling me more about his job with Hardy Crushing. The owner, Ferdie Barren, had a girlfriend in the apartment complex around the corner from my place. Ferdie's accountant, Terry Murdoch, also lived in Halston and was letting some of the crew rent rooms from him. It saved them each $75 a night in motel fees. Murdoch didn't sound like a bad sort. He let Riley borrow his wheels when he needed to get around, he had a huge house with a pool table and big backyard, and he had kids who, Riley explained, "thankfully only visited every second weekend." I got that feeling about the kids again. My date sounded like he didn't know what a kid was.

"So how old are you anyway?" I asked, holding my breath.

"Thirty-one. Why? Does it matter?"

My jaw slipped for a second, but I quickly recovered. Thankfully he didn't ask my age and I didn't volunteer it. Did a six-year difference matter? I searched deep (ha) into my heart and at that moment I didn't care if he was 21. I liked him and I liked even better how he was looking at me!

"No, not a single bit."

"So when did the break-up happen between you two?"

"Who, Billy and me?"

Riley nodded.

"Wendy was two and Warren one when I placed them onto my hips and walked out of our trailer. I hope they were too young to remember the break-up." I smiled a bit, despite myself. "It wasn't violent, merely a loud verbal thing with a lot of windmilling hand gestures.

"I had a job at a video shop but that's a whole other story of the first two years after leaving Billy. Then the HEW hired me to open their new store five years ago. This job gave me the financial stability to completely close the chapter on the haywire life with Billy Sands. Or so I'd thought."

We both had a good chuckle. It sounded so funny when

telling this man about it. Last time I'd checked, it hadn't been that funny.

"I'm trying to stand on my own two feet, although some days it's a pretty wobbly picture. Real life and extra bills have a habit of sticking their feet out and tripping me."

I finished my beer and begrudgingly admitted I had to run. I gave Riley my home, cell and work number on the back of a drink napkin, before we stood and made our way to the exit. The pool wenches waved and blew lewd smooches at Riley as he laid a twenty beside the cash register and we headed out the door.

The evening air was brisk. Overhead, the moon was rounding to an almost-full one. The cloud partially covering it rolled away.

Riley followed me over to Billy's truck.

The Levi Man leaned down and kissed my cheek, a quick, short peck, not giving me time to react. He said he would try to see me again soon, but no promises. His job kept him extremely busy. He then walked over to a motorcycle that sat by itself in the parking lot. On the side of the tank, I could just make out the drawing of a large gold snake.

I had a rough night between my aching palm and trying to keep one eye on the dresser pulled across my bedroom door all night. I couldn't wake Bill up when I returned so he spent the night on my couch, his snores reassuring me there wouldn't be another attempt to get back into my pants. I never said Billy wasn't attractive or that we hadn't had our moments when married; I'd said he was an irresponsible, unrealistic "Boy Wonder" that refused to grow up and help parent our kids. Or had I said that yet? At least the divorce was finalized, so that was one wish come true. Funny that I spent two years trying to get free of his lying ass and the next five trying to track it down. Divorced or not, a little thing called child support kept us attached better than our vows ever did.

The first year after our separation, Billy and his latest girl-friend moved into the apartment below. It was time to get out. The now-leaky house that I own was purchased with money borrowed from my parents. After four years, I mort-gaged the house to pay back my parents, thinking that be-tween Bill's child support payments and my new job, I could meet my obligation, but I was starting to sink. Interest rates jumped while wages stayed the same. Add to that those emp-ty promises from Peter Pan and that spelled foreclosure.

But I now had $1100 in my hand and two blank cheques. Life was definitely going to be easier this week!

I was out in front of the house before 6:15. Ann was always early; it was the overachiever in her. But that morning I was ready, hoping to explain the white truck in my driveway be-fore she waltzed in to see for herself.

We pulled on our High Viz vests and started trotting down the road. It was light enough without flashlights but still cool enough for thin gloves. We had a circular route that took 40 minutes; a good trail, carefully picked to avoid any dogs that might come shooting out after us. I had been bit in the calf by a dog I was running from when I was a kid. Now I wet myself if one even tried to lick me.

"Whose truck?" Ann asked as we rounded the first corner. Her grin was wide.

"It's not what you're thinking," I puffed back. "It's Billy. He fell asleep on my couch."

"Mm-hmmm." Ann grinned again, more like a Cheshire

this time. "Taking a ride on the old train, are we?"

"Cut it out, Ann." I squinted my eyes at her, a signal I was being dead serious. "He came by to see the kids, not me. But he did give us some money. I can make some bank payments today."

"Kath, I told you, if you need money to tide you over, just ask me." She slowed her pace to meet my struggling one. She wasn't breathing hard yet. I sounded like I was in hard labor.

I shook my head. "'S all okay. I got 'er. We're fine. Thanks."

Because I was finding it hard to talk and run, Ann carried on the rest of the conversation. I learned all about the mating habits of bears. A new book she was reading. Could we be more different? My idea of a good book had sex in it too, but not with bears.

We finished our run and I signaled good-bye as she headed off to her Audi. I headed into the shower, making sure the door was solidly locked first.

I came out to see Billy enjoying a bowl of cereal with the kids. "I paid for that," he said to them, pointing at the box. Wendy mentioned her tummy felt better, gave us each a hug and left for school. Warren gave his dad a fist noogy and then ran behind her, promising to remember to get off the bus at the dentist's office. He was to walk home with a friend if Vespio's taxi couldn't be rounded up.

"Thanks, big guy," I called after him. He was a brave boy. It might be a 30-minute hike uphill with those grade three legs of his.

I turned on Billy the moment the front door slammed.

"They say it was a white truck that picked Judy up at the Sev on Saturday morning. Your truck is white."

My ex stood up to his full height, towering over me.

"It wasn't me." His voice was borderline hostile.

"Prove it then. Where were you, Bill?"

He sauntered toward the hallway. "I don't have to take this from you," he said over his shoulder, and he walked out the front door.

I pantomimed a nasty flag code I'd learned in Girl Guides at his back.

Twenty minutes later, my morning got a bit better with a phone call from the *Halston Today* newspaper saying I could have the job of selling ads. I left the house much earlier than usual and walked to the newspaper office, where Nancy, my new boss and the paper's publisher, gave me some huge newspaper-size blank sheets with numbers and lines on them. I was to sell the advertising spots to the local merchants who would be holding their St. Patrick's Day sales soon. Sounded easy.

After visiting a dozen businesses in and near the mall, I had most of the ads sold before making my way to my usual job.

Work started at HEW with a $1500 stereo sale and almost as much in accessory sales. Cha-ching.

Despite all that, there was some sadness when glances down the mall failed to show any sign of Riley. Yes, I know what he'd said.

It was just before lunch when I smelled before I saw a bag from Mr. Sub enter the store, attached to Neil!

Riley who? I thought. A visit from Neil worked just as well.

"Hi," he said. "Thought you might like some lunch." He grinned at me and I quickly stowed my surprise and smiled back. I was super hungry and whatever was in that bag was making my mouth water. "I never realized you were in here by yourself all the time. No wonder kids see this place as an easy mark."

My smile slipped. "Kids think what?"

Neil tried to backpedal. "What I mean is, it would be easy to steal from this place if you were distracted." He lowered his eyes from mine.

Distracted? Was that what I'd been? Was he implying something about Riley and me, as if that was why it was so *easy* to shoplift here? I suddenly wasn't so anxious to be fed anymore. My hands flew to my hips.

"Neil Thomas, in the first place, I . . . I . . ." My finger poked the air toward Neil's head, which instantly drooped and hung down like a hound dog. A very adorable hound dog, mind you.

My heart lurched. Didn't I recall that stance from whenever my mother had read *me* the riot act? This poor man had obviously been kicked by women before and was getting ready for it again.

I took a slow, deep breath. "Do you have something you want to say to me?"

He raised his curly head and walked up to within an inch of me. He smelled of spicy aftershave that reminded me of all the Westerns I loved to watch. He bent his freckled nose toward mine and my heart fluttered wildly as I wondered for a moment if he was going to kiss me. I steadied myself, wishing, raising a little higher on my toes.

He opened the bag still in his hand. "Would you like a meatball or a Louisiana chicken sub by any chance?" His grin looked a little uncertain.

I lowered myself and came to my senses. Okay, so maybe the attraction was only one-sided. But still, it was no reason to be busting his chops. This guy had gone out of his way to help me with those two characters yesterday and today he was here bringing me lunch. What was up with me?

I took the Louisiana chicken from him. "Any hot sauce?" I asked in hope.

Neil tossed me a packet of sauce and a wink. That was three winks from three men in two days. Kiss or no kiss, car or no car, things were definitely starting to look up in my life.

CHAPTER FOUR

Thirteen was the number of tries it took to catch Lana between her constant phone calls.

"Can you come in at four and close for me today? I have a few fires to put out."

I heard a snap of gum in my ear.

"What kind of fires? Will there be firemen?"

"Down, girl," I told her. "Not those kind of fires. My car died two blocks from my home and I'm worried the neighbors will either plant flowers in it or paint it to match their house if I leave it too long."

Another snap of gum. "Whatever," she said.

"Did you hear Judy's been missing since Saturday?"

"Unh huh, and I heard it had something to do with your husband. Is it true?"

I expelled some air before answering. "Of course it isn't. Bill, my *ex*-husband, just rolled into town. He came to the house. Saw the kids, gave me some cash. It's all good. Judy's with friends. She's lost track of time, partying her teenaged butt off."

"That's not what I heard. Judy's friends are really worried.

None of them are missing and they say Judy wouldn't have left town. Even the guy she's seeing is freaking out."

It was suddenly hard to catch my breath; like someone had kicked me in the stomach. "All of her friends are accounted for? Even the lowlife she was hanging with?"

"All of them. What other fires are you putting out?"

"I'm meeting a mechanic at four to look at the car. Then the bank and some groceries. Can you come in?"

A double snap. Lana was going to milk this. "The mechanic is Jackie?"

"Yes."

"Done that. No firemen?"

"No, but there's a new crushing crew in town. Some pretty hot guys around that I've never seen before. Have you done, I mean met Billy before?"

"Can't say that I have. Maybe that new cop in town would be impressed if I pumped your ex for some word on the Jude-stir."

Such a choice of words. You go, girl. "At four then?"

She was already changing.

Remember the fake gushing downpours of the old black-and-white movies? Well, they were real in Halston. I stood drenched beneath a lopsided umbrella waiting beside my car to meet Jackie Carmichael, a "cheap" backyard mechanic recommended by Billy. My chariot looked sad and broken, the duct tape peeling back in places. Jackie rumbled up in his Camaro and pulled on a ball cap before hopping out into the fresh puddles on the ground.

"You're all wet," he said.

"How observant. I had to walk. Hopefully you're as quick with the diagnosis on my car."

Jackie felt around for the hood release and with one hand, raised the Sunbird's bonnet. He poked around for two seconds.

"Timing chain's shot," he told me. "You need a new one."

"Is that bad?" I asked, my voice slightly weepy.

"The part costs about a hundred dollars. I can buy it and put it in but you have to pay me the money first. The labour for the installation I owe to Billy. I swapped him my canoe for his river boat and I'm working off the difference. Billy said to tell you to take another five hundred off what he owes you."

He laughed at this until he coughed.

"Let me guess. It doesn't cost that much to put a timing chain in a car?"

His smirk confirmed my theory.

"How much is it usually?"

He stopped laughing. "It's cheaper than going to Franklin Motors and paying real money to get it done, that's how much it costs."

He had me there, except Franklin's did wash your car if you had it serviced.

What was I thinking? I could save a month's worth of groceries for the price of that free car wash. I sighed deeply. "Let's do it, Jackie!"

It was a good decision because rain was in the forecast all week. I was going to need a vehicle to buy bigger water buckets for the living room. For now, Sharon was running over on her lunch hour to dump the ones that were there.

I was relieved it wouldn't cost much out-of-pocket money to get the car fixed. This meant I could still make a house payment plus get groceries. Jackie gave me a lift to the bank where after paying for his part, I walked around the corner to the supermarket.

I hadn't been so excited about shopping since living with

my parents and using their "magic credit card" – the kind that made everything I bought "free."

This felt the same. Though the money was rightfully ours, it still resembled blissful pennies from heaven. I grabbed a cart and within minutes it was brimmed with foods we hadn't seen in months like bacon, cheese and an entire chicken.

I arrived home by taxi to discover Bill's white truck once again in the driveway. My smile faded. Why did I always forget about the strings that came attached to this guy?

Warren launched himself at me the minute I struggled in the door with some of the bags. Bill was flopped on the couch watching cartoons with Wendy. He had a beer can in his hand and my GOD DAMNED phone attached to his ear.

I didn't say hello.

"Get off that phone," I yelled. Both kids looked up. They didn't hear me yell much. Bill had heard me yell ever since I'd met him, especially when it came to the phone. I had lost groceries to long distance phone calls more than once.

I received a grin. "Okay. Good talkin' to ya, bud. Maybe see you sometime this summer. Hey, how's your sister doin'? Is she still single?"

"Billy!" I bounced a box of pasta off his forehead and he yelped, straightening up immediately. I was a crack shot when it came to aiming missiles at this man.

"Okay, okay, got to go. It's that warden again. Talk to you soon, guy."

He hung up.

"What's for supper?" he asked, rubbing at the red mark on his head.

Sheesh!

I managed to get Bill out the door and the kids settled down for dinner just before eight o'clock. Later than usual, but there was a lot to unpack, particularly with the kids squealing at everything they pulled out of the shopping bags. "Bananas! Look, Mom, juice boxes. Look, Wendy, cheese stix. Look, Warren, tampons."

It was during our favourite meal of fish sticks and Caesar salad that I remembered my son had been to see the dentist. "What did Dr. Paul have to say, honey?" I asked.

Warren flashed a crooked smile at me. "Braces," came the answer. "He asked me if you got a second job yet. If you did, he said you should call him."

How much did braces cost? Bill's niece had to get them and her parents paid out $4000 – about a truckload of loonies from a Swear Jar, I figured. I looked over at his smile. Maybe those teeth weren't as crooked as . . . but they were. Warren's teeth could win prizes for "most puzzling arrangement."

I reminded myself there would be a second pay cheque coming in another week on top of my regular pay cheque and Bill's cheques. Help was on its way. If I could just keep my sanity open and my cheque book closed until then.

A call after dinner to the Charlies' home was answered by Sharon.

"Is it too late to join the search tonight?"

"Hi, Kathy, no, it's not late, but it's been called off. A lightning storm started and so it resumes tomorrow."

"Is there any word? I'm assuming no one's heard from Judy yet."

"Well, there's some news, but I'm not sure how hopeful it is. The police are busy tracking a lead in Vancouver where a tipster said Judy had been seen. The five-thousand-dollar reward money posted by her grandparents yesterday has brought in hundreds of leads. They all have to be investigated."

"How's Janice holding up?"

"She's living on coffee and sleeping pills. Not a good mix."

"I hate this," I said. "I'm just so scared for Judy. What am I going to tell the kids?"

"I wouldn't tell them anything if you can help it."

I agreed that might be best and asked Sharon to give Janice my love. We hung up, but not before I noticed a miniature rascal scoot away from around the corner.

"Warren!"

He zoomed back.

"Did you hear what I just said on the phone?"

His head nodded hard enough to sway his thick sandy hair into his eyes. "Is Judy going to die?"

"Oh, no." I scooped him into my arms and nuzzled his cheek. I carried him into the front room where Wendy had camped on the couch. Her cheeks seemed flushed again.

"Wendy, I have something to tell you both." I set Warren down on the couch beside her. "It's about Judy."

"She's dead," Warren blurted. "Dead, dead, dead."

Wendy's face crinkled and her eyes dilated. "No . . ." she cried.

Warren studied her face and then mine. He appeared puzzled, not quite understanding what he'd said.

"No she's not," I said, reaching for their hands. "Judy is . . . is . . . well, we're not sure where she went. She could be away visiting someone. She hasn't called to say where she is and so her family and her friends, we're getting worried. But everyone is trying real hard to find her. I'm sure they will."

They didn't look convinced.

"You just have to believe that they will. Okay? It's important."

I gave them each a hug.

"Hot chocolate anyone?"

I managed to sell two mugs.

It was still early so I spent the next hour working on drawing up the final advertisements I had sold for my new job. I took the information each business had given me and wrote it onto the blank newspaper sheets. I added notes saying I would like a picture of a shamrock here, or a leprechaun there, where colour should be added or not to each space. These were called the spec sheets. I would return them to Nancy, who sent them to production in Spencer. There, Tammy would work her magic and return the ads one-by-one on individual sheets for me to take around to each business to review. Any changes were sent to Spencer again and the spec was to be reproofed by the business until it was right. After approval, a billing sheet was handed in and at the end of the month someone would cut me a cheque.

I considered marking off the days on the calendar.

Mini called at seven p.m. in crisis. She couldn't choose between wall paint colours for her latest kitchen makeover. It was the Merkleys' tenth wedding anniversary coming up and they had a huge wingding affair planned. Mini wanted the house to be the rave of the century.

Ann picked us up in the Audi. I had to admit the leather seats smelled nice. I reminded Warren about his seat belt, which merely involved a sharp look to get his attention. Click. He threw me a flying kiss. I pretended to grab it and sent one back to him. He keeled over like it knocked him flat.

Ann drove through Halston for 10 minutes to the eastern outskirts of town. Kenneth and Mini's little rancher had been under renovations for months. Mini had an eye for interior decorating and Kenneth had given her full rein. To a point. He did have a stubborn streak and went to great lengths to convince Mini they needed blinds instead of curtains. She came home one day and there were blinds installed on every window in the house. The curtains remained, just stood on the outside of the blinds.

"The Big 'C' means compromise, not control, in this house," Kenneth loved to say. Case closed. He never stayed angry; he just found ways around Mini, which wasn't an easy thing to achieve.

With paint chips in one hand and glasses of fine French merlot supplied by Ann in the other, we got to the task at hand.

Within five minutes we all decided on the same colour, pale Kelly green for the kitchen walls.

The next tasks were to apply black mud packs on our faces, slip our feet into our foot baths and tuck into the gourmet baked Brie Kenneth had made for us before heading off. He didn't say to where and Mini had a lasting frown on her face long after she kissed him good-bye.

What was up with that?

Wendy sat on the couch stroking her satin pajama pillow, trying to keep her back to us. Her one arm curled up toward her face. I felt bad she figured she had to hide her habit. I didn't like the thumb sucking, but what was the difference between that and my sucking on a glass of red wine after work? Comfort was comfort, right?

Her tummy was sick again and she was definitely running a fever. The table behind her was littered with used tissue, empty apple juice containers and a bag of potato chips. No matter how sick my kids were, they always had an appetite for potato chips. Right now Wendy was being mesmerized by Darth Vader. Kenneth loved anything to do with shooting or guy battles, and *Star Wars* was the safest thing out of his DVD collection for her to view.

Warren was watching as well, but insisted on "manning"

(he loved that word) the wine glasses. Our "waiter" was paid in jelly beans or butterscotch mints whenever he remembered to swoop by and check on us.

"So where did Billy get all the money?" Ann demanded, crunching down on a cracker after she spoke.

"Does it really matter?" I grabbed my glass of wine and took a large sip.

I got "the look" from my sister. "Okay, it matters. He says he's been working, and that's what Riley said as well. Riley met Bill on the job in Prince Grange and said they would be crushing in Halston for a long spell."

Mini leaned forward, watching Warren make a great production out of filling her wine glass to the brim. Mini pushed her bowl of candies toward him. "Take 'eavy," she told him.

She probably meant "take tons." "One," I told Warren.

Like a squirrel, Warren grabbed and scooted from the room again. Mini glanced over at me. "What's up with you and this Riley? I thought you were hot for Santa."

"Isn't this amazing?" I asked them. "From famine to feast, although there hasn't been a banquet yet."

Mini and I cracked up.

"What does that mean?" boomed Ann's voice.

I ignored her. "They're so different," I said as I licked the cheese off my fingers. "Neil is your high school sweetheart, possibly moldable, possibly the keep-around type, while Riley is a treat you should give yourself if you ever get the chance. Like having an overnight fling with a hot young rock star. Something to look back on and remember when you hit the rocker stage. It's a stalemate between who has the best backside." I grinned, feeling cracker crumbs in the corner of my mouth. I wiped them off. "I do feel like a pig, dreaming about two men while you're still so footloose," I said to Ann as I drained the rest of the wine in my glass.

My sister leaked an indiscernible smile and swiveled her chair away from me.

Hmmm?

I looked to see if Mini had noticed Ann's response but Mini was no longer paying attention. She was frumped in her overstuffed club chair, her chin resting on her massive bosom. I had seen that pose all too many times.

"Hey, Sebastian. You in there?" I whispered to her. No answer.

Sebastian, once he came forward, usually took his sweet time showing Mini what he wanted her to see. Mini would go into a sleeplike trance and then the King Fruit of the Loom would show her weird movie clips or pictures he flitted across her dream stage. She was supposed to make sense of them, interpret them. But Mini sucked at charades. She also sucked at paying attention to detail. At least there wasn't talking involved! I could only imagine her trying to decipher that!

"Sebastian try and pull 'is 'air out once. 'E gets so frustrate with me. But 'is 'air can't be pulled out. 'E forget 'e's dead. At least that is one thing I 'ave up on the old queen."

When Sebastian decided Mini needed to know something, he just snapped his fingers and she was out. One time she was driving her car to town when she went into a trance. She hit the ditch and continued through it for two hundred feet before the vehicle stopped. She and Sebastian had a big fight when she came out of it. She could have been killed. "I would have shown you that," Sebastian countered. They didn't talk for weeks.

Mini could summon Sebastian any time she wanted, she just couldn't see anything in the past or future until he put her in the trance. And you couldn't rush him any more than you could rush a cross-dresser past a size twelve ladies shoe sale.

"Um hunh, uh ha," mumbled Mini in a sleepy daze. Her head of curls bounced back and forth like she was watching a tennis match.

"Jesus!" she screeched, bounding to a standing position, no small feat considering her size. I'd never seen her move so fast. Mini's body began shaking like she was having an earthquake. "Crrrap. I hate snakes," she cursed as she brushed something invisible from her arms.

I quickly agreed and worried about what that old pouf had shown her this time. Where the heck was this snake, anyway? And why was Mini brushing it off her arms? Maybe this wasn't about a trouser snake?

Mini stared at me, the whites of her eyes glowing from the black mud, like the old lawn-jockey Sambos.

"You better watch your derriere, Kathy," she said, shuddering hard. "That is one mean snake that's going to pop out and exclaim to you. *Mon Dieu.*" She made the sign of the cross. "I sure 'ope I'm not around when it 'appens, either. And don't yelp for me when it does."

Ann and I both leaned forward, trying to keep our voices down from the kids.

"What snake?" my sister urged.

"The one that is going to choke Kathy," Mini said, wrapping her hands around her own neck. "Sebastian show what look like the Garden of Eden with Eve and the snake and the apple, and the snake is choking Eve, who look a lot like Kathy.

"Then he show the apple in your 'and. Wait! There is a pile of apples stacked up beside you, all turning to dust. Whatever that means. I don't know why 'e can't just tell me. 'E knows I don't do games. I tell you, one of these days I am not going to do Sebastian!"

"He hopes," I told her, rolling my eyes and calling for Warren by jingling the candy dish. "Time to head home, buddy," I told him. "Just let Ann and me wash up."

As I cleaned off my face, I started thinking maybe I'd been mistaken about Sebastian being jealous. This snake sounded real and dangerous, which not only scared me, but made me very tired.

In the morning, Wendy was still feeling sick. Billy phoned and offered to stay with her as he was working night shift and could stay until five p.m. Her fever remained constant and she complained her "bones hurt." It was a typical run of the flu, something half the kids at school got every year at this time. Last year it was Warren's turn. I was thankful it wasn't both of them at once. Flu or not, I still phoned the doctor's office as soon as they opened. Billy said he could take Wendy in at 11 o'clock, the earliest my friend Dr. Keswick could see her. I took a chance, trusting he would follow through.

Lana was on an all-day shopping jag in the big centre of Prince Grange with her girlfriend. That meant I was again stuck at my post at HEW. I spent most of the morning unpacking freight. The new line-up of boom boxes had arrived a week early and the place was ceiling high with merchandise to be unwrapped, priced and displayed. At least it made the day fly by. I also had to put up the St. Patrick's Day sidewalk sale posters on the three different mall entrances and read the ad copy for mistakes before getting it back to the newspaper office by 6:30.

I phoned home at lunch time and there was no answer. Bill and Wendy must have been delayed. Tired of unpacking boxes, I spent an hour on the CD order to be faxed the next day. It was almost two o'clock when I next poked my head up. Ringing the house again received no answer. Although this probably meant nothing, I was a little concerned because it wasn't like Dr. Keswick to be so far behind in her schedule.

I found the number to her office and spoke to the receptionist.

"Yes, they were here, Kathy, but they left over two hours ago."

I tried the house again but got no answer. I phoned Mini at her home. No answer. Arrgghhh. It was so frustrating being stuck at work when I needed to be elsewhere.

Sometimes being desperate called for desperate measures. I telephoned the first knight in shining armour that came to mind (and that I have a phone number for). I called Neil at the District of Halston office.

"I'm really sorry to bother you at work," I started, "but I'm really worried about my daughter Wendy, who is not well, and is possibly being dragged around town by her father. You wouldn't be able to see if they're in town, maybe drive around and look for his truck? It's a very new, white GMC half ton extended cab with no tailgate."

Neil was quick to help. He had two kids of his own that came to stay with him on weekends. His daughter looked older than Wendy by about six years, but still. He would know how I was feeling.

"I'm actually on my way downtown to the hardware store, so I'll take a few more minutes and cruise the restaurants and other shops. I'll give you a call as soon as I get back. You okay?"

I tried to sound okay and hung up quickly so he could get going.

I spent the next twenty minutes biting what was left of my nails down to stubs. Who needed a manicure when we had perfectly good teeth?

Neil phoned me back with the bad news. No sign of them. He'd even driven by my place. Maybe they'd gone shopping in Spencer, our neighboring town?

That had to be it. They would be back shortly after I got home from work.

After closing HEW I dropped off the advertisement proof to the newspaper office upstairs and then had Vespio taxi me to Jackie Carmichael's to pick up my car. Vespio waived his usual fee. He had a soft spot, he said, for "damsels in distress." I thanked him more than once.

As forlorn as it was, my chariot looked pretty grand to me. Oh, to have wheels again! It fired right up with my remote starter and I drove home to discover no Warren, either.

I imagined he was also with his father, but still I phoned Warren's teacher.

"Mr. Sands picked Warren up from school at three o'clock. That's okay, isn't it? I mean you two have joint custody, don't you?"

"For now," I said begrudgingly, before disconnecting. It was sinking in that any dealings with Billy would always end in worry; that this would continue for 10 years. It sounded like a prison sentence. Ten years of Billy just popping in, doing what he wanted on his own terms with our kids. Being disruptive and belligerent and irresponsible and . . . and . . .

A small pile of papers on the kitchen table caught my eye. Billy was a perpetual scatterbrain and constantly lost or forgot things. I sifted through it: an old pay stub, a letter demanding payment for a credit card, an expired coupon for a free hamburger. No clue there.

I paced the front carpet until I worried a pit might form; still no sign of the kids or Bill. Maybe they'd been in an accident; they were in surgery, possibly jail. One never knew with Billy. He considered shoplifting "borrowing," although he never returned anything he stole.

I phoned the clinic, the Spencer hospital, the RCMP. When I called Mini and asked her to rustle up Sebastian, she phoned back to say he had been insultingly blasé: "I don't see anything so for Pete's sake tell Kathy to quit biting her nails and let me get some sleep."

"Spirit guides need their sleep?" I asked, amazed he'd known about my fingernails.

"You know Sebastian. 'E might be dead and only a fig in my 'ead, but 'e still considers it 'is duty to look good. You should 'ave seen 'is electric blue pajamas, green night cream and orange cloth sunglass. It was scaring. Now *I* won't be able to get sleep." She ended the call after trying unsuccessfully to ease my worry.

I wanted to scream at the walls. I couldn't believe any of this. First Judy, and now my children. Where had everybody gone?

And more important, was everybody okay?

Even in the comfort of your own home, darkness could be a frightening thing especially when you were overtired, stressed and continually watching for yet another snake that was going to jump out and kill you. To console myself I settled onto the couch and watched for the hundredth time the home movies of the kids when they were toddlers. Warren falling into a puddle, Wendy opening the dryer door, sticking her head in, her diapered bottom sticking out, hollering "da-goy, da-goy" and relishing in the echo.

By the time the call came I was openly weeping into a pint of ice cream – a tub saved purely for extreme emergencies.

"You're eating ice cream, aren't you?" said Billy without even a hello.

I sat up quick enough to give me an ice cream headache. "Where are you?" I shot back, one hand on my temple. "Where are the kids?"

"Whoa, lady. The kids are here, they're sound asleep in the truck, and all is fine."

"Where are you, Billy?" Frustrated, I slammed my left hand on the counter, almost fainting as it was my wounded one that had barely started to heal.

I heard him laugh. "I thought I'd exercise my joint custody agreement and take my kids for a while. Maybe for the year. And you know what that means, don't you?"

"What?"

"That I won't be paying you a dime anymore. You might as well rip those cheques up that I left because I won't be putting any money into that account. I'll need it to buy gold bricks for the kids." He chuckled at his own pathetic joke.

"You can't do this. You can't simply take our kids without my consent. What about Wendy? She's too sick to travel. What about school and all their clothes and all their things?"

"Wendy's fine. I've been giving her stuff that's keeping her sleeping which is probably the best thing for her and—"

I cut him off. "Billy, what did Dr. Keswick say? And what the hell are you talking about?"

"We're just going on a little holiday for now and we'll deal with all that other stuff later. I gotta go. I'll call tomorrow and let you talk to the kids. Been sweet talkin' to ya, good lookin'." And he disconnected.

Damn, I wished I'd had caller ID on my phone. But it was one extra expense I couldn't afford. I tried star 69, but was told the number was not available. I had no other working numbers for Billy and no idea where he'd called from. He could have driven to anywhere by now. West to the Pacific coast was four hours, up north toward Alaska another 10 hours or east to Prince Grange only three. The latter was the gateway to Canada and the United States. Where had he taken the kids? What about his job? What about everything?

The only thing I could think to do was call Neil again. He answered on the first ring and was at my house less than 10 minutes later. It was like he'd been waiting for my call for help.

A second glass of wine seemed necessary for all the advice I was getting and as I poured, my phone jangled. I snatched at it, hoping it would be Wendy or Warren, but it was Mini, her voice edged in French panic, which sounded very loud and high-pitched.

"Kathy, *ma cherie*, oh, *mon Dieu*, are you watching the television right now?"

"No," I told her, "Billy has taken the kids from me again. He said possibly for a year. I am right in the depths of despair, Min, and Neil Thomas was kind enough to come over to talk." He was watching me; I smiled reassuringly.

"*Maintenant!* Turn it on!" she demanded. "Channel two. CJBV news." She waited as I picked up the TV remote and turned on the television.

Channel two was called "peasant vision," as you didn't have to pay for it. Cheap or not, it was the only local news channel in an area that waited for Wednesday's newspaper to come out. Locals named the *Halston Today* "Halston Last Week." You get the picture. That's why we relied so much on the spread of gossip.

Spencer local Hattie Deckland stood daily before her cameraman, faithful sidekick and purported lover Steve Ducell, and boldly reported where no reporter had been before. She hoped.

Hattie was in a large muddy field, the wind wafting and tugging at her wavy, blonde hair. It was difficult to hear over the whistling noise and the flapping of her windbreaker as she pointed to trees behind her. It wasn't the most professional of broadcasts, but it was all we had. All three police cars from town were also behind her. I moved closer to my television. That field looked familiar.

I cranked up the volume. The nineteenth victim of the highway had been discovered. A young native girl's body had been dumped into a shallow grave on acreage east of Halston. I looked closer at the scenery shots. Holy Banana, Batman! That was Mini and Kenneth's place.

It would be hard not to recognize the 12-acre parcel of land that stretched out across two haying fields, bordered by rolling woodlands and a creek that bustled this time of year. A railway track dissected the entire package, making a walk through the vast area easier to access on foot.

My second thought was, *Oh my God. That wouldn't be Judy?*

Hattie reported the body had yet to be identified and the name disclosed to the public, but then the sweet, smiling face of my missing babysitter appeared on the big screen. I dropped the remote in my hand.

"No," I whispered under my breath. "Not Judy!" Nausea rose up into my throat and I had to plunk myself down in a chair and put my head quickly between my knees.

Neil picked the remote off the floor and turned the volume up even louder.

Hattie continued, saying that 18-year-old Judy Charlie had been missing from the Halston area since early Saturday morning. Family and friends had been combing the area by foot, helicopter and with dogs but she had yet to be found.

"The police are refusing to disclose whether this victim bears the pattern of the last four murders. According to police, the missing women cases in the past eight years have had a disturbing connection where the female heads had been slightly 'disfigured.' The police continue to refuse disclosure of the nature of this significance."

"Disturbing . . . disfigured?" I shuddered from head to toe with my head still between my knees.

"The body was found when two local teens crossed this field on their ATVs." I heard Hattie interviewing the kids. I tuned them out.

My worst fear had come true. How could it be possible? She wasn't hitchhiking.

Judy left her car at the party, my brain confirmed. *How did you think she got to the Sev?*

She hitchhiked, I answered.

But she was seen at the Sev. What happened to her after she got into that white pickup they said was Billy's?

It was *Billy's.*

Could someone else have been driving Billy's truck?

You are so naïve, Kathy. How many times has this man taken you for a ride?

No, he wouldn't do anything to hurt anyone.

He hurt you with Linda. And if he's so innocent, why has he taken off with the kids?

My mind started going faster with more conclusions. It became a blur of voices and I pressed my hands against my ears. My vision landed back on the television and I removed my hands.

The photo they showed on the news was one of Judy's recent graduation pictures from the package she'd received only last week. I had asked for a larger size to put on display in our living room. Her straight black hair neatly framed her chiseled cheekbones and her chestnut eyes. She was a beautiful young woman, full of promise and direction. How could she be dead?

My memory funneled back to the first time we met. She was 13 and only starting to babysit. I hadn't been confident about leaving my four- and three-year-old kids with her when Billy had an open revolving-door policy. But Judy had

taken them to her mother's home and they had spent the
time colouring; safe from harm or from Billy's meddling for
an afternoon. They hung the spectacular pictures on our
fridge with magnets. I still had them in a folder in the office.

A clipped interview with the RCMP spokesman for the
area, Tom Shields, came on in which he said they had leads,
but nothing concrete had come from them yet.

The story switched back to reporter Hattie holding her
flailing hair back with her fingers. "A private investigator,
Ted Perdue, has been hired by some of the families of the
missing women to dig deeper into the cases, but still to date,
there have been no detained suspects or arrests."

A sad smile. "We will report on more details as soon as
they are made available. The family has yet to be notified before the name of the deceased can be released."

The camera picture fell sideways and they were off the air.

Mini was beside herself, ordering me to come over *"depeche
toi!"* She was drowning with grief for the young woman, and
the reporters were camped on the porch waiting for someone
to come out. Kenneth was nowhere to be found.

Mini never once called the girl Judy. I took heart at that.

I grabbed my coat, apologizing to Neil as I ushered him
out of the house. I declined his offer to accompany me over
to the Merkleys' place. I was badly shaken, but I could still
drive and Mini would be hurt if I brought anyone to see her
right now.

I sped through town knowing I wouldn't get a ticket. Halston's three cops would be preoccupied with this tragedy.

CHAPTER FIVE

I threw a pillow at my alarm for waking me up too early. Might have helped had I reset it. I had been at Mini's until midnight when Kenneth walked in. I decided to let them work things out in private. Mini had told me how exasperated she was with his disappearances.

Glancing out the window, my tired eyes took in the intimidating black clouds. Another drizzly, rainy day. At least the water buckets weren't dripping away yet. Big positive thought.

Waking up to an empty house was so discombobulating. There was no one to tickle out of bed, or to chase to the bathroom to get washed up for the waiting bowls of cereal. Wendy's and Warren's little beds were still made up from the day before. Their stuffed toys and particularly Warren's drums were waiting for their hands to bring them back to life. As much as it drove me nuts, I would welcome the sound of Warren bashing away on his new set of skins.

I was still reeling from the young woman's body being found yesterday. Mini and I had consoled each other, saying it wasn't Judy Charlie. Hattie said the identity had not been

confirmed or the family notified. Judy's family lived here in
Halston. It would have been confirmed by now if it was her.

At least we hoped?

I checked to make sure the drip buckets were freshly emptied in the living room before getting dressed. I phoned Sharon, affirming she still didn't mind emptying them when she
went home for lunch, before dragging my butt to the store.
It beat sitting at the house waiting for what, I wasn't sure.

Before Mini's call last night, I had a few minutes to talk to
Neil. It had been helpful. He knew all about separation
agreements because he'd recently been through one and because the courthouse was a part of the District of Halston
building. Court was held every Tuesday in an adjoining
room so the District handled the forms and paperwork for
small claims court, etc. He advised me to get help.

"No," I told him. "No lawyer. I have more pressing things
to spend money that doesn't exist on. Like shingles and braces."

"Then at least apply for sole custody of those poor kids.
You don't have to have a lawyer. The only problem will be if
Billy gets one. Some of those spin doctors can really turn a
case around. You may end up losing, worst-case scenario, of
course. I'm just making a point."

My jaw dropped. Billy having sole custody of the kids until they were 18? Billy being in charge of where they lived, of
getting their teeth fixed, their medical paid? Of teaching
them right from wrong and about being the best they could
be?

I had lived through Bill's ideas on those issues and there
was no way our children, his kids or not, were going to turn
out anything like his devil-may-care side. Bill treated bills
like they were optional. And he always opted to ignore them.
He thought the medical profession was a snake-oil set-up.
He was way too cheap to get a lawyer. Wasn't he?

Neil saw my look of doubt. "Otherwise, Bill is going to keep doing this to them and to you. Do you think they like being wrenched away from their mother and their friends? From their own room and their stuff? Well, no more than you or I would."

I had to agree but what was the best way to do it to be fair to everyone?

After waking up to another early morning in my soundless house, I made my way to the District's office before Neil's shift started. In case I changed my mind, I told myself. I picked up a small claims form for the $2500 Bill still owed (following my math, not his, meaning I only knocked off $400 for the car repairs) and also a form to apply for an application to vary the Order of Divorce. Our divorce paper stated that joint custody had been agreed upon and sanctioned by a judge. That paper had been filed in court to make it a binding contract.

The biggest problem I saw once going over the forms was how to deliver the notices to my ex. He must receive a copy of my intention to take him to small claims court and then another to say that I was applying to get the custody rights changed from joint to sole. I wouldn't stop to think of his reaction to all this. It was too nerve-racking.

The filing and service fees came to over $300. It was explained that unless I was indigent (which I basically was, but not according to the law; you couldn't be "broke" if you had two jobs and a home), I had to cough up these fees in advance. The good part was that for another $100, I could have a sheriff personally track that white ass of Billy's down. I daydreamed the scenario to a full-feature action movie, with Billy slammed into a brick wall before being dragged to court in handcuffs; a gun pressed against his temple. I'd skip six months of lunches to have that happen. More if I could take a video.

Still, it was a pipe dream. The money had officially slipped through my fingers for the month.

At home I set to cleaning to keep my mind off of everything. I grabbed a green garbage bag, went into the kids' room and discarded any refuse like holey socks or broken toys. I removed a dried-out grilled cheese sandwich carefully stuffed under Warren's pillow. Like his mom, he had an emergency favourite food stash. I moved Wendy's new Barbie camper van from under the kitchen table to join the drum set in their closet.

I stripped the bedding and put on fresh sheets, cleaned the carpet and wiped the walls before quietly closing their door. I was hiccoughing and my eyes were leaking like waterfalls. This sucked.

I called my sister, but Ann couldn't understand why I was so distraught.

"You get a free break from your little soldiers and you complain? Now is the time to get ahead. You can work extra hours. Make the day pay!"

We agreed to meet in the morning for a run. At the very least it would help clear my head and possibly slim down that new bulge I was getting from stress-eating. In case I ever got to play this doctor game, I told myself. As if he'd heard something, I no sooner hung up and the Levi Man called.

I gave Riley directions to the house over the phone and within the swish of eyeliner and a dab of mascara he was here, a bottle of red wine and a box of mixed dark chocolates in hand. Oh-oh, one of my favourite combinations in life. What a way to cheer me up!

I was thankful I'd spent so much time cleaning the place. Other than an assortment of pictures scattered around the walls and tables, there wasn't the usual evidence to trip over that declared the kids were first and foremost in my life. Riley seemed child-phobic so the far-fetched idea was to ease this bachelor into a possible future role around them slowly. One dose at a time.

I couldn't help but admire his butt as he went into the kitchen in search of a corkscrew and glasses. A picture of Neil's backside floated to me – he had a fine butt as well. Different: rounder, higher. Grabbable. I shoved Neil out of my mind.

"The drawer closest to the fridge," I called as I pushed play on the CD changer. "Glasses are in the cupboard beside the stove."

Riley had the glasses filled, his feet up on my coffee table, nice and relaxed like he belonged there while Bob Seger played in the background. I snuggled in beside him.

He smiled at me; the man was movie star material. A sigh escaped my lips.

"Is Billy still around?" he asked.

"Huh?" I bolted upright from my cuddled position. This was the first thing he wanted to talk about when we hadn't seen each other in days? He wanted to know about Bill? Not my injured palm – which still hurt, by the way – my job, the kids or my favourite colour?

"What, you don't like people asking about your ex?"

"No, I just don't see why that has to be the first thing you ask me. But speaking of him, have *you* seen Bill around?"

Riley sipped his wine and opened the box of chocolates, extending the assortment toward me first. "He didn't make it to work last night and the boss is looking for him."

I chose what I hoped to be a caramel before staring Riley straight in the eye. "He called yesterday and said he was going on vacation." I didn't mention for how long. It was too horrible to even think about. "He also said he would call me tonight so I could talk to the kids, but I'm still waiting." I bit into the chocolate and experienced two seconds of bliss before the depression returned. I reached for another one.

Riley put one hand on my thigh as he bent over to put down the box down. A tingle at the touch spread up toward my centre like snake venom. Oh right, the snake! I was on high alert, trembling with delight from a mix of fear and anticipation. Riley had said there were all kinds of snakes. Was I about to see his? And that thought reminded me . . . I checked my breath on the sly. Nothing but chocolate. Good. I twisted toward Riley. "Now I have a question for you. What's with the snake on your bike's gas tank?" I was all ears, even though 80 percent of my brain was concentrating on where Riley's hand was. Would it try to go higher? And if it did, would I let it?

"That's not my bike."

He had my full attention. "Whose is it?"

"A guy named Terry Murdoch, aka Snake. I've been staying at his house while we're in town. Bill had been staying there too. Now Billy and his gear have disappeared. The boss is none too pleased. And neither is Snake."

Snake! I wondered if *he* was Sebastian's snake, and if so, why would this stranger want to strangle me? What had Billy said to the guy? I hadn't been vicious or horrible to my ex, unless you considered badgering worth killing someone over.

"So what's the story on this Snake guy?"

"I dunno. He's been here for a while. Bought a place on a dead-end street called Church Way; one of the new ones they're building in the area. You can tell his place isn't a church, though, because it's surrounded by a six-foot fence, razor wire and security cameras."

"How do you know him?" I asked.

"Through the crushing outfit. He's the boss man's accountant and he's giving us a place to stay for a few bucks a night. We save a lot of money."

Oh, right. Riley already mentioned that the night we met at the pub.

"So do you and Bill share a room, or do you have your own?"

"I have my own room upstairs and Billy sleeps on a pull-out in the family room downstairs."

"I see," I said, when I didn't. The doorbell rang and I happily stood to answer it.

My surprised facial expression was hopefully complimentary at the sight of Neil standing on my stoop. A bottle of wine was tucked under his arm and he extended a paper bag with what smelled amazingly like egg rolls. I *loved* egg rolls.

Could I handle this with the orgasmic delight of the chocolate and wine I was already having? Talk about welcomed distractions.

I invited him in, not thinking that I should have said I was busy. But seriously – send home a handsome man with wine and Chinese food? Did you think I was crazy? This would be a moment to relive for the rest of my life.

Neil immediately sent a male-dog-pissing-match glare at Riley, who pulled his feet off the coffee table to scramble to attention.

"What's he doing here?" Neil asked, jerking his thumb toward Riley.

"I was invited," Riley said before I had a chance to reply.

Neil looked at me, a pout on his lip. "Should I leave?"

"No! No, it's okay; it's a big living room. Stay, here, take your coat off. Can I open that for you?" I reached for the bottle he held out.

Neil followed me into the kitchen, bending down to breathe into my ear. The fine hairs on my neck shivered with pleasure.

"I'll go if you really want me to."

I excitedly shook the grease-spotted bag he'd brought. "Chinese?"

His face said he knew he was staying.

Nobody wanted to end the party, particularly me, who couldn't make a decision between who she wanted to stay or go. They were both so incredibly polite and charming, especially from the viewpoint of an aging, attention-starved mother.

It was hard trying to hold my gut in all night though.

Perhaps I had a bit too much to drink because I woke up at two o'clock in the morning to the phone ringing. After pushing off the blanket covering me I discovered both men were gone. I must have fallen asleep on them.

I picked up the receiver. "'Lo . . ."

"Where's Billy?" hissed a distant voice.

"What?"

"You know where he is. Tell me," the voice insisted.

"Who is this? And why are you calling me at this time of the night?"

"Tell me where he is or you'll be sssorry."

I hung up the phone but it immediately started ringing again. The sound rattled me in the dead of night. I didn't pick it up, going instead to check that the doors were all locked. My goose bumps were as big as blueberries.

I counted ten rings before the caller gave up. "Shit," I said to no one in particular. To heck with the Swear Jar; I was all alone. I glanced around. The men were gone, but hey, it wasn't all bad. I picked up the brown paper bag Neil brought over and shook it. There was still one egg roll left. Stress always made me hungry.

It was cold but who cared? I bit down hard on one end of the roll just as there was an ear-splitting crash. Glass flew through the air, sprinkling my outstretched arm and unprotected face. A red brick skidded across the living room carpet. A writhing, wriggling ten-inch snake was tied with string around its middle to the centre of the brick and when I saw it I tried to scream. I hated snakes! As I sucked in air to holler, the egg roll caught in my throat and I choked. I coughed and coughed but couldn't dislodge the lump of food in my throat. I whacked at my chest. Thump, thump. No use. I felt the purple rise in my face. I bounced up and down and paced around the room. The seconds were like minutes and before long I thought my head was going to explode. My temples were pounding and I couldn't breathe. I panicked, running around the living room like an overexcited springer spaniel. I clawed at my throat but nothing was working. In desperation, I leapt up on the couch and threw myself down onto the corner of the armrest, simulating the Heimlich maneuver. I read somewhere that this move could have saved Mama Cass, who choked to death on a ham sandwich. I hadn't read about how much it would hurt! Good thing or I might not have tried it.

"Ufffff."

A greasy piece of egg roll shot from my mouth and hit the coffee table. I gasped in great gulps of air. It took time to settle down and when I did I noticed for the first time there was writing on the brick.

"TELL" was all it said.

It didn't take a genius to figure out who had sent a snake as a message. I tried the phone book and then operator assistance for a Terry Murdoch, to no avail. His number must be unlisted and Riley had never given me a number to the house. Or his cell phone, for that matter.

I tried phoning the RCMP, but the call was transferred to another larger community called Tessak, some three hours away. I was told an officer would be by closer to morning, unless I figured this was life threatening.

Say what? Hadn't I just been threatened? Wasn't there a snake possibly still trying to get at me from beneath the roasting pan battened down with the three heavy books piled on top? What if the snake managed to ditch the brick and the roaster and slithered up my pant leg and killed me? Actually, judging by the size of it, it would have to get on a chair to bite me now that I had my knee-high winter boots on for safety's sake, but who knew how high a snake could lunge?

The senior RCMP officer in town, Corporal Andrew Currie, took 40 minutes to attend and after lifting my roaster up, had a good laugh at what he called a "harmless little garter snake." He did, however, seem very concerned about the damage done to my front window and the evidence of fine glass still sprinkled on my face.

"Little shits," he said under his breath. If I'd been thinking straight, I would have nailed him for swearing and demanded a loony for the jar. But I wasn't. I was busy wondering why he imagined this was the work of young kids. Had he not been listening about this Terry Murdoch?

After taping a square of cardboard over the hole, Currie drove me to the clinic to have a nurse look after my skin before returning me to my place. After making sure it was secure, he gathered the snake and brick and left me to try and get some sleep before I had to head to work.

Fat chance, I thought, with visions of snakes still crawling in my head.

The phone was ringing as soon as I had my keys in the door at HEW; I déjà vued because once again it was before opening hours. I ran for it, already warmed up from my morning jog with Ann. I kept an eye out for where the receipt tack was, my hand squeaking out a little remembrance throb. I still had a scab over the hole in my hand. It looked like I had tried to crucify myself.

"Hello," I answered. "Halston Electronics World, Kathy speaking."

There was a one-second delay and I whirled around, fearing another brick would fire through the store's front window, but nothing happened.

"Mommy?" came Wendy's sweet voice. She sounded tired. She sounded too far away and she sounded about one hundred hugs short of a load.

"Baby, is that you?"

"Hi, Mom," piped Warren's voice on the same line. They must be in a place with two phones.

"Hi, guys! It's so great to hear your voices. How are you?"

"Great," shouted Warren. "Mom, there's a Laundromat here with a free game centre and everything. It's like way, way wicked. You should see the swimming pool out back too. Dad says they will put water in it so I can go swimming every day here if I want."

A pool? A Laundromat? Were they at a motel?

"All right, all right, cowboy," I said. "I'm glad you're having fun. Can you tell me where you are?"

"Dad says to tell you we're on the moon," and he let off a roll of high-pitched giggles. How much soda was this boy on? It was a continual battle between Bill's parenting and mine. He would return them after a prolonged "visit" strung out like little sugar junkies. It took an hour to corral Warren into the bath last time.

"The moon, hunh? That's super, but does the moon have a name?" Why would Bill want to keep the name of where they were a secret? I thought of the brick's message and began to wonder if Bill was hiding from more than me and the police. If that was the case, were my kids in danger? I tried not to panic.

"Daddy said we are at Uncas," Wendy whispered. "But I

don't know where that is because we were sleeping and woke up when we got here."

"Hi, Wendy, honey. How are you feeling?"

"I'm all better now, Mommy. Daddy gave me a bunch of those aspirins that I like, the grape ones that . . ."

And just like that they were gone. But not disconnected.

I could hear them talking to their father, who was telling them something I couldn't quite hear. Then I did.

". . . a bad mother. She doesn't want you to come home. She's too busy working and playing with her new boyfriends. You guys are much better off here with me. Don't call her anymore."

I started yelling, "Wendy, Wendy, pick up the phone . . ." until I was hoarse. It seemed like an hour, although it was more like 10 minutes. The line began to drone, signaling it was dead.

People walking past the store stared at me in alarm. I gave a feeble little wave.

It was okay. Everyone knew I was a single mom; heck, half of the people walking past were single parents at one time or another. This town had a regular spouse-swap every spring, so although they look shocked, no one came in to ask what was going on.

I quickly called Ann and then Mini to let them know I heard from my babies and that they sounded okay. What a relief.

I phoned Neil at work. I admit I mostly wanted to hear the sound of his voice. It would have to suffice for a hug these days – a sexy man's deep baritone. I told him about what happened after he left. He said Riley tried to wait him out, but when he suggested they both leave together, Riley took the hint and they headed their separate ways.

I paused, hoping an invite would come for dinner, or for

some reason for us to get together. We both listened to nothing but breathing for a whole minute, which was an eternity for me.

"So, I, uh, I'll probably see you around, then," I stammered.

He agreed.

And that was that.

Crap! I hit the wall with my good hand. Why hadn't I asked him over for dinner, for coffee, for help cleaning the oven, *any*thing? I smacked my forehead.

It would be too embarrassing to call back, having to go through other staff to reach him. The tongues were probably already wagging at every hair salon in town.

It seemed like the day would never quit, but my phone fiasco with Neil somehow revved me up to take charge of other things.

Uncas. What could that be? My search engine said the word meant "tribal chief"; nothing about an actual location. I called the telephone operator, something I did when I couldn't think of anyone else to help. One time I learned how to smoke char. Another solved the mystery of how to turn Patches' fog lights on.

But six operators in a row had never heard of any such place or thing.

I grimaced first before phoning Billy's sister Amanda, who hollered at me loud enough for the next group of people walking through the mall to hear. "Don't ever call me again!" I was going to take that as a "probably never heard of Uncas" as well.

Amanda unnerved me enough to call it quits with phoning Bill's family. I switched gears completely and hit the list of advertisers I had been given for my other job. I sold a $1000 full-page ad after the first 10 minutes. Tim Smith, the general manager at the Cana Forest Products mill (and coincidentally Sharon's husband), had a great advertising budget but was jaded by the constant screw-ups of the last ad rep. He accepted my promise to triple-check every detail. Five more calls netted more money in my pocket. *Look out, Warren — here come those braces,* I told myself. At the same time, I grew sad remembering I would need my son's mouth here to put them into.

Where the hell were they?

I'd have to put a few extra loonies in the Swear Jar when I got home. Enough to make sure we threw a grand party when they returned, with pizza and games and, what-the-heck, sodas!

If they ever made it back, a little voice deep in my heart murmured. My eyes clouded up at the thought.

At four o'clock a jittery young man came in. I'd seen him around town on occasion, usually at the bakery. Not bad looking, late twenties, dark, disheveled hair, needed a shave. I let him walk around the displayed floor stereos for a few minutes before I headed over.

My sales strategy was to never ask a customer if they needed help. They usually said no, even if they did. I began by talking about whatever the customer seemed to have their eye on. A short icebreaker; a cheap, free advertisement for the manufacturer.

"You're looking at Halston's hottest and most kick-A stereo system, a Damon 1400-watt seven-channel super pounder. It comes with an Elite Blu-ray disc player, a double auto reverse cassette deck, multi-pack CD player, iPod dock station and a surround speaker system with 150-watt downward firing subwoofers

The man listened to the spiel and nodded his head in long

bobbing arcs like he was newly born and having trouble keeping it upright on his neck. He then pranced around the display, gliding his hands all over it, and bouncing up and down like he had a jumping bean shoved up his backside. He wiped at his runny nose with the back of his hand.

He was pretty funny to watch as he floated over to the speaker section, asking what would give him the most "wicked mother f$%#ing sound?" He said this so loud spittle flicked out of his mouth. He wiped the back of his hand across his lips. He also wiped at his runny nose again. I hoped I wouldn't have to shake that hand.

"It's prime flu season," I said sympathetically, receiving a hee-haw reply.

With all this odd behavior I was beginning to think the worst; that Ron Gweek, as he called himself, was what we in the biz called a "timewaster." If there was another salesman around, we would tap our watch, meaning we were with a long-shot sale and were free if a better prospect popped up.

I started peering around to see who else was in the store when out came a multi-coloured wad of bills from Gweek's front pant pocket. It was about six inches thick – a doubled-up mass of paper. He waved it at me and the ends fluttered up and down. A mouldy, musty smell hit my nose, like the bills had been buried for a spell. It sure looked good, regardless, and I was sure it would still fit in the cash register.

"So how much are we talking for those speakers over there," he pointed toward the two he last draped himself over, "and this big old stereo package here?"

My autopilot mental calculator flicked on. When it came to making money, my pencil was razor sharp. Even sharper when my son needed braces.

"With tax included, you're looking at fifty-two hundred dollars even." I looked for a reaction. Gweek didn't blink.

"Say five thousand even and you deliver and install it."

Yippee! Before I remembered the spittle and nose wiping, my hand shot out and we shook on it. Well, I shook Gweek's swinging wad of cash, as he didn't seem to get the handshake concept at that moment.

What a deal! We delivered and installed our systems anyway, so I was happy, the Gweek looked happy and we both did a little happy dance right then and there. I swear it was infectious. Happy, happy!

I began to write up the sale while Gweek dictated his address: 3100 Heritage Road. He flapped his pile of cash like a flag as he spoke.

It didn't bother me when he said there wasn't a phone number he could give me. Remember, happy, happy! Sure, yes, I'd be there as soon as we closed at six.

When I finished writing, he pushed the money wad toward me and said, "Here, take what you need." A wink followed. What was it with people winking at me? Was I causing eye disorders? Or should I reciprocate?

I winked back. Better to be safe at this stage of the process. I handed him his receipt and the rest of the wad, put the cash owed in the till and then he was gone. Poof! Just like that.

I did a second little dance and then couldn't help but sit down with a piece of paper and write all this down. I added up my regular paycheck, the $1100 from Billy, the advertising money and my commissions so far for the month. I had a column for the incoming and one for outgoing. For once the incoming was winning!

It looked like we were going to survive after all. Not quite enough for a new roof but definitely some spot repairs come summer. I was feeling brave enough to phone Warren's dentist for a quote. And maybe one day I could think about applying for that sheriff's ass-whupping for Billy. Go for sole custody. But not yet. Not with so much else to pay for first.

After I piled all of Gweek's stereo pieces together it was time to lock up. I phoned the Charlies and someone named Erna said the searches were over. They had covered the town and surrounding areas. Nothing had turned up, no news yet. Yes, she would tell Janice I was thinking of her. Please call again.

I made another quick call to Ann to see if she wanted to get together later for dinner. I could use someone to rehash this depressing news about Judy with. I refused to believe the body that was found was hers. Janice would have called me.

We agreed to meet at the pub at eight o'clock to split one of their famous Shelly salads. They were too big to eat alone and sharing one justified the price of a glass of beer. I finished by telling Ann about the big sale I'd made. She was properly impressed.

I locked up the store and threw the keys into my purse – a big Phat Baby knock-off loaded with fake blingy metal parts and a chain for a handle. It was the gaudiest purse in the world, except it could pack a bottle of wine *and* a bag of cookies on top of my usual necessities when called for. I named it my Big Black Hole. You could lose a whole cake in there!

I pre-started the car with the remote but it didn't help much. The seat didn't depress when I hopped in. The weather seemed to be going backwards. Spring must have given up and we were returning to winter. It made me even sadder than I was a minute ago when I was thinking about Judy.

The shop had a rear delivery door so I drove around to get the stereo pieces. The darkness hung like a thick backstage curtain. Thank goodness for the security lights on the mall's roof so I could see. The trunk didn't take long to stuff so the backseat and the passenger seat got piled to the roof. I packed a large roll of speaker wire and some clippers into my purse before grabbing a big hammer from the repair work bench and tossing it in too. Never knew when a girl might need a hammer.

Billy's face flashed into my mind. I blinked twice and the image dissolved.

At the last minute I remembered to pack the town map, compliments of the District, because even after you'd lived here your entire life (which not many of us had), you still didn't know street names. Even the main street was called downtown and no one remembered it as 9th Street unless you owned a store there. That counted for six people.

I flipped on the car's interior light. The map showed Heritage Road heading up past the Wander Inn bar (nicknamed the Zoo for very obvious reasons) toward the Christian All Saints church. I scrutinized the map, pulling it up to the overhead light. At the very end of Heritage Road was a road that seemed more like a cow trail. The mini writing on it said "Church Way."

The street Riley said he was living on with Snake.

I left the car radio turned off as I slowly cruised beyond the Zoo. I needed some silence to think. I was traveling at old-lady speed, in no hurry to get to where I worried I was going. I also hoped the shaking in my right leg would stop.

The show homes on either side of the street lit up with modern motion-sensor street lamps as I passed. Being so new, they still had dirt piles for lawns. I gathered no one lived in them yet as no interior lights were on. There were no vehicles or bikes or usual people paraphernalia, so I was sure my guess was right.

I read the even numbers on the houses until I hit 3090. Then I ran out of houses. The only other thing I could see was a church on my left and a massive concrete wall that was topped with barbed wire on my right. It resembled a penitentiary. Were they trying to keep people out or someone in? I drove closer. My headlights discovered miniature cameras

mounted in two different places on this side of the barrier. I
saw a barred gate and puttered closer to it. There were numbers on one side: 3100. Beneath the numbers someone had
painted a large gold snake.

CHAPTER SIX

I was too spooked to get out of the car and wander around so I sat there listing my options. One was to say to hell with this sale, my commission and roof repairs and head straight to the pub. Or I could go in and see what this Snake guy wanted with me. He had threatened me twice and quite frankly I was getting tired of it. What was the point in hurting me? I was probably the best chance he had of finding where Billy had moved to.

A mini pep rally sounded off in my head. Yeh! Who did this Snake think he was anyhow? He couldn't just throw garter snakes and bricks through people's windows. Did he think I was a pushover? Something inside my head laughed at that. *That's what Billy thinks, so why wouldn't Snake? They're friends, remember?*

That made me mad.

I tried reasoning with myself. The stereo receipt copy, which had this address on it, was still on the counter at work. Someone would discover the last place I went before being murdered. I swallowed hard. Don't think like that. No one was stupid enough to bring me here to kill me.

I opened my purse and took out the hammer, grateful I had thought to snag it. I slid the head of it through a belt loop on my pants. You couldn't see it with the suit jacket hanging down over it. I did a checklist for anything else that could be considered a weapon in this big black pleather-hole. Pliers, check. Hair spray, check. Perfume, check, cork-screw, well, maybe check, ball point pen, overdue library book, plastic lunch container, make-up kit. Maybe I should just swing the bag at his head if I needed more than the hammer?

Feeling well armed, I peeled myself out of the warm security of my car. I carried the speaker wire and my purse separately so I wasn't walking in empty-handed and sidled up to the gate, giving it a hard shove. It didn't budge.

Roarrr! A giant brown and black blur with big long dripping fangs leapt up in front of me. Two snowshoe paws jammed their way through the gate's bars and I stumbled backwards, emitting one sharp, startled yelp. The long jacket would now be hiding more than a hammer. My underwear didn't feel so dry anymore.

A growl that was more like the rumble of thunder came from the most unimaginably massive Doberman. Even my worst nightmares wouldn't have pictured one so . . . so . . . truck-sized. I bet it was named Godzilla or Shredder and it fed on salespeople. Gone in two bites like those brownies I loved.

Spotting a doorbell buzzer from where I sat on the cold earth, I straightened, brushing my fanny off, and hit the button.

Floodlights illuminated a door opening and a man's voice yelled for "Prince" to "Shud-up."

So this was where the Prince of Darkness lived. I shivered but not from cold as I could feel beads of sweat lined up to roll down my forehead. My right leg began to shake again.

The Doberman pulled its weight backward and disappeared at the sound of the voice. I heard the door open and close again and then there was someone half walking, half bouncing down a cement pad walkway toward me. Gweek. He pushed open the gate and floated over to me. I wasn't sure whether I was relieved or not to see his scrawny frame.

He said hello and bounced over to my car. I quickly followed.

We each grabbed a large speaker and headed back up the path toward some stairs.

"Is this your place?" I asked, walking behind him.

"Nope."

He had nothing more to say; seemed like he'd met his talk quota that afternoon at the store.

Inside the fenced area a black van with a grey stripe around the middle sat parked on a paved strip of driveway. I kept looking for the dog, but he was nowhere in sight.

"Do you know someone named Riley Wells?"

No answer.

We headed up the stairs and inside what looked like the rear entrance to the house. We were now in a large kitchen. At the sound of the screen door slamming shut behind us, the Doberpony called Prince came tearing at me from around a corner. Great gobs of spittle flooded from his mouth like he was salivating just imagining how I'd taste. I recognized the symptom. I did the same thing before biting into a dark chocolate Carmelmilk bar.

I held the three-foot speaker up in front of me like a shield but thankfully Prince's nails couldn't get purchase on the floor's slick linoleum and he merely froze in space spinning his legs.

"Eeep."

I hoped that my parents would at least be sent some of my parts once I was ripped in half. My mother would be especially pissed if there wasn't at least a salvageable piece to fuss over.

Gweek grabbed the thick studded collar not a second too soon as the animal's paws finally connected and it sped forward. The dog's weight spun the man for a minute, but Gweek gained on it and managed to drag it over to a door that, once opened, showed stairs leading downward, probably to the basement. He kicked the dog's behind and then closed the door after it.

"This way," he said to me.

I followed on wobbly legs down a narrow hallway. The passage opened into what some people called a living room. Here, it was more of a dead room; a wildlife mausoleum with mounted and stuffed animal skins scattered around the room. Brown, glazed eyes from caribou, elk, sheep and deer followed me across the thickly carpeted area. There were standing stiffs of a wolf, a moose and one huge grizzly – claws extended and teeth bared. I could almost feel the breath on my neck.

I spun slowly around the room. Along the entire back wall was a stuffed boa constrictor, its head standing out from its body by about a foot. It was glaring right at me with unblinking yellow irises. My skin began to crawl in different directions, trying to leave without me, I figured.

"The pieces can be piled in here," Gweek said before turning back down the hallway for another load. I ran after him.

The last to come in were the speaker stands and I sent Gweek out to get them while I started assembling the rest to put into the pre-made stand. As I piled the CD and cassette player on top of the amplifier, I caught a slight movement out of the corner of my eye. Did I just see a tongue flick out of that snake's mouth? I looked at it again. It stared at me with those all-engulfing eyes. I couldn't be sure, but was my hair now standing straight up in the air? I watched, horrified, as a forked tongue slid out of the constrictor's mouth and darted back in again.

Jeepers, Mother Jemima, Fudge! I snapped to my feet, grabbed my purse and blasted as fast as my legs would carry me back down the hallway. When I was two steps from the kitchen and from the door that would lead me outdoors away from here, an arm shot out of nowhere and pulled me straight through the wall. Or it looked like the wall. Turned out the door to another room had been wallpapered to appear like it wasn't there. But it surely was.

The man still handling my arm was short, barrel-chested and I figured at least 250 pounds. He had red hair that was years overdue for a cut and a full red beard to match. Rings of skulls and jewels adorned every finger on his hands.

"Hey," I yelled. "Let go of me." I tried to wriggle free but the hand only clamped tighter. It went right around my entire arm.

The man dragged me to stand before him.

"You must be Katherine."

I gave him my best you-better-not-mess-with-me look and tried to say, "Who's asking," but all that came out was a dry squawk.

"Awkk."

So much for my bravado.

"Ssssso," he said, drawing the word out like a hiss, "are you ready to tell me what I want to knowww?"

Fearing my voice was still gone, I merely shook my head in a defiant no.

The books say you should never show an animal your fear, but then I remembered I already smelled like pee. No wonder Prince had been so eager to take me down. I hoped Snake didn't have the same sensing capabilities.

"Where is your Billy?"

My hair flew around my face as I shook my head again.

Snake's left hand threatened to cut off any remaining blood supply in my arm. I wondered if this was what it felt like when a hungry boa constrictor had you.

The hammer! I used my free hand and pulled it from my belt loop, swinging it toward the hand that held me.

Snake reached up and stopped the hammerhead's path with the palm of his right hand. He wrenched the tool from my grip.

"What's this? You're trying to hurt me?" He made a surly face.

My voice felt as if it might work. "Like you aren't trying to kill me first," I said, a bit garbled, but at least it hadn't come out sounding like a high-pitched scream.

He let go of my arm and I reached up immediately to rub some blood back into it. My fingers on that side had gone numb.

"I had hoped we could have a reasonable conversation. Now, where is your husband?" His voice was menacing. "You are going to tell me where he went."

That was reasonable? "He is my EX-husband, thank you very much, and I don't know where he went. I'm trying to find him myself. He took our kids and I want them back."

"He's your ex-husband," Snake repeated. "He said you were his steady ride."

His ride? I took a step closer to the door I had just come through. "He hasn't ridden this horse for years."

Snake's face slid sideways, which I think was the equivalent of a sneer. "He has your kids. They will phone you and when they do you will phone me." He thrust a business card at me. I didn't take it so he shoved it into the top pocket of my pants.

I hated this man even saying the words "your kids." He was dangerous and undoubtedly slimed everything he talked about. What was Riley doing living with a man like this? I didn't care how much money he saved from motel rooms. Yeesh. Had he no scruples?

Oh right, as if I was one to talk. Last I remembered, I had been ready to play doctor with Riley even though I hardly knew him. Some scruples.

How did I do this? A man was standing before me threatening my life and I was busy harassing myself for being too easy? My mother had achieved her life's goal!

I forced the glazed look from my face.

"What exactly do you want to see Billy for?"

Snake's eyes narrowed until they were slits. "I ask the questions here, bitch."

I turned to leave. "I don't need this," I emphasized. "I'm expected somewhere for dinner, and you can install that stereo yourself. I don't work in rooms where big snakes are licking their lips at me."

"Hey," he yelled, grabbing my arm again. "You don't go nowhere until I say you do."

Okay. Whoa. Now that was one way to piss me off. Nobody other than my mother can talk to me like that.

I swung my purse, this time in a much smaller arc, and connected with his eyes. That wouldn't have hurt so much, except the fancy doodads on the purse strap went straight into his eyeball. He let me go and his hands whipped to his face. I ran and got the heck out of there. I had no idea where Gweek went but he wasn't there to stop me. I raced back down the hall and ripped open the back door, flying through the gate while hitting the auto-start button on the keys I had stuffed in my jeans. I was in and gone in a flash. A glance in the rearview didn't show anyone chasing behind, but I burned rubber anyway. It's a wonder I didn't get a flat tire.

My heart was convulsing as I barreled through the side streets on my way to meet my sister. Adrenaline was pumping through me like liquid fire. I had saved my own life, I was sure. I was one kick-ass mother! I did a mental back slap and grinned like Sylvester did every time he swallowed Tweety Bird. Who knew I had that in me! I had never felt so alive! Or, I had to admit the truth, terrified. My mind flashed an image of the monster snake eyeing me up. Jesus! That must have been Sebastian's snake! Lucky I got out of there!

The business card was sticking into my hip bone so I pulled it out and turned on the overhead light. All it had on it was a phone number beneath a . . . Oh crap! A Hells Dragons logo. Damn. A feeling crept up my shoulders. It was one I knew well. The "in way over my head and I'm going to drown" feeling.

A flashback residual of Life with Billy.

Ann didn't arrive at the Happy Mac Pub for another hour and by that time I had four gin martinis under my belt. That meant I was a babbling brook of gibberish. I think it was Mae West that said, "I love a good martini, two at the most. For three I'm under the table, and four I'm under my host."

The host was almost Riley, who showed up mere minutes before Ann. I was only too embarrassed to remember sticking my tongue in his ear before I slid off his lap and wound up under the table. I hoped I wasn't headed there on purpose and had merely lost my balance.

Ann ended up pouring me into my car and driving me home. She hung my car keys on a holder beside the door and walked me to my bed. I didn't recall anything more except the room spinning until I woke up with someone else's head on my shoulders. At least I wished like hell it was someone else's head.

I took it for granted that Ann had marched the ten

minutes back to the pub before taking her own vehicle home. We took turns doing that for each other when the situation arose. Being a two-bar town, the police only had to drive by and notice your vehicle parked there long enough to get impaired and then follow you home. I think we had more DUI per capita than we did people that voted.

I made it to work on time. Thankfully the phone wasn't ringing as I dragged myself in. I put a double pot of coffee on and disappeared for a quick pee. I noticed I had my under-wear on inside out. Good grief. I managed to fill my coffee mug even before the coffee machine stopped dripping – I needed something to wash down more tablets from the first aid kit. I didn't think this was the day to try to dry swallow anything. It might come back up faster than it went down.

I flipped the sign over to read "Open" and then sat behind the counter with my thick head in my hands. Why was it when we're down, we beat ourselves up even harder? "The floggings will continue until morale improves" was a sticker I once read on an outhouse wall. How true.

I didn't care how much money Gweek had spent in our store, I wouldn't be dog food or snake appies. And there wasn't anyone else I would expose to the danger there.

Okay, I did care. That commission alone could mean a big difference in my family's life.

But I was not going back to set up that stereo. Gweek could just march it right back to the store and I'd give him all that money back. Somehow. I would simply explain to Head Office that I had been threatened. They would surely understand! My heart sank. As if.

But Gweek never showed or called all day. So it was a fair-ly dull Thursday until I noticed two long legs striding toward

me in those straight boot-cut Levi's. Mmm. I smelled the
cool air on Riley's shirt as he glided up to the counter. He
leaned into me like we were old lovers.

Think he took my tongue in his ear the wrong way?

His hand reached out and flicked my chin.

"Have dinner with me. Tonight." It wasn't exactly a question.

The look on his face might be suggesting he was on the
menu. I had to swallow hard before answering. One didn't
want to seem too eager. Right? Besides, and most important,
this man was living with a Hells Dragons member who had
threatened me more than once.

But, "Sure, love to, when, what time?" fell out of my
mouth before I could stop it.

"Your choice, lady. But decide quick. I have to run. I'm
not supposed to be here."

I countered with myself that I would give Riley a chance
to answer all my questions during dinner. Besides, I had
turned to mush at the word "lady." Talk like that in this
small town was possibly banned in the 50s. People spoke to
their women like the truck drivers and cattlewomen that they
were. Call them a lady and they'd fall off their tractors laughing.

I was not laughing. It had shivered my timbers. Right to
their core.

We agreed on seven at the Pleasant Valley Restaurant.

I chose PV's because it was the best place in Halston to
have a private dinner. We had a lot to hash out. The front
part of the place was a diner for truckers and the coffee
klatches or anyone trying to catch a quick bite. But behind
the section containing the washrooms was an even larger
room where a cozy dining area was set. This room had red
velvet curtains, a nice brick fireplace, flowers and a candle on
every linen-draped table. It remained secluded and away

from the beaten track. A couple might have a chance to get to know more about each other. Not to mention the menu boasted things like Dungeness crab, prime rib and fresh salmon. I didn't get out much, so this was going to be a big treat.

Worrying about what shape I would be in the next morning, I decided to use one of my first sick-leave passes and get Lana to open for me.

I picked up the portable phone and dialed. Lana's answering machine clicked on.

"Hello, dah-ling," she cooed. "If this isn't Saks calling, leave a message and I'll think about getting back to you. If this *is* Saks, yes, please send it all." I rolled my eyes while listening to the familiar beep. Lana had Saks taste but a Wal-Mart budget like the rest of us. But not everyone knew that. It was all about "perception," she told me, her rhinestone rings waving. Mommy might have money but Lana was expected to make her own way in the world. Or at least until Daddy took pity that her credit cards had melted from overuse.

"Hi, Lana. This isn't Saks, it's Kathy. Do you know if you were to work from nine to one tomorrow you could buy both the new mixed pop *and* the summer music CDs you've been pawing? Call me as soon as you get this."

I hung up and no sooner turned toward the back of the store when the phone rang. It was Lana. She had been screening her calls as usual. Yes, she could be at HEW at nine in the morning, if only I did her one little "wittle" favour. Could I give her phone number to the stud that had been looking for Kathy the last time Lana worked?

"You know, one of the rock crusher ones you told me about. His name was Riley. Is the Billy you mentioned that hot looking, too?"

Dead silence from me; I wasn't sure what to say.

"Word has it you've hooked up with Neil Thomas, isn't that right?" she fished.

Man, the rumour mill was working overtime. I wondered if they'd moved us in together yet. And had I decided it *was* Neil over Riley yet? Or Riley over Neil? Both men made my heart flutter and my knees go funny when they came into a room. Was there a statute of time on choosing? According to my barracuda part-timer, there was and my time was up.

"Sure, I can do that. Next time I see Riley, I'll make sure he gets your number."

As if!

"Oh, and thanks for the tip on this new crew 'to do'. There's four of them, five if you count the boss."

"He has a girlfriend," I informed her.

"So? I don't want to *marry* the guy! Sheesh."

Crap.

Lana had me beat hands down and four cup sizes up. She was a cute little bleached blonde, with perky body parts that stuck out in all the right places. She was always on deck with full make-up, Pamela Anderson eyelashes and big pouty lips. Men got whiplash when they walked by her.

"Good then," said Lana. "See you at one. Don't be late. I have a dress fitting at Mauvery's at one-fifteen."

Oh wow! How did she manage that? Mauvery Flintlock rated right up there with the best hair colourist in town when trying to get an appointment. It was impossible unless you were God, had personally talked to God or went to Mauvery's church. Which we didn't. Yet. I had considered joining last year in desperation when I blew out the zipper in my favourite jeans. It had been a bad week and one row too many of cookies.

Lana could at least sew on buttons, where I was hospital-ized for multiple puncture wounds and a blood transfusion if I even approached a sewing kit. Never mind hemming a pair of pants. If Lana had an appointment with Mauvery, I would be there for her! Maybe she would put in a good word for me?

At this point, that meant more to me than any issues over the men in my life.

I raced home after work and tore my closet to shreds. By 6:45 there was a Mt. Everest of clothes hurtled on my bed, which I collected and stuffed onto my closet floor before shutting the door. I'd deal with the mess tomorrow.

I decided on the backless emerald green dress that Mini insisted I buy because it matched my eyes. Not to mention the cut dropped 10 pounds from my waist and the bra shelf assisted my "girls" to stay in the proper area of my body while riding free. Without that shelf, there would be a few extra lumps floating around in some pretty unnatural places on my torso.

The above-knee hemline showed I still had pretty good legs. I managed to find a pair of nylons with only a small hole in the toe that I repaired with clear nail polish.

Wobbling in a dusty pair of extra-high black heels, I checked the mess looking back at me from the bathroom mirror. It got scarier the closer I got to that dirty "F" word of forty. My face looked square with the flat hair. I rolled in some hot curlers and skimmed some eyeliner and brown eye shadow on and then tried to outline my lips with a shade pencil. I rubbed it off. I looked like I'd been stung by a bee. I ran the lipstick around my lips and brushed some mascara onto my long lashes.

After pulling out the curlers and hair spraying myself almost to affixation, I smiled for the first time at the woman looking back. I was a stunning peacock in full plumage!

I finished with a blob of clear lip gloss that tasted oddly of bacon. Wendy, I thought, and smiled. Then I started to sniffle. God – *gosh,* I corrected – I missed those two.

It took a minute before I managed to straighten up and mop the fresh tears. I reminded myself I could still apply for sole custody. I could show Billy that he couldn't act like an irresponsible human being. That he couldn't just swoop in and steal the children away like this. Surely a judge would see the truth in our situation? This was a temporary thing, I told myself. The kids were merely vacationing with Billy, and if karma was real, the damned dipshit would choke on a burger and the kids would be calling me soon for a ride home.

I gladly tossed a twoonie into the Swear Jar on top of the fridge on my way out the door.

CHAPTER SEVEN

I had never seen the PV restaurant so busy. The parking area was jammed and I had to park Patches so far from the door that I lost sight of the entrance. Old Mr. Wringer was hobbling toward me and witnessed my half somersault from a patch of ice. The resulting flash of my underwear got me a toothy grin and a tip of his ball cap.

Riley was standing just outside the double doors that went into the dining part of the restaurant. His black hair was neatly combed to the side and his beige suede sweater had a fresh line running down the centre like it had been recently washed and folded.

His eyes bugged in his head as I came toward him. Was I still flashing? I quickly ran my hands around my torso, but everything seemed to be in all the right places.

We said awkward hellos and exchanged quick polite pecks on the cheek. Well, mine was quick. His lasted way longer, before he opened the door and ushered me in. By that time my knees were weak. If I had known he would nuzzle me like that I would have worn something more solid. Like a mattress on my back.

I started to make my usual beeline straight to the back where the upper level and fireplace were but quickly stopped. All the tables on top had been pulled together horseshoe-style for a meeting of about 30 people. It often happened in our small town. Weekday dinner meetings, so you didn't have to rent a hall to gather in.

My neighbor Sharon, in the capacity of mayor, appeared to be running the show from the centre table. To her far left was Mini, who was waving at me like a windmill. I gave her the Queen's nod and excused myself for a minute from Riley's company, climbing the three stairs to her table. I noticed Judy Charlie's mother and grandparents and gave them a quick heartfelt squeeze of the hand as I passed. The rest of the people I didn't recognize. Most of them were natives and it looked like they were from out of town. As I said, we could recognize people from "away" pretty quick.

I nodded at Sharon, who was welcoming everyone at her adjoining tables to the meeting, before I knelt beside Mini's chair.

"What's up?" I asked.

"I was supposed to call you and tell you about this meeting," whispered Mini. "But I knew you 'ad a passionate date and didn't want to spoil your chance at getting laid."

Some whisper. Everyone at her table turned to see whom I had lined up to do the dirty dance with. Riley was still standing down below, looking innocently around for a table. It was suddenly very warm in the restaurant.

A loud buzz of chatter started. I couldn't hear what Sharon was saying anymore. I saw our mayor look around to see what had gotten everyone's attention. She bent her ear down to her husband, Tim, who sat beside her.

"Kathy is planning to do that new guy tonight," he told her, pointing down at Riley.

Sheesh – why not get a megaphone!

Mini continued, "It's a Missing Women meeting. We're going to 'ear from the investigator the families bought on more we can do to discover Judy. They're saying unofficially it was not her body found on our property. It was someone else! But that's not confirmed."

She whirled a pen around her pudgy fingers. "Kenneth 'ad to go out so I came in your place. That way you can concentrate on your evening. I'm taking notes and will fill you in on all the details first thing tomorrow, *mon cherie*."

The recent victim had not been Judy! What a relief, I thought, while still feeling terrible for the young woman and her family. Who was she?

I thanked Mini, gave Tim an exasperated glare and headed back down to where Riley was waiting. I would have loved to sit in on the meeting. If Mini had given me the choice, I would have met Riley another time. But she had obviously known that and taken the decision out of my hands for a reason. I really did need some action in my underwear. Guess it wasn't a secret any longer. Five years was a long time ago and a whole other story. (The two years after I'd left Billy was an adventure best left for another time.)

And of course I could wait longer. If I had to. But things had been going so well in my favour lately. One could only hope.

I didn't begrudge the people at the meeting their place around the fireplace, but it sure deflated my romantic feelings. *Or are they even romantic?* I asked myself. Maybe this was simply lust at work here? I glanced nervously around my shoulders. And could everyone tell? We were getting a lot of looks.

Riley and I seated ourselves on the lower floor level by the window at one of the last two tables available. I told him what Mini had said about Judy. He patted my hand, gave me a polite smile and said it was wonderful news. Then he hid behind his menu.

Why did I get the distinct feeling he already knew? But how? I worked in the mall, chinwag central, for Cripe's sake. If anyone knew it would have been me.

Still, good news made me hungry and I was already starving, so I brushed my silly idea aside and opened the menu. Because Riley insisted on treating, it was a toss-up between the sole or steak. On my dime, it would have been between grilled cheese and a side salad.

I was about to ask Riley what he was ordering when the bell over the restaurant's back door clanged. In slinked Lana, a white faux fox draped around her neck, and Neil Thomas draped across her shoulders.

I must have looked gob-smacked because Riley reached over and gently pushed my chin up to close my mouth.

What was she doing here with Neil? Hadn't she just asked me to give *Riley* her number? Didn't she say that I was supposedly an item with Neil? What was this? They were both dressed up so it had to be a date. I mean, why else would they be here together?

I looked away, then immediately looked back. Oh crap. They were headed right for our table. I thought of ducking, but twice under a table that Riley was seated at might convince the rest of town that the rumours from Happy Mac's had been true. I held the menu up high enough to cover my face and closed my eyes.

"Well, look who we have here," trilled Lana in her loudest "everyone notice me yet?" voice. "Hi, Katherine." She looked over at Riley. "And here's that handsome young *crusher man* that came looking for you. I think it's time we were properly introduced."

Lana held out her hand to Riley like she was Scarlett O'Hara and expected it to be kissed. "Lana Bowles. At your service." She dipped forward, further exposing two bulbous mounds ready to pop from the top of her dress.

From the look on Riley's face, he could see right down to her netherworld. Sheesh.

"Riley Wells," he said, standing up and shaking her hand. "Pleased again." He 100-watted her.

Beam up the chopped liver there, Scotty. Get me out of my misery.

Meanwhile, Neil nodded in my direction, a curt "Kathy" on his lips as he wandered over to the centre of the room to take the last table. He seated himself with his back to us.

Lana finally quit fussing and dipping and gesticulating for Riley and then turned on her heel, walking very slowly, swinging her butt like a pendulum toward the table Neil had taken for them.

It was very distracting trying to eat and pay attention to Riley while trying discreetly to watch what was happening at the other table. For me and everyone else in the restaurant. Lana acted like fresh nectar, pouring herself all over Neil. She had dragged her chair so that she sat almost on top of him, her thick thigh half on top of his. I wanted to shout, "Get a room," but then I didn't want to seem like I cared. Because I sure didn't. If Neil wanted to boink a phony, promiscuous *girl* barely older than his daughter, then he could just get right at it. But don't come around looking for attention with gifts of Louisiana subs anymore. Men! They were so infuriating. I crossed my arms.

As for my date, all Riley seemed interested in was Billy. He asked about his previous jobs, people we knew, places we'd lived. He inquired three times, only in different ways, if I had heard from him. He said their boss, Ferdie, was frantic.

"So, hire somebody else. Trust me, Billy *can* be replaced," I said rather haughtily.

"I think the problem is he's the only one trained for the tower job, plus he took a special course on maintenance and the crusher is overdue."

I had no answer to that, but I didn't want to sit talking about my ex-husband with someone I considered a potential candidate for things my ex-husband used to do to me. If you get what I mean?

I said no to dessert and Riley left to pay the bill while I watched Lana tying a knot in her cherry stem with her tongue. There was more than one sigh across the room when she pulled the successful task from her mouth.

I couldn't leave soon enough. When Riley returned, I stood, grabbed my purse and stormed past Neil and Lana.

"Don't be late opening the store tomorrow, Lana," was all I could think of to say. Then I added, "Or I'll be late for you. Remember your fitting!" I was happy to see a cloud cross her face.

I glanced up to give Mini a farewell wave, but she seemed intent on listening to the man who was speaking to their group. I made a mental note to call her for details first thing in the morning.

Riley and I drove back to my place where a bottle of white wine was chilling in the fridge. Going to his place was obviously out of the question so I had prepared.

He did say he had seen the stereo equipment piled in his living room after work yesterday and had taken the time to put it together himself. Snake and Gweek hadn't said anything about anything. Not even thanks.

I asked him about all the stuffed animals and the boa.

"You mean Crunch? Yeh, that's a bit creepy, I must admit."

"Crunch?"

"Yeh. Terry feeds it rats and watches it crush them before it eats them. Pretty twisted."

"So why do you stay there?"

Riley shifted on the sofa, his gaze taking in the pulled front drapes. "I have my reasons. It hopefully won't be for much longer." He brushed his fingers across the top of the backless area of my dress. Things inside the bra shelf fired straight out at attention. Alert! Alert!

My full wine glass slipped from my fingers, spilling on the carpet. I bounced off the couch like a kangaroo for a paper towel. I felt so awkward. It had been a long time since anyone had touched me like that. But nervous or not, I was determined to get on with it. This was like falling off a bike, right? I simply needed to get back on and ride.

Except that this rider didn't look the same with her clothes off as she did with them on. Once that bra shelf slipped, things kind of went where they wanted to. There was a muffin top that would make the donut shop proud ringing around my waist. How was I supposed to ride "a bike" while holding everything in place? Maybe I could push stuff up and out while hiding the roll with my elbows at the same time? Or maybe I should get smart and ditch the lights after I got the wine mess cleaned up? That thought cheered me up.

Riley was on the floor ready to help. He mopped everything by himself. Okay, that could be fun. It had been light years since I'd had a rug burn.

I got on the floor beside him just as he stood. He tossed back his own glass of wine with a "glook" sound, pretended to yawn and headed toward the door.

I did an amazingly fast armpit sniff while his back was turned. Did I miss something?

I didn't walk to the door with him. I just stood there. Stunned. Crazy. Ready, although things inside my dress were returning to normal state.

"I can't believe I'm so tired," he said, his beefy biceps flexing behind his head as he stretched. "But I'm up at two, work from three to three and only power napped for a few hours so I could take you to dinner."

My grin was frozen to my face. "I understand. Gee, you must be exhausted. Well, thanks for dinner, then."

He threw me a wink, blew me a kiss with his hand and stepped out into the brisk night, giving me a clear shot of his delectable butt as he went. My nipples didn't even bother to respond. They were in as much shock as the rest of me. Talk about your crossed signals.

I went to the door to lock it and noticed a black van parked right across the street. I'd seen it before but wasn't sure from where. It had a grey-coloured decal around the middle and there was a light glowing from inside, like from a pen light or something.

I never gave it another thought, busy inspecting my breath to see if maybe that had been the problem.

After double-checking I had locked the door, I went through the house one room at a time to make sure there were no surprises waiting. I realized Sebastian hadn't had any recent premonitions and the choking because of a snake had come and gone (I hoped, unless someone was still going to feed a giant boa through the outside vent into my dryer. Note to self: skip laundry for now). But one could never be too careful, especially in light of my recent troubles.

Before I went to bed, I again checked the kids' room, taking a big sniff of the stale air. A scent drifted to me of dirty socks and old chewing gum and rubber and plastic and sweet, cuddly, warm bodies that I missed more than anything in the world. I wiped away a tear and crawled alone into bed.

I woke up to a sunny but cool day. It was +12C, not as frigid as last week, and chances were the bouts of snow had ended. It was the fifth season of the year, called "Muck," a phenomenon we had to endure for a solid month. I would say 50 percent of women shoppers at the Super Price were in rubber boots with a half-pound of dried mud on them. Great exercise. It was like walking with weights on. Good for the butt muscles, I'd been told.

I rolled out of bed, having had enough of the tossing and turning all night. I kept seeing snakes wrapping themselves around me as I tried in vain to reach out for Wendy and Warren. The more I reached, the more snakes that wound round my legs and down my arms.

The creepy-crawly feeling persisted even after having scrubbed my appendages until they hurt during an extremely long hot shower.

My usual breakfast of oatmeal, raisins, sunflower seeds and skim milk kept me full until lunch, when I often defeated all that goodness by having something stupid like fifteen cookies (a full row). I'd then spend the rest of the afternoon trying to talk myself out of the next rows. Which never happened. Today I got smart and made myself a sandwich. With the kids gone, I was afraid all the new food in the fridge would spoil. So it was an apple sip box, a ham, pickle and lettuce sandwich, four Fig Newtons (unfortunately raspberry and not chocolate), two cheese sticks with a chunk of pepperoni and a banana. I pictured Wendy and Warren saying, "right-eous" and high-fiving each other over such a lunch. It was enough to make me cry again.

Mini called as I washed off the counter, reminding me of last night's meeting that I'd missed.

"Feeling fulfilled this morning?" she chirped.

Sheesh. Why was a single person's love life of such inter-est? I kicked myself. That wasn't fair. Mini was a good friend. Of course she was interested if I'd had a hot romp.

"Nope, it's still an empty nest here, on all accounts."

Okay, I forgot, Mini sucked at word games. "Nothing happened. I'm still desperate, chaste and pure. Well, as pure as a single mother can be at this stage of her life."

"What did you do?" she asked. "Or not do?"

"It wasn't a case of either. He came in for some wine and then he got tired and left."

"Oh, so you did tire him out first."

"No, not that kind of tired, Mini. He was tired, tired."

"Around a lusting, needy woman 'e 'ad bought dinner for? I don't get it, 'e couldn't twist this if he tried. It doesn't add."

"Well, it doesn't and he did. But I don't care. I have other things to worry about. So tell me more about the meeting last night."

"That's why I called. It was quite explaining. Sharon promised to be useful as mayor for the case and the local government peoples promised as useful from Ottawa. So they are going to widen the search for Judy. They 'aven't given up that she is alive. The investigator is convinced the bad man keep the girls for an expanded time before he kills them. If that's the case, we just 'ave to find where 'e 'as 'er invisible."

"I think you mean hidden," I said absentmindedly, being happy to hear some positive news. It was the first piece of hopeful information since Judy had gone missing. I crossed my fingers and said a quick silent plea for her. *Keep her alive.*

"When can I help?" I asked.

"Most of the searches are in the daylight, and you're working then. But you can 'elp by keeping me company in the evenings while I make soup and squares for the volunteers that are out in the woods calling Judy's name. They're not leaving any bush or stone unshaken. They're going to find 'er, Kathy. I 'ave a good feeling about this, and so does Sebastian. Yesterday 'e showed me an abandoned camera with an unloaded pickup camera standing by itself. I didn't see anyone or 'ear anything. There was no river or lake that I could see, only the camper and a number fourteen."

"Camera? You mean camper? A campground?"

"Yeah, that's it!"

"Holy crap, Mini! That's huge news. Have you told the police about this vision?"

"I did, but you know how much they love 'earing from me. I'd 'ave a better chance of getting somewhere with that reporter 'attie Deckland."

I perked up. "That's not a bad idea, Mini! If you get the media on board, calls might come in about anyone having spotted an abandoned camper in a campground somewhere. It's worth a try!"

"You might be right," Mini told me. "I'll call 'attie this morning. Oh *merde*," she said. "I might end up on television. Quick – what pants do I own that don't make my derriere look like *un montagne*?"

"Oh, Mini. Your butt doesn't look like a mountainside; it's more like wild wilderness. Besides, why would they be filming your butt?"

"You're right," she laughed. "Okay, what could I wear that doesn't make my stomach look like . . ."

"Mini, for goodness' sake, make the call! It's for Judy. Quit worrying about what you look like!"

"You're right. I'm on it. Come over when you get ticks."

"Time," I auto-corrected. We hung up.

I packed my lunch into my cloth carry-all then picked up my purse from the floor and dug out my car keys. I hit the remote start as I reached for my coat, thinking the car didn't need a lot of time to warm up, when a huge *boom* filled my ears and the front picture window imploded into the living room. Once again bits of glass sprayed across my carpet. The piece of taped cardboard covering the previous hole hit the back of the living room wall. The glass half-moon on the front door also blew in and showered me from my butt to the top of my hair. Luckily I'd had my back turned to it.

Were we at war? Had another tree fallen and hit the house? Was there another brick?

I looked out of the new hole in my front door, feeling the cold breeze sting my warm cheeks, and saw a huge cloud of smoke coming from around what was left of my car. Patches, or something that might resemble her, had flames licking out from where the hood once sat. A huge cloud of billowing, pungent smoke rose up from the twisted metal, the smoldering seats and tires. There didn't seem to be a windshield or any glass left where it should be. Heck, I couldn't even find a trunk or a steering wheel. Wait, what was that in the flower garden?

I opened the front door and took one step toward the stairs when another *kablam* blew out at me. I flew backwards into the house. I lay in the entranceway, both stunned and stinging. Holy Fuh-dgesicle. My car had blown up! Twice! My next thought was, *What if I had been in it?* My knees liquefied and when I tried to stand, I collapsed back down onto my floor. I sat there in a drooling-idiot mode until Sharon came running over.

"Holy crap, Kathy. What happened?" she hollered. What a good thing as my ears seemed to be stuffed with socks.

"I don't know. I pressed the start button on my car's remote and the next thing I knew it was raining glass and then the car was burning and then what was left of it . . . it blew up again!" I knew my voice was shrill but I could barely hear it, even in the narrow hallway.

Sharon helped me to a standing position and I felt the blood slowly return to my legs. I peered out again at what had been my car, our beloved Patches, now a scrap of burning metal. I gagged. I thought of the hundreds of times all of us rode around inside of that car. I turned and fled to the bathroom and emptied my stomach to the toilet.

Sharon stood in the bathroom doorway.

"I don't understand. Were you having problems with the car?" she asked.

"No," I managed as I wiped my mouth off with a sheet of toilet paper. "I'm having problems with some*one*."

This was a small, friendly town. The worst thing that happened here was finding your husband with his trousers
around his ankles in front of a man-eating babysitter. People
didn't threaten people here. They had sex with them. They
didn't throw snakes into your house and they sure as hell
didn't blow up your car!

A large gathering of Jewel Street's residents had surrounded the smoking vehicle and I could hear a fire truck already
wailing up the hill. I brushed the glass from my hair as best I
could and pulled out my toothbrush to redo my teeth. I
planned to get right up and into Corporal Andrew Currie's
face this time.

The corporal was all ears, giving what I had to say a chance
instead of brushing it off as a childish prank. It helped I had
the mayor standing beside me. Sharon wouldn't get the run-
around.

He said he had visited Murdoch, who denied knowledge
about a snake tied to a brick. Currie hung his head, making
me think he and Snake had shared a little laugh about the
crazy woman on Jewel Street.

"What an imagination," they would have said.

As if that wasn't already written on any file ever made on
me.

A few years back while dicing cooked chicken, I thought I
felt worms crawling on my hand. Without thinking, I tried
to flick them off with the sharp knife only to discover there
were no worms. By then two deep cuts into the flesh between my thumb and first finger gaped. Two quick little
flicks got me 25 stitches at the clinic, where eyebrows skyrocketed as I recounted what happened.

Everyone also remembered the hysterical mother that

rushed a younger Warren into the clinic, convinced he had serious internal bleeding. Turned out he'd eaten beets for dinner at a friend's house the night before.

Really, I was quite harmless. But now someone was out to harm me, which didn't make sense. Did Snake want to know where Billy was or not? How could I tell him if I were dead?

I told Currie about the black van that had been parked outside my house last night. I also said to check out my new mechanic, this Jackie Carmichael, who had been working on Patches recently. He would have had an opportunity to wire explosives under my car. Why he would have done that was anyone's guess, but he'd had dealings with Billy, so who knew? I left Currie with my remote starter and ignition key, which were now useless to me, and I left the house.

I was angry. Angrier than I'd been since I couldn't even remember, but I was sure the memory would have involved Billy. Someone had just tried to kill me. And what if they had succeeded? What would happen to Wendy and Warren? What was happening to Wendy and Warren right this minute?

Coming so close to death made you remember that life was too short. If I wanted changes in my life, it was high time I made them happen. It was time to walk the talk.

I marched to the courthouse, a brisk ten-minute venture downhill, which helped clear my head. And my ears.

Once in front of the clerk, I wrote a cheque for $106 to small claims court (there went the grocery money for next month) to collect the remaining $2500 Billy owed us. I didn't care anymore what he was going through personally or what he would do without money for a while. The kids and I had been down that road far too long ourselves.

The second service fee was to make an application to the court to vary the Order of Divorce. I was going for sole custody of our children. I'd had enough of Billy pirating them away and disrupting their lives. To heck with everything Billy had told me. It was time for *me* to grow up and take charge of my life and our kids' lives. Was I divorced from him or not? It was time to sever this cord all the way through.

It was an actual physical pain, though, as I wrote the second cheque out to the Crown for $300 (that I crossed my fingers would be accepted by the bank). The good news was this included the services of the sheriff's office, who would track down Billy like the dog that he was, and serve him papers demanding he get his butt into a courtroom to settle this once and for all. And while he was here, I could get the kids back and Snake would get Bill and quit trying to kill me. Everyone would be so bloody happy. Okay, wrong choice of words.

I walked over to the mall and popped my head in to say hello to Lana. Actually I wanted to see if she was hungover. She was looking vamped right out in stiletto heels and a clingy, semi-clear mini-dress that could have doubled for food wrap. I hoped Riley didn't come by while she was there, especially when she leaned over the counter the way she was doing to get the phone.

"It's for you," she sang, handing it over.

I put the receiver to my ear. "Tell meeeeeee," hissed the same voice I had heard the other night. I was sure I had listened to it over and over in my last dream as well. And I knew who it was.

"You don't scare me," I said not very convincingly. My teeth were chattering and my throat had gone as dry as the burned-out coffee pot I could smell roasting away in the back room. "You'd better watch yourself."

"You too and a little reminder, I don't work alone." He hung up.

Lana's face expected an answer. I was half tempted to tell

her it had been Riley. That he was actually a very bad guy and she should stay clear of him. But that was too mean, even for me in the mood I was in.

What I did say was, "Did you have a good time last night?"

Lana pulled her hands in and checked her fake nails. "Actually, no, I didn't. Which is funny because Neil was the one that called and invited me out, you know? I thought you two were like, an item. But he said you weren't."

I just stared at her. She seemed to be telling the truth.

"We had dinner and then he dropped me off at my place and left."

I still had no comment for her.

"I think he likes me, though. He let me order the lobster."

I let that hang for a second, hoping she might realize how ridiculous it sounded.

"Never mind, it doesn't matter," I said. "He's right, we're not an item. We're just friends. But there's something else, and you're not going to believe any of it," I started.

Lana pulled herself up on the counter and swung her legs.

I explained in great detail how my car had blown up in my driveway.

"Wow," was all she said as she blew a bubble with the gum in her mouth. "Sucks to be you." I was pretty sure she was being earnest. She plopped off the counter and looked at her fake Gucci watch.

"You only got twenty minutes and I'm outta here."

Oh right. Her fitting appointment. I would get no breaks for tough times today!

I gladly left her and the smell of burning coffee behind and ran across the hall to the insurance agency. That's the beauty of a small town. Practically one-stop shopping.

Veronica Sellers was the local agent for ICBC (Insurance Corporation of British Columbia). We used to work out at the same gym before the kids arrived and my workout became lifting diaper pails and cases of formula. She was as horrified as I'd been to hear my car had blown up and you could see her fingers itched to hit speed dial to all her friends with the news. That's the ugliness of a small town. Of course, she had to milk me of all the details first.

"Is your hair singed?" she asked. "It is! I can smell it! Look at your eyelashes!" Her face scrunched into a frown.

How bad did I look?

"Did anyone get hurt? Was there something wrong with your car? What did the police say? I heard Jackie Carmichael did some work for you. Is he being investigated?"

Why was she looking for more drama than the explosion? Hadn't it been enough? Sheesh!

After the third inquisition ended, we went over my insurance policy. Thankfully I was covered for what was left melting down in my driveway. It seemed when Billy had transferred the insurance from our last joint vehicle onto the "family car" he let the kids and me have, he hadn't realized he had paid for collision as well. (Apparently an explosion counted as a collision.) A "minor" deductible payment would get the windows and the clean-up paid for thanks to the bank's insistence on house insurance when I remortgaged. The deductible wouldn't have to be paid until after the repairs were completed. Maybe I would find a third job by then?

My mother entered my head. "You wouldn't have such large holes to crawl out of if you didn't dig them so deep." What would my parents have to say about this mess?

I mumbled silent thanks that they wouldn't have to know about it. I certainly wasn't going to tell them and I was fairly sure Ann wouldn't either.

After leaving Veronica I hurried over to the HEW to relieve Lana. Princess Lana had her coat on and was prancing at the door like a four-year-old desperate to pee.

"I might need you for a day or two next week, as well as on Friday," I told her. "Any problem with that?"

"Only if lover boy doesn't need me," she whipped at me as she sped out the door.

I stopped moving like I'd hit a wall. Whoa! Lover boy? How quick Lana's mind had jumped from "I think he likes me" to having a new pillow partner. Did Neil know what he'd gotten himself into? I couldn't stop myself from making a dagger-stabbing motion with my fist. Then I realized I must have missed something. Lover boy? So they MUST have done it! Neil had done the nasty with my home-kit-bleached employee. If he'd dropped her off right after dinner, then when did they have time? On the car ride from the restaurant to Lana's apartment? In the restaurant? Before the restaurant? I was starting to seethe.

Okay, so Lana *was* a friend of mine, but she was also nothing but a floozy when it came to men. Even she admitted that so I wasn't saying anything behind her back. Women aren't quite that bad. Okay, so maybe we are, but not to an employee you needed to spell you off. Okay, okay, at least not in your outside voice!

I pulled my coat off, opening my lunch bag and spilling the contents onto the counter.

What? I saw a note taped to the counter top that had Riley's name on it and a phone number. It was not addressed to me; no line at the top saying, "Riley was by. Please give him a call." It just said "Riley 845-5192." Must be a cell phone number.

So Riley had been here after all. And given Lana his phone number. Fudge. It must have been that shiny cellophane dress she'd been wearing that got him. That man-stealing hump-o-matic. I envisioned the entire thing – Lana bent over this counter top while Riley slipped in behind her.

Eeewww. I grabbed my sandwich off of it.

This was a big bad day. I scooped up my lunch and piled it on a box marked Kenwood Amplifier (chances were they hadn't screwed on that!) before going to the back to wash my hands. I caught a look at myself in the mirror. Cripes! My hair *was* singed! My eyelashes were blunted black coal stubs and my bangs seemed a whole inch shorter, making me look slightly third-grade-ish.

This was a VERY, very, big, bad day.

CHAPTER EIGHT

I gobbled my sandwich, thinking it funny I should have an appetite after almost being detonated into charred chunks. Even the fact that Lana had scooped me with the two men in my life hadn't dulled my hunger. I didn't usually take rejection so well. But hey, wave food in front of me at the right time and I'll flatten you like a bug on a windshield.

Mini roared in looking especially agitated, her eyes bugging from her head. A trickle of perspiration ran from her brow.

She rattled off in French, her arms waving like thick fans. My hair lifted in the breeze.

My look of puzzlement made her realize her mistake and she tried again in English.

"Your car gets blown up and you 'aven't called me?" She marched up like she was going to slug me. "I've called everything trying to find you. Lana said you would be here now." Mini softened for a minute. "She says she got an appointment with Mauvery for a dress fitting."

You could hear the admiration for Lana in her voice.

I stood up from where I'd been half leaning on the counter.

NOT JUST ONE 121

"Sorry, Mini. I think I'm still in shock. My head is not on straight yet and I've only now had a chance to catch up to my butt that's still trying to go somewhere. But I think I managed to get everything I needed done. Except find that scallywaggart ex of mine."

"Oh, *mon Dieu!*" she burst out. "Look at your poor eyeflappers. Let me get my miracle bag."

"You mean make-up bag."

"No, I mean miracle bag! Your glow *au naturel* looks scary enough for 'alloween." She fished a cosmetics case larger than my purse from her over-shoulder satchel.

As Mini worked on my face with a pair of sewing scissors and her many magic wands, I filled her in on the car blast and the snake on the brick.

"You are *absolument* kidding me! A snake? And you were choking? That's just what Sebastian 'ad . . ."

"I know, I know. Sebastian was right. I'd been hoping he'd been wrong because he didn't see anything about money in my future and Billy handed over a big wad of it."

Mini ignored that. She seemed to be holding something back, which suddenly burst out of her mouth.

"You're on the news!"

My eyes went wide. "How could I be on the news? There weren't any cameras there when I left. No sign of Hattie Deckland or Steve Ducell."

"Well, you were. It was the big story on lunch hour and they showed your 'ouse with the windows absent, and then the wreckage smoulder and then a picture of you. It looked *plus vieux*, er . . . old, from the newspaper. You had a funny 'airstyle and you looked a lot 'eavier. Probably you were thick with a baby birding, *au possible*."

"Birthing," I corrected her, my heart not in it. And crap, I remembered that picture. I had been embarrassed for months after the newspaper had printed it years ago. I had been sitting in a water-dunking tank for the kids' daycare fundraiser. The picture had been taken right after Warren hit the big round button with a softball for the fifth time in a row. The pin beneath my seat had released and down I went, again. I was dragging myself wearily back up to the seat while looking like I wanted to kill my own son. My hair was spiked like a natural tomahawk and there were dark circles of mascara under my eyes. My soggy jogging pants balled and bunched around my waist so I looked huge. And no, I had not been pregnant.

Aaarrrgghhh. Any picture but that one. Was there no justice in life? I imagined all the people in town who would laugh at it.

Neil Thomas.

Riley Wells.

And worse, Lana and Linda.

Damn.

I wasn't home for two minutes when the phone rang. I rushed to catch it, hoping it was the kids, so I was doubly slammed when I lifted the receiver to hear:

"Kathy Leigh Griffon! What in the blue blazes have you got yourself into this time?"

There was no doubt it was my mother and there was no doubt she wouldn't pause for me to answer. Without thought, I lowered my head and studied my shoes. An old habit from my high school days when being lectured on what time a respectful girl *should* be getting in on a Saturday night.

The receiver vibrated in my hand. "I can't BELIEVE I had to watch my daughter's picture, which by the way is a TERRIBLE picture, on our very own news station. Isn't there enough bad news in the world without you adding to it? And why didn't you tell us you were pregnant? You know you can tell Dad and me anything. To have to find out like this! The entire city of Appleton has called to say . . . isn't that? . . . and what is she up to now? . . . to which I had to answer you're DIVORCED and now PREGNANT by God-knows-who and add to that your car has been blown to SMITH-EREENS and . . ." Her voice trailed off. I heard hiccoughing and then my dad's voice came on the line.

"Here, Helen. Use the paper bag again." Then into the receiver he said, "We're on our way, kiddo. Sounds like you could use some rescuing. Got the luggage all packed and we land in Spencer on Sunday night at seven thirty. Can you come and pick us up?"

I stared into the phone. They were coming? And hadn't they just seen my car had blown up?

My mother, Helen Griffon, was a four-foot modern-day David. Her Goliath was my father, six-foot-three Reginald, or Regi as he preferred, Archer Griffon. I'd always figured my brother, sister and I had been adopted because there was no anatomical way my parents could do what the Encyclopedia Britannica said they had to do to have children. At least not while standing like the naked people in the book were.

My mom spent most of her time babysitting our dad, her "oldest child," who recently lost his tire shop in downtown Appleton, New Brunswick. I say lost because he didn't sell it and he didn't retire from it. One day it just belonged to someone else. My friends back east say there was a card game involved, which was more than I could ever get out of my mother on the subject.

Regi was a poster child for attention deficit disorder. He had the patience of a four-year-old, thought stop signs and red lights were suggestions and as legend went, took a chain saw to a wall in his motel room to make "adjoining rooms" for him and his hunting buddies.

My father once called me "nosy" after I found magazines
with naked pictures under his sofa chair. He said that children like me were often found abandoned.

This was the man coming to my "rescue."

"Don't come, you guys. Really, I'm okay. It was nothing."

"Nothing," my mother wailed from the background,
"nothing is when you trip and stub your toe or you lose your
snow boots on the way home from school."

"That wasn't me! That was Ann!"

My mother came back on the line. I pictured her grabbing
the phone right out of Dad's hand. "Don't tell me what I do
and don't remember, young lady. It was you because they
had white pom-poms on them and you howled for a god-
damned hour in the Levine's boot shop until I bought
them."

Good memory, Mom. Too bad you didn't also remember
that Ann got all my hand-me-downs, not that there was
much left of them from a snow-climbing toboggan racer that
used her boots as brakes.

"I'll find a vehicle," I managed, "and I'll be there to pick
you up. Have a nice flight. Oh, and Dad, you can't pack
your own booze on board anymore. There's a liquid ban so
you'll have to buy them from the little cart when it goes by."

"Well, we'll just see about that!" he said and then disconnected.

My father hated being in closed spaces for too long. With
three flights and nine hours of flying to get across Canada to
the Spencer airport, I wondered what condition he was going
to arrive in. I pictured him being led off the plane in handcuffs. It was all too possible.

I let out a huge, rattling groan.

◆ ❖ ◆

It was Saturday and usually Lana worked so I could have the weekend off. I phoned her and said I'd changed my mind. I would work the shift in case I had to appear in court later or run off and rescue my kids or possibly be committed when my parents drove me insane. I was paid the same either way but I didn't want to overextend my luck with getting Lana in to cover a shift.

I couldn't believe Mom and Dad were coming all the way across the country when it wasn't even Christmas and no one had died. Yet. I cursed myself for the thought.

Could things get any worse?

I walked to the mall, planning on checking out the car dealership at the other end of town after work. I would need to find something as soon as possible. I looked for Neil for our usual wave exchange – not that I was going to give him the usual wave but was merely seeing if he was going to give me one – but he wasn't there. His truck wasn't in the District parking lot, either. I checked my watch. Ten to nine; he was either running late or had taken the day off. Maybe Lana had been too much for him and he was recuperating? Or they had both taken the day off and were shacked up somewhere.

I tsked in disgust. At him, not Lana. It wasn't Lana's fault. Lana was perpetually in heat. A born bitch with a natural thrumming motion built into her walk. It drove men nuts.

I walked to the *Halston Today* offices on the second floor of the mall and picked up my first pay cheque for the advertising. I kissed the thin piece of paper that said "Pay to Kathy Sands $550"! I headed back downstairs to the east end of the mall where the ATM was. The bank machine gobbled the cheque from my sight faster than I could have spent it. That was a joke because as soon as I hit the deposit button, that money *was* spent. Nice handling you for seven minutes.

The first order of business at the HEW was to sell myself a

call-display telephone. Thankfully my credit card was good for another few purchases. I then called Telus and forked out for their telephone package that included the call-display service. I winced at the price, but it was necessary. I wanted to be ready in case Billy or the kids called again.

The store got surprisingly busy, but I figured a lot of the traffic was due to my car being blown up. Everyone in town wanted to know more about it. Or at least get a look at my singed hair and lashes. Mini had cleaned me up but she could only do so much.

No one I asked seemed to know anything about this Snake fellow though, or noticed his house on Heritage Street. Being out of the way like that, not everyone would have had a chance to walk by or been terrorized by Prince leering at them through the gate like they were souvlaki-on-two-sticks.

After three hours of being grilled, sometimes by people I didn't know, I started getting fed up. At least pretend you're here to shop, people!

I was a celebrity that would remain on the hot seat until the gossip-grapevine found someone else to take the heat. That wasn't usually hard in a small town. My misfortune had let an accounting firm being sued over an $800,000 embezzlement charge off the hook. Without any thanks from them, they were out of the limelight! What I had to hope for now was someone's gambling addiction or steamy affair to be discovered.

I thought of Kenneth's unexplained disappearances and shut my mental trap.

The sheriff's office called. They had traced Billy's social insurance number and were finding no sign of employment anywhere in British Columbia. They were going to broaden the search nationally. I gave that about as much hope as I did miraculously waking up ten pounds lighter. It just wasn't gonna happen. Billy's first choice was to work under the table. He hated paying taxes. And obviously child support.

I told the sheriff to check with my ex-husband's ex-girlfriend Linda, the appendage-attachment. Maybe she'd heard from Billy? The man had no scruples when asking for space on someone's couch or for a "temporary" loan. Not that you'd ever get paid back in money. You would end up with a broken-down 20-year-old snowmobile on your front lawn one morning, or a free load of gravel that you did not want in your driveway. But . . . everyone always fell for his earnestness the first time. Luckier ones fell off of anthills while some of us fell from so high up, we should have had parachutes.

The sheriff said he'd be in touch if he received any news.

It was disappointing and a slow process, but I still figured hiring the sheriff was the best $100 I'd ever spent. He was actively pursuing Billy – and therefore where my children were – on my behalf, while I could concentrate on my jobs. It made me feel less guilty for not doing what I really felt I should do. Quit work and try and find those kids myself and bring them back to their friends and their school. But deep down, I knew quitting work would send us nowhere but backward. How could I afford to keep my children with me if I didn't have a job? It was a vicious circle.

I wished the sheriff luck and meant it.

The day got better. I was on one of those natural selling highs where I could have sold steak to a vegetarian. The bread maker Mrs. Wilson was eyeing up was exactly like mine. So I mentioned I would throw in my best recipes if she bought it. Sold. If Henk bought two more CDs to add to the five he had in his hand, I would throw in a free one. He grabbed 16. It felt good and the time melted away. I did feel horrible after joking to one elderly couple the microwave they were eyeballing could do everything but empty their garbage can. After they bought it, I thought I heard her say something about washing laundry in it.

Right before closing, Mini called and in a breathless voice demanded I drop everything and change the usual satellite channel over to the local news.

While running to the remote control, the phone still attached to my ear, she asked if I'd seen Kenneth. Was he in the mall? Had he been by to say hello?

"No, haven't seen him lately," I answered. "I can call you if I see him."

She said to not "border" (bother?) and reminded me to watch the news.

We hung up and with remote in hand, I walked over to our wall of televisions on display.

At first I thought she wanted me to see how bad I looked on television. I figured they were still running the story about my car being blown to pieces. But it wasn't about me.

The televisions were all set to watch a movie played through one central DVD player. It showed truer colours that way. But we were also hooked up to satellite and at the push of a remote, the National News broadcaster began speaking from 26 different televisions. The man was commenting on a story about the Hells Dragons in Vancouver facing off with another gang from Washington State called the Banditos. Good, I thought. They could kill each other and save the taxpayers the money from the police having to do it. Maybe there would be fewer drugs on the street without those guys around to bring it in.

The gang news was followed by a story on the young woman's body being found in Halston. I turned up the volume and the four people shopping in the store stopped talking to listen.

A picture of our missing Judy flashed onto the screen. Had they found her? Was she alive? The report was coming from Hattie Deckland, who was once again talking in front of the Merkleys' back field where the body had been found.

The deceased woman had been officially identified as Kitty Tyson from Hazelton. Her high school picture appeared on the television screen. She was a cute, moon-faced girl of 16, last seen almost a year ago hitchhiking to Tessak. Her tearful parents came on begging for tips or more information.

My heart bled for them. I shook my head in despair. What they must be going through! At least they now had some form of closure. The Charlies were still in their hell of worrying and hoping. Was Judy alive? Was she dead? Every second of every waking hour went to waiting for any new clues.

I hoped this meant the search for Judy would be vigorously renewed. Where was she? What reason could there be for no one having heard from her for so long? She was not a runaway. Was she buried in her own shallow grave somewhere? After this much time, I couldn't help but think the worst. Tears slid down my face.

It seemed I was not alone. Hattie continued by saying the RCMP would be combing the Merkleys' grounds for any more signs of "foul play" regarding this incident or the disappearance of Judy Charlie.

The camera switched pictures and there was Mini, looking wooden and robotic. She was standing behind her recliner chair in her living room so all you could see was her head and neck.

Hattie's voice introduced her as a local "psychic" with breaking information on Judy's whereabouts:

"I think she's been kidnapped and is in a camera in an abandoned camera-ground somewhere. You must discover her."

The picture panned back to a puzzled-looking Hattie, who added, "Ah . . . I think you mean 'in a camper in an abandoned campground.'" Hattie finished the piece by adding Judy was last seen getting into the pickup truck of another local. Police were now looking for and asking the public's help with finding — and here they flashed a picture of my ex-husband on the screen — "Billy Sands."

I tried to call Mini back, but the line was busy.

The fresh air that hit my face after work at 6:15 lifted my spirits somewhat. The days were definitely getting longer now we were headed the right way toward the summer solstice. The sun was still above the tree line as I headed to the sole car dealership at the edge of town.

All I could think of was Judy and Billy and how I had to talk to my ex right away. He could probably clear this up with a phone call. Bill had said it wasn't him that picked Judy up at the 7-Heaven on Saturday morning. It must have been someone who looked like him. Surely he had a better alibi than "I was sleeping"?

I wondered if he had any idea the police were looking for him. Billy wouldn't hurt a fly, of that I was sure. Yes, he could torment the hell out of me, seemed even to enjoy doing it, but he had a heart as big as a room and would give anyone (but me after we separated) the shirt off his back. Sexually assaulting women? Kidnapping teenagers? Not even a slight chance! They were after the wrong person.

I had phoned ahead and talked to my friend Grace Tucker, a saleswoman at Franklin Motor Products, simply called Franklin's by everyone. Grace had been to a few of the merchant association meetings I had attended. After the first few glasses of wine, our hair came down and we fell into swapping a few man-horror stories. She was fun and likeable, and we became fast friends, so I trusted her enough to not only buy a vehicle from, but to use words like "desperate," "anything will do," "budget," and then "desperate" a second time in case she hadn't heard me the first time.

Grace had pulled a 1996 Dodge caravan around front of Franklin's for me to look at. I oohed and ahhed at all the cup holders – Wendy and Warren would be impressed. It smelled good and looked okay, having had a new paint job. Not the best paint job, either. The color looked unreal, like a sandpapery eggplantish shade. Very amateurish. I'd seen better paint-by-number work.

But it started right up and the few rust spots over the wheel wells didn't jiggle like I thought they might. We piled in and I took it for a test drive. It seemed to handle fine. I gulped at the mileage being 281,770 but Grace said this beauty had lots of life left in her. The passenger-side airbag didn't work. It was a minor drawback, but a livable, affordable (wink) one. It had been in a little, wee accident, Grace said, but who needed an extra airbag? "Totally overrated," she told me. I highly doubted that, but for the price, it was something I could overlook for now.

As a good friend she was even going to throw in some new floor mats to cover the wine-stained driver-side carpets. All I could think of was having something to pick up my parents in the next night, so we shook hands and went in to sign the papers and transfer the insurance over from Patches.

Once inside my new wheels, I felt a little better. I was mobile again, and although I wasn't going anywhere but to an empty home, it still felt like I was moving forward positively.

My driveway had millions of charred, peeled paint bits stuck into the muddy earth beneath. The auto wreckers had removed the blown and twisted carcass of our beloved four-door friend. I sighed a gloomy farewell, knowing it was headed to a metal scrap heap. Hey, maybe we would get it back one day as part of a can opener or a corkscrew. The thought made me smile; a luxury lately.

I went into the house, which had a new door and front window already and walked straight to the kids' room. I opened their door and took a deep breath, then closed it again. I wanted to try and preserve their life force that still reverberated between the walls. I sure missed those two. The house felt so lifeless.

I unboxed my new call display phone and plugged it in. I pulled a glass from the cupboard and poured some water from a jug in the fridge, then jumped about a foot when the doorbell rang. No one ever used the doorbell. I opened the door to see Riley in all his hotness standing before me, a bottle of Maple's in his hand.

Oh-oh. How did he know?

Maple's Irish Cream happened to be at the root of many of my worst memories. Or lack of memories to be more precise. It was the quickest route to removing my inhibitions, my cares and my panties. It took only a third of the bottle for me to wonder why I needed to wear *any* clothes.

But damn, I was thirsty.

I couldn't tell you all the details of what happened next because I don't really remember, but suffice to say that when I woke at 6:30 in the morning there was an almost empty bottle of Maple's on the nightstand and a trail of my clothes that led from the living room to my bedroom. The window above my head appeared to be steaming. Riley was nowhere to be seen, but the pillow beside me was still depressed and a pair of men's boots were at the foot of the bed. I figured he hadn't gone far.

I hugged my naked self beneath the sheet. I wasn't feeling so lonely at that moment. I was feeling pretty darned won-

derful, actually. Had I really kept up with a 31-year-old? Did
I hear birds singing somewhere?

I licked my dry lips. It felt like there had been a sandstorm
in my mouth overnight and I needed a glass of water. I
pushed back the sheet and padded *au naturel* down the hallway. On my way to the fridge, I had to pass the tiny cubicle
that doubled as an office and there stood fully clothed Riley
rifling through my filing cabinet!

"What the HECK?" Wait. Was that my outside voice?

Riley whirled to face me, snapping shut the drawer
marked "Family" he had been pilfering through, his face
looking as surprised as mine must have.

"Good morning. How are you feeling?"

"Surprised," was all I could manage.

"I can explain about your clothes in the hallway," he said,
stepping away from the cabinet, trying unsuccessfully to keep
his gaze at my eyes. "You wouldn't keep them on even when
I insisted. Nothing happened between us last night."

My heart fell. What? I hadn't had sex with this man?
What was wrong with me? I glanced down and seeing nothing too grotesque, looked back up. Better yet, what was
wrong with *him*?

"I stayed with you as you kept repeating how lonely you
were. I didn't think you should be left alone in the condition
you were in. I'm in here looking for something to read," he
said. "I couldn't sleep."

I pointed to the overflowing bookshelf behind him. "And
none of that would have worked?"

He sighed like he had been beaten at a game. "I want to
help find Billy for you. He must owe you money for support
or whatever for those kids? And I was hoping to find out
more about him in here, maybe find a few clues of where he
might be."

I didn't know what to think because the letters GUILTY

were stamped right across his forehead. That drawer held all
the legal papers I kept of my life with Billy. The marriage and
divorce certificates, car insurance photocopies, and pages of
notes I had recorded about all the crazy things Billy had done
over the years. What was Riley talking about? And how
would he know Bill owed us money? I had never mentioned
it to him.

"Get away from that cabinet," I told him, my voice icy
clear. "Get your boots and get out of here. Now." My em-
barrassment at not being good enough for him to have taken
advantage of me took control. I had wanted to be taken advantage of. Now I was feeling stupid. Old. Naked.

My parents always told me I was a quick draw with the
rose-coloured glasses. Someone please shoot me!

CHAPTER NINE

Ten minutes later, I watched Riley's lean frame climb aboard the Harley. Seeing his leg swing up and over the saddle like that still made my stomach flutter. I was a sick woman.

The flaming snake on the gas tank glowed slightly in the hazy morning light and I waited in my doorway as he rode out of sight. He never looked back.

I went in and made a huge pot of coffee and decided to help myself to some of the eggs in the fridge. I couldn't remember the last time I had felt like cooking breakfast. It was seven o'clock and I was famished. I held the bathrobe tighter around me, and as I reached across the frying pan there was a knock on my door. I grinned, figuring Riley had returned to apologize. I was irresistible and he was going to come in and . . .

I opened the door with my housecoat slightly ajar, trying to look my vampish best, to RCMP Sergeant Candace "Tart" Bartlett and the rookie cop Constable Joe Lyons beside her. Lyons' eyes almost dropped out of his head.

I grabbed my lapels shut and stammered out a questioning "Good morning, Officers?"

"Good morning, Kathy. We're here to ask you some questions about Billy Sands. Do you mind?" said Tart as she stepped her way past me into my hallway. Lyons blindly followed her.

Hey, what happened to the rule that RCMP had to be invited in? I hurried after them and scooped my socks and jeans off the carpet, wondering where my underwear was hiding. "Coffee, anyone?" I threw the clothes into my office and closed the door. Had they seen Riley leave?

"That would be great," came the reply. And without skipping a beat, "We know that your ex-husband Billy Sands has left Halston," Tart said, "but can you tell us where he went?"

The million-dollar question of the day. "What's he done now?" I said as innocently as possible from the kitchen as I poured out mugs of java. I returned to the living room with a tray of coffee and condiments to see Tart's raised eyebrow.

"What's he done before?" she asked.

I glared her down. "Nothing. And I have no idea where he is. I'm looking for him myself."

"Okay." Tart sniffed at her coffee and then put it down and added some sugar. "Do you know what time exactly that he left town?"

"No. It was on a Monday though. He took my daughter to her appointment with Dr. Keswick at eleven."

"And that was the last you heard from him?"

"No," I said slowly. "He phoned from wherever he is, but he wouldn't tell me where that was."

"And he has your children?" Lyons interjected. Tart gave him a scowl.

"We have joint custody, so yes, he took the kids."

"And you don't know where they are?" said Tart, her eyebrow once again raised.

I was slowly getting the point. Right. How could he get away with that? I was their mother, joint custody or not. Of course I should know where they were. It was all so maddening. But what chance did I have of laying down the law with this man until I got this court thing settled? And would a court be able to bend Billy Sands to do what was right for our children?

"Does he drive a white 2008 GMC club cab?" asked the younger cop.

I nodded my head. "With no tailgate."

"What is his shoe size?" asked Tart.

"His shoe size?"

"Footprints at the crime scene," blurted the rookie and Tart shot him a look that should have drawn blood.

"The crime scene?"

"We're investigating the death of Kitty Tyson."

I sucked in my breath. "And you're asking questions about Bill? Whatever for?"

Tart seemed to mull over what she was going to say but Lyons was quick to dish everything out. "A witness saw his truck leave the area near where the body was found. That was on the Saturday, the day Judy Charlie went missing."

I felt a chill creeping up and wished my visitors were gone.

"I think you're barking up the wrong tree."

"His shoe size?" repeated Tart.

"I don't remember."

"What sort of boot does he usually wear?"

"I couldn't tell you," I said, which was not quite a lie. Of course I knew, but I couldn't help an investigation into a murder rap against someone not capable of committing the crime. That meant the cops were on the wrong trail and someone out there was murdering these women. Possibly right under their noses here in Halston.

I changed the subject quickly to Terry Murdoch, aka Snake, and the threats against my life.

"It's all under investigation," said Tart.

I looked over at the rookie expectantly.

"Murdoch owns that black van you saw the night before your car was bombed." He was beaming at the good news he was able to give me.

I rewarded him back with a smile of my own. A connection between the bomb and Snake. Gotcha!

"It's all under investigation," Tart crossly reminded Lyons. "We can say nothing more."

Fine, be like that, Tart, but my confidence was already boosted.

After the officers left I went to my fridge door and quickly pulled off the photograph hung there with a magnet. It showed a two-year-old Wendy trying to stand up inside one of her daddy's size 11 brand new brown leather cowboy boots. The same ones he still wore.

It was all too much. I couldn't believe the mess that had whirlwinded around my ex-husband. Everyone was looking for him; me, the sheriff, Snake, Riley and now the cops – this time for Judy's disappearance and possibly for a murder!

I quickly showered and dressed before pouring a glass of juice and fishing through the phone desk for my address book. It was high time I got on the bandwagon and brought that sorry-assed excuse for a man back to this town, even if it took my every last can of soup in phone bills.

◆ ❖ ◆

I started my long-distance phone marathon with Billy's mother. Mrs. Carmen Sands lived in Ft. Laredo, Florida, in a small pensioner's shack with her sister Mildred.

Bill's father had passed away seven years ago and every truck driver between Prince Grange and Prince Ruden had attended the funeral. I had never seen so many people packed inside a church. Caleb Sands had been the friendliest, kindest man you had ever met. There were many elderly women openly sobbing beside his coffin. It must have been embarrassing for his wife, if you catch my drift?

When I called Carmen in Florida, she played dumb, not wanting to say anything at all about Billy. I asked where he was and she talked about the weather. I asked if she'd heard from her grandchildren and she told me her goldfish died last week. I finally wished her well and hung up.

I next tried Bill's sister Amanda again. We used to get along so well, I couldn't believe she wouldn't help me find the kids.

"What the hell do you *want*?" came a very angry huff.

"I'm trying to find Bill," I said as quickly as I could, fearing she would hang up again. "He has our kids and I need to talk to him. It's important!"

"Well, you should have thought about all that before you left him. Don't call me anymore."

My ear was ringing from the sound of her slamming down her phone again. What stories had Billy been filling her ear with? I could only imagine. Sigh.

I went to the kitchen and poured the last dregs of the coffee pot into a cup and then zapped it in my microwave. I got the almost empty bottle of Maple's from the bedroom and tried to encourage the last drops down into my mug. I stuck my tongue in the bottle's neck. Cripes, I was pitiful. I forced myself back onto the couch and made the next call.

I had a bit more luck with Bill's sister Tanya in Alberta,

who clearly did not want to talk either, but was too polite to hang up.

"I'm not supposed to be talking with you," she murmured softly.

"Tanya, it's really urgent that I contact Billy. Something terrible has happened in town and I have to get him to come home."

A pause of silence. "I don't know exactly where he is, Kathy. But if he does call, I will at least ask him to call you. You know, I think this family has been very unfair to you. If he'd been my husband, I might not have stayed with him either."

Yes! It was a start. I was very happy for small favours. For any favours. "Thanks, Tanya. I'm so grateful." I left her with my home, cell and work numbers.

Bolstered, I phoned every name in my address book of friends or acquaintances I had kept after the divorce. With no luck there, I went to my office to get out the written notes I had kept. I pulled open the cabinet drawer and discovered the entire folder on Bill was gone! I opened the other three drawers, thinking Riley had possibly misfiled it earlier when I'd caught him in the cabinet. But it wasn't to be found. All the journal entries and data I had on Billy were missing. And I know exactly who had them.

I plunked myself down in my office chair. Was Riley tied up with Snake somehow? I tried to think it through. What did I really know about this man besides what he'd told me? He was from London, Ontario. He was living at Snake's house. Snake was the accountant for Hardy Crushing but he was also rumoured to be selling drugs. And he had given me a business card with the Hells Dragons logo on it. Snake was trying to kill me for some strange reason, because he wanted to find Bill. Why did Snake want to find Billy so bad? Did Snake have something to do with Judy's disappearance? And where could I find some answers about where Bill was?

I needed to check out the last place Billy had lived. Unfortunately, that was at 3001 Heritage Drive. The place where a Prince from Purgatory and a snake named Crunch also lived. Not to mention Snake himself.

Being no further ahead, I put all thoughts aside for the time being. Everything would have to wait because – and I checked my watch one last time – I had to get my butt to the airport to pick up Mom and Dad. I grabbed lunchmeat and a square of cheese from the fridge and snatched my purse. I made a clumsy sign of the cross and said a silent prayer that their flight had been hijacked to Tahiti or someplace warm. Maybe they'd forget where they were going by the time they got a few cocktails into them.

It didn't work and there they were at the Spencer airport, standing by what looked like a dozen bags all neatly lined up on the sidewalk. So they were moving in to stay for at least a few birthdays? I wondered who I had wronged in the past to have attracted such rotten kismet.

I piled the bags and my mother into the van and grabbed the weaving back of Dad's jacket. I wrenched him away from a group of young girls he was explaining how to hypnotize lobster to and got him into the rear seat. As soon as we left the curb he reached around for a certain bag and extracted an almost empty miniature bottle of yellow mouthwash.

"My scotch," he told me, grinning mischievously. "I need a little 'topping off.'" He was snoring happily 10 minutes later.

Well, it was better than I'd hoped for. No handcuffs or SWAT teams to remove him from the aircraft as I'd imagined.

It was another 40 minutes before we reached Halston so Mother and I made polite conversation, both knowing I would get the full barrel blast when we got to my place. My mind was going 200 mph trying to think of how to derail and distract.

Luckily there was a line-up of messages on the new call-display machine and I held my hand up to my mother in a "wait" gesture and let them play.

A message from Mini still worrying over where Kenneth was disappearing to for hours at a time. And a side note that Sebastian had only now warned her about the car explosion. "A little bit late again. Sorry," she said. "We 'ad been fighting over *Days of Our Lives* again. I insist on Oprah and so 'e got in a spit and 'adn't come through for days. 'E said 'e knew you don't die. Like I should be fine wid dat? I got so mad at 'im I tried to choke myself."

I smiled despite the horrible image I got.

Someone named Claire LeDune had called and not left a message. I wrote down the number from the call-display screen.

A message from the sheriff's office about a court date. They could squeeze me into the roster in two days for small claims court. At last!

Mr. Gordon, the Twain principal, was asking where the kids were and when to expect them back for class.

The insurance check for the car was ready and where would I like it forwarded to?

Sharon had called to see how things were going and was there anything I needed help with?

Another bottle of Maple's, I thought to myself. Without the man attached.

Warren's dentist was the last message. He wanted me to call back to discuss the future of my son's "impression on the outer world." And the future of my pay cheques, I added a little grudgingly.

I called back Claire LeDune and left a message on her

machine saying I was returning her call. I would try again
tomorrow to reach her. I hoped she wasn't the Rug Specialist Company phoning for a free cleaning consult. Annoying-
ly common around here.

By now it was almost 9:30 at night and my mother, with a
four-hour time difference behind her, was fading fast. I suggested we have the "talk" in the morning and walked her to
the spare room. My dad was already snoring like it was a
competition and he was determined to take first prize. Luckily my mother had a good supply of heavy-duty sleeping pills
with her. She would need them to stay asleep beside that
racket.

I closed the door behind them.

Once snuggled into my own bed, I pulled the pillow Riley
had used over to my face and took a big smell. It was like he
was still there. I tossed the pillow right off the bed. I wasn't
sure that was what I wanted anymore.

I managed to dodge the mother bullet again in the morning by rising early and leaving a note. I had some advertising
suggestions to take around to the second sawmill in town
and to some of the other trades like Inland Kenworth, Fin-
ning and White's trucks. These places opened early and I figured the best time to get in the manager's face was before
anyone else got in their face for the day.

I had on my power-selling outfit – a short khaki skirt with
a matching jacket, a white scoop-cut blouse and my brown
calfskin boots. Hopefully I could avoid the muck long
enough to make a few sales. I dabbed some lipstick and mascara on and fluffed my hair into the messy style they were
wearing today. Only on me it wasn't a style. Just a statement

about the bad hair life I was having. I dragged it back into a ponytail and told myself to quit looking in the mirror. That would help.

With portable coffee mug in hand, I scrambled from business to business showing my ideas, picking up cards for logos, getting the okay to approach employees responsible for ad content. It was a lot of racing around.

I managed to see everyone I needed before heading to the mall for my "real" job. I looked across the parking lot for Neil, more from curiosity than routine, but he wasn't there. I felt a slight pang of sadness. Oops, stop that, I told myself. Neil was a Bimbo Boinker!

The store remained empty until almost 10:30, when Riley came striding in, that same wide grin on his face like he had a secret and he wasn't going to share it. I didn't smile back.

My hands went to my hips. "Where's that file you stole from me?" I said, my lips snarled back. I felt a bit rabid.

His smile slipped a notch, but not much. He walked over to the store's open door and pulled it shut, turning the lock until it clicked. He flipped the sign over to say "Closed."

"What exactly are you doing?"

Riley crossed the room to where I stood. He reached for my hands but I drew them back.

"You look so sexy when you're.angry."

"You're working with Snake, aren't you?" I hissed.

His eyes went wide before he burst out laughing. "Honey, nothing could be further from the truth." He reached over and grabbed my hands before I had a chance to move them.

"Listen to me," he said. "It's time I told you something." He looked all serious so I calmed down a notch and focused my hectic attention span.

"I got permission this morning from headquarters. I am now allowed to tell you that I am working undercover for the RCMP. I'm on a case against Terry Murdoch, or Snake, as you know him." His grip tightened on my hands. "I can only tell you this because we need your help."

I tried to jerk my hands back but he held onto them. "Calm down," he said.

Oh, if those aren't the worst words anyone can say to a woman who is pissed off. I kicked my leg around, aiming for his head. He quickly dodged, laughing at me again.

"Ohhh." I was seething. Where was a gun when I needed one? I had spent an entire evening bedding down beside a liar? Who was a cop?

"Let me go," I snarled between gritted teeth.

"Kathy, Kathy, really, relax. I need to ask you an important question."

"Like what?" I fired back. "Do I always act like that around men I don't know? Why don't you take that question and shove it right up your . . . ," trying not to swear, my mind blanked, ". . . sass."

I was hopeless at chastising.

He chuckled again, somehow enjoying this show. I felt smoke coming out of my ears and couldn't seem to stop it. I wriggled my hands some more and he finally let them go. I spilled backwards, nearly missing a stack of radios.

"I need to ask you to go away with me for a couple of days. I've been subpoenaed for a special-ops court case in Vancouver tomorrow. I want you to come."

I just stared at him.

"Snake is really gunning for you. It's not safe when I'm not around."

"As if you're always around," I scoffed.

"Honey," he said, his eyebrows knitting together in a serious squint, "I've always been somewhere close behind you every second of every day since I got here."

Oh crap. I thought of the ride home from the pub with Ann the other night when I was blasted. We had to stop so I could open the door and throw up on the curb. Had he been witness to that as well?

"I'm not going anywhere with a liar," I said.

Riley stepped back from me. "Okay, fair is fair. I would have told you earlier, but I couldn't. We need your help tracking Billy down and we figure because he has the kids, he is eventually going to need to get in touch with you. And when he does, we want to find out where he is. Meanwhile, I'm here to protect you. But I can't get out of this court case. It's vital that I appear."

"So you're going to just leave me here simply because I don't want to go? How can I go? I can't just go like a yo-yo?" Uh-oh. I wasn't making sense anymore. I was obviously flustered.

"You could get Lana to run the store."

"And what about my parents? I presume you know they're in town, if you've been following me."

"Your parents will be looked after by the local guys, Constable Lyons and Corporal Currie. They'll be fine."

"Well then, Currie and Lyons can look after *my* sass as well!"

Damn. I hadn't wanted to make him laugh again.

"And with such a cute *sass*, I'm sure they will." He pulled a deep frown. "Okay. I'm only going to do this because we know Snake is leaving Halston for two days. He and Gweek are headed to Tessak tonight. There's some kind of gathering of the Hells Dragons going on."

Tessak was only a two-hour drive west of Spencer, toward the coastal city of Prince Rupin. Far enough, yet still pretty close to us!

More Hells Dragons? "You mean Snake isn't the only one?"

"There is a chapter in every town between Prince Grange and Prince Rupin. Most stay under the radar, but not this get-together. There's trouble brewing. Big trouble. We've got it covered by the Tessak detachment, so I need to get to Vancouver and now is the only time." He looked at me pleadingly. "Sure you don't want to come?" He lowered his voice, and those long eyelashes of his. The ones I had a flash-back of kissing not more than 48 hours ago. Fudge. I envi-sioned a hot scene in a lovely hotel room, the lights of the city glittering. The way Riley was flirting, it looked like there was still a chance.

Then my mind crashed to me trying to explain this ren-dezvous to my parents.

They were just getting over the fact that I wasn't pregnant. "Yet," my father had warned. My mother in this scene had a brown liquor-store bag up over her nose, inflating and deflat-ing to regulate her hyperventilating while my father stood beside her smacking the largest flat BBQ flipper in the world that he'd once swatted me with. It stung like hell. He didn't look afraid to use it on me now that I was an adult either.

"I'm sure. See you later." I turned my back on him, straightening up the headphone rack the kids continually winged around. I was trying to get a grip on everything he'd said. I wasn't as mad about the fact that Riley was a cop as I was that he'd lied to me. And okay, I got that too, undercov-er meant undercover, but he could have told me he wanted those papers in my filing cabinet and I would have given them to him. Or would I have? I was getting so confused.

Well, good. I was glad he was headed out of town. I need-ed some time to think.

When I got home after work, Mom said we were all going to Ann's house for dinner. Excellent timing, because we still wouldn't have time for "the talk." I changed out of my power-selling outfit into a more relaxed garb of jeans and fleece sweater. Dad had heard there was a female dancer at the Zoo bar in town and wanted us to go. He didn't call her that, though. He called her a peeler. I said it sounded like she had leprosy. Was she a vegetable and going to take her skin off? Going for a little carrot bump and grind, Dad? Sheesh. No, we were not going to see the peeler.

Ann welcomed us in past her fur-ball, Miss Puss, who had come to see what the ruckus was in her house. The cat took one look at us and her nose shot into the air. Riffraff! She stalked off indignantly without even a greeting.

Ann served the cutest little toast points on which she had piled a lovely egg salad with watercress. She then herded us into her dining room for an amazingly delicious and perfectly medium-rare prime rib roast. I sound astonished because I was. My sister cooked everything in her microwave. The potatoes before the pre-cooked BBQ chicken and then the frozen corn. But tonight, she served oven-cooked fare, including a turnip puff, brussels sprouts in a hollandaise sauce and Yorkshire pudding. I hadn't ever figured she knew what that was. Where had she found the time to learn all this? Was there someone new in her life she was trying to impress? I got a sudden sick feeling in the pit of my stomach, but immediately brushed it away. No way. Never would happen. I let it go.

My mother would not shut up with the raving. Ann was astounding. Ann was brilliant. Look at the perfect table setting. The adorable salt and pepper set. Weren't these the lightest Yorkshire puddings, Regi? Then Dad chimed in. He had never had roast beef done so bloody perfect! She could be his chef anytime, anywhere. What a girl!

My teeth fillings were starting to hurt from all the screaming in my head. All right, okay. So the last meal I had made him was jarred spaghetti. Next time I would try a little harder.

My sister didn't "do" dessert, so it was just after dishes were done that Ann said she was sorry but she had to head out at nine for a meeting. We were more than welcome to stay. She would see my parents tomorrow after work; she'd come by my place. Mom said it was her turn to cook. I licked my lips. Off the hook yet again. This was all perfectly fine by me.

I used Ann's phone in the kitchen and called Mini, asking what she was up to. Maybe we could swing by for a visit tonight, put that Mom lecture off even a little longer.

Mini said, sure, come on ahead. Kenneth had made her favourite apple/peach strudel for dessert and there was still lots left over. So we said goodnight and thanks to Ann for the spectacular meal and headed out.

You could smell Kenneth's strudel from outside their home. Mom asked about the yellow police tape that still hung off the side driveway to the Merkleys' place and I had to explain about Kitty's murder.

Mom hadn't heard about it yet and couldn't wait to get out of the van to corner Mini. Thanks for taking the heat off, friend of mine!

As we walked in the door, Kenneth was busy putting on his jacket and boots.

I introduced him to my parents, and he shook their hands, apologizing that he had a meeting to go to. But he'd be back by 11 at the latest, he promised.

"Way past this horse's bedtime," said my dad. "Got any scotch?" he asked.

Mini took Dad's hand and led him into the bar in the kitchen. My mother was hot on her heels.

I had a minute alone with Kenneth.

"What's up?" I asked. "Where exactly are you off to?" I didn't mean to sound so concerned, but I was feeling really sick.

"Just out." Then he whispered in my ear, "It's a secret." And walked out the door.

Crap. My own sister. The vision of Dad taking the flipper to me was nothing compared to what I'd do to my sister if she was having an affair with my best friend's husband. She wouldn't, would she? Ann could have any man she wanted. I was surprised she wasn't after Neil or Riley already. But she wouldn't be if she already had someone else, would she? Could I shoot my own sister? I needed to talk to my brother. He would know what kind of trouble I'd face if I did.

My mom was in the kitchen grilling Mini on the gruesome details of the Hazelton girl's murder. I couldn't stand to listen to it or be reminded of the fate my beautiful young babysitter might have faced as well. Dad was sipping his drink while watching the Canucks hockey team "beat the tar" out of the L.A. Kings, so I slipped into an overstuffed chair and finally got a chance to relax and think about my own troubles.

Work had been so busy, and now with this new advertising job and the St. Patrick's Day promos I was losing sight of what really mattered the most. I needed to see Wendy and Warren. Where were they? Where or what was Uncas? How was I going to find Billy? What could I do that wasn't already being done? I racked my brain and then a light went on. It was a small light, but it was on.

Billy was such a slob. He always left something behind wherever he went. Like the pile of papers left on my kitchen table. That meant there was a good chance he'd left a clue at Snake's place as to where he had gone. Riley mentioned Bill had lived in the downstairs family room. A man would spread out in a place like that. And knowing Billy like I did, I figured there could be something down there. Maybe something Riley would have overlooked but that I might make sense of. It was worth a shot.

But how would I get past the dreaded Prince of Darkness? I didn't want to end up being a sales-burger. I played with my lip. I needed to put that dreaded doggy down, but it wasn't in my nature to hurt him. I had to put him to sleep. The little light in my head grew brighter. Then it became a full-strength stadium floodlight! Sleeping pills. I could slip one of mother's pills into a small pocket cut into some meat and toss it at him. Then I could wait and see if it conked him out or not. If the dog was outside. If the dog was inside, I would have to wait and deal with that tomorrow.

Normal girls looked forward to dates with men. Me, I was looking forward to knocking out the beast of Satan and trying to avoid a ten-foot unstuffed boa. How my life had changed.

CHAPTER TEN

We no sooner walked in my front door before Mom began "the talk." I didn't realize I was "too old to be running around" by myself. And that I had slipped into the "what is this world coming to" category. I nodded to hear my mom was quite shaken by her daughter's car having been detonated to fragments in the driveway. What if I had been in it? What would she have told her neighbors?

"Your children have been kidnapped by that good-for-nothing father of theirs and you have no idea where they are or how to get in touch with them. Their grandparents are here. What are we supposed to help you with if the kids aren't here? Do you realize how much money it cost to fly from one side of the country to the other?"

My dad didn't think I'd noticed but he'd poured himself a hefty scotch and was trying to hide at the far end of the couch while I was being "tuned in" on how to live my life.

I mumbled, "I can still hear you," as I left the living room and went to the kitchen. Her voice continued to trail behind . . .

". . . and your babysitter has taken off without phoning you . . ."

I mixed Mother's third rum and cola of the night very heavy-handed. I looked over at the call display on the phone, noticing that the person named Clair LeDune had called back. Phone tag. I'd have to try her again tomorrow.

". . . and you have more bills than you have money coming in . . ."

"Here, Mother," I said, delivering her the drink and repeating, "I can still hear you," as I headed down the hallway, her words, ". . . and when are you going to learn to stand up to these people . . ." at my back as I slipped into the bathroom and found her travel kit. Inside was a vial marked "Triazolam" – her sleeping pills. I took one blue pill and stashed it in my pocket before returning to the front room.

Mother had finished her drink and within seconds I had matching bookends snoring away on my couch. Funny that Mother bothered with sleeping pills; a bottle of rum a week would be cheaper.

I transferred the sleeping pill into the pocket of my black jeans before putting on a black T-shirt and black hoodie. I looked dark, almost invisible. I swathed a favourite black scarf around my neck just to add *some* glam to this bleak outfit before squirming into black cowboy boots with sensible heels.

I went to the fridge and pushed aside the package of steak in favour of a one-pound package of hamburger. No way would that dog eat steak on my dime. Meat was a treat in this house, and I didn't feel so generous toward something that would just as well eat my leather boot as it would an expensive piece of meat.

I rolled a big blob of the hamburger into a meatball, pushing the sleeping pill well into the centre. I tossed it into a plastic baggie and then my purse. The note I left on the table said, "Back by midnight. Forgot I was to feed someone's dog." I left out that optimistically it would just be a meatball and not my arm or worse.

I quietly left the house and drove up the darkened streets slowly, feeling my heart thud faster the closer I got to Heritage Street. When I got to the top of the corridor, the lights in the church were on and a few cars remained in the parking lot. Damn. I was hoping no one would be around to witness my criminal activity. But I was too pumped to turn back. What was I supposed to do at home, at night, alone in a bed with all this excess energy running through my veins? I could easily hurt myself.

I pulled the van further away from the last street light and got out. I walked to the gate and sure enough, there was Prince waiting to welcome me. The giant canine torpedoed himself at the gate, his long chain stretching from the back fence maxed to its very end, his thick neck straining at the collar which choked him as he barked like a crazed ogre. Gobs of spittle flew, his teeth were bared and his hackles rose higher than my hair, which now stood on end.

My right leg began its usual cowardly tremor. I ignored it, pulling the wrapped meat ball from my pocket. In my excitement, I tossed it baggie and all through the gate. Prince caught it and gulped it down in one motion. I didn't hear him swallow, but it was gone. I used my penlight to check the yard. It was definitely gone. I fretted someone might later find the baggie and wonder about it. I glanced around the yard. It was a minefield of over-stacked poop mounds. Not to worry. No one was cleaning up after the beast. Could you blame them?

I went back to my van and climbed in. Now was the waiting game. It took one pill twenty minutes to knock my mother flat. She could be mid-sentence when she went. It was hysterical, as if someone flipped a toy switch on her back. I'm awake. Flip. Now I'm not. Powerful stuff.

I checked my watch.

Twenty minutes goes very slow when you're sitting in a van in the cool spring air. Especially when you're about to break into a house. The adrenaline was pumping and I wanted to jump out and run wildly around the neighborhood a dozen times. I was wound up tighter than Warren on sugar cubes.

But the time did finally pass. I took the hammer that was still in my purse and put it through my two front belt loops. I put my cell phone in my pocket and grabbed my mini pen flashlight again and I was set to go. I walked slowly up to the gate and there lay Prince, his tongue lolled out of his head like a red runway carpet from hell.

I figured I had lots of time to check this place out. That dog was out cold!

I was juiced. I was going to do this. This was the plan. It was time to do something positive for myself. I wanted to find Billy and this was my best chance to do it.

I pushed at the gate but it was locked. A big chain hung around the bars and a lock the size of my two hands dangled from that.

Phooey!

Another expletive – a real one this time – fell out when I gazed up at the razor wire. I had to find another way into this fortress. I decided to investigate the perimeter of the fence; its tall walls showed no sign of an entry. It was when I tripped over a root that I finally peered down and saw what I needed. Prince had dug an escape hole beneath the fence. He couldn't go through it because of the chain, but it existed and seemed big enough for my slim 120-pound frame to squirm through. Okay, I was closer to 140, but what do you care? It was a 20-pound muffin top!

I wiggled head first into the hole and hoped nothing else

would come running at me from the other side. I had a moment of panic when my butt got a little stuck. I cursed the chocolates Riley had brought over. How could they work that fast?

Once on the inside, I cautiously stepped around at least 40 mountainous piles of doggy doo. What did they feed that thing? Oh right, salespeople like me. The way he had scarfed down that plastic bag, I half expected to see a whole tie or a suit jacket in one of the piles. I walked up the back steps and found the door locked. No surprise there; that's what the hammer was for. Being on a dead-end street I assumed no one would hear a window being broken, although I wasn't prepared for it to be as loud as it was. I also didn't plan on ripping a hole in my butt as I tried climbing through the window. Ever try it? You have to do a push-up, which I am terrible at, so at the last minute I twisted to rest my backside on the window sill, not realizing a glass fragment was still attached. Ouch! Throbbing pain stabbed at my rear. It felt like I'd need stitches but how could I explain what I'd been doing? I didn't think "I dunno" would cut it so I would live with the scar and for now, the pain.

I clambered the rest of the way in and plopped down onto the kitchen floor.

I was in.

The place was stealthily quiet. And dark. What did Snake do with the boa when he went away? Take it with him? Lock it in a cage? Give it the run of the place? I trembled at that thought before forcing myself to snap out of it. The plan. Positive. Best chance. Right.

I made a quick trip down the hallway to the living room area and shone the penlight around. The stereo was all set up in the corner like Riley had said. The stuffed animals were still on the walls, minus Crunch. I looked around the entire room. No sign of the snake. He might have gone with his master. I pictured him on the front seat of a truck all buckled in between Snake and Gweek. Maybe?

I crept back to the kitchen and opened the door to the basement where I knew Billy had been staying. I creaked my way down to the carpeted floor, thankful I wasn't trying to break in while people were sleeping. I was being loud enough to wake a zombie.

The room opened into a den with a regulation-size pool table in the middle and a couch and chair off to the side. A large mural covered the entire back wall – a scenery shot of a dirt road covered in fall leaves. A small box with a blinking red light was on it, tucked back into the far corner at the west end of the wall. The whole room smelled musty. I eyeballed the pool table, which took up most of the basement. How had they ever got it down those narrow stairs? I prowled around it, seeing nothing out of the ordinary. The legs didn't appear like they detached and neither did any of the railings.

A small kitchenette was in another corner of the basement with a bar set up to cut it off from the rest of the room. The ultimate family place. Piles of toys filled white laundry baskets along another wall. I saw balls and Tonka trucks, Barbie dolls and My Little Ponys. Board games half pulled apart, a plastic bat and giant bowling pins. I circled the couch and coffee tables. Again, nothing out of the ordinary. But I used to clean a house that my ex-Neanderthal lived in and I knew dirt wasn't just surface deep. I lifted the skirting around the couch and chair and peered at the books and bits of popcorn beneath. I hauled the cushions off the couch and stuck my hand down toward the springs. I found the usual bits of fluff, pens, and a twoonie that I stuck in my pocket. A free swear word, I told myself. I checked the stuffed chair the same way. I finally found something in the leather rocker. Crammed in the back was a white paper pamphlet. I pulled it out and un-

scrunched it. The words on the front read "Adoption Disclosure Unit." The inside contained details on how to track
down a birth parent, sibling or extended family and a web
site for more information.

I slid it into my pocket. I didn't think it had anything to
do with Billy, but it was all I found.

I wandered over to a shelf of reference books and was sort-
ing through them when I heard a voice coming from upstairs.
The hair on the back of my neck lifted and I stifled a scream.
Who the heck was in the house? I heard footsteps overhead
and realized I had quit breathing. A sudden steady beam of
light popped on under the door at the top of the stairs. Holy
crap! Had Snake and Gweek returned early? I whipped my
head around, frantically searching for a good hiding spot in
case someone came down. The room was very exposed for
anyone descending the stairs. They would get an aerial view
of behind the couch or chairs. Was that a closet at the back
by the bar? I ran to it, pulling it open. Something fell out at
me and I held out my hand in front to stop it from bowling
me over. I let out a tiny scream. It was Gweek. A very purple,
dead-seeming Gweek now lying bent over at my feet.

I heard the door to the basement creak open and the light
overhead flicked on.

I shoved Gweek back into the closet and went in after
him, closing the door behind us. I stood there in the darkness, trying to be somewhere else.

I heard each step as someone clomped down the stairs.
They moved slow and sure and I knew they were searching for
where the sound of that scream had come from. My heart was
knocking in my chest so loud I was sure they would know exactly where I was. I could feel heat coming up my body before
realizing it must be Gweek leaning against my leg.

Wait a minute, why would Gweek be so warm? And why
was Gweek moving up my body?

Holy bananas! That wasn't Gweek. *Crunch* was in here too!

That was my last thought before the snake had finished wrapping itself all the way around me and I began to feel a quick tightening. I opened my mouth and screamed like I had never screamed before. I didn't care who found me in the closet; I was being squeezed to death by a boa constrictor. I felt my ribs start to hurt and then worried they were going to snap. I was a tube of toothpaste being squeezed and soon my brains would come shooting out the top of my head! My face was piping hot and pulsing and I wondered if this was what had happened to Gweek. I hoped my eyes weren't going to bug out like his. It looked terrible. I thought about what my mother would say. I was still screaming when the door was yanked open and hands reached in and pulled me out.

It was Neil. He was hitting at Crunch with a giant flashlight, but the colossal snake was not loosening his stranglehold on me. It only made him squeeze harder. The room swirled and swam around me. Nothing was solid. The world was liquid. I couldn't breathe. I thought about the kids and hoped they were as warm as I was. I watched from a dream as Neil finally grabbed the snake's tail and bit down on it. Hard.

My chest loosened a notch and I struggled to get in a sip of air. Neil bit down hard again and the snake unwound even further, enough for me to get almost a full breath in. The last thing I remembered was how handsome Neil looked in that shade of red he was wearing.

When I came to, Neil had me propped up on the couch. I glanced nervously around for Crunch or Gweek and was glad not to see either of them. Neil's face was full of concern, mixed with what might have been called anger.

"How are you feeling?" he asked.

"A little crushed, but I think I'll be okay." I pressed on my ribs and felt the bruising. "Ow."

Neil ran his hand through his hair. He had such beautiful, thick, full hair. I wanted to run my hand through it too. Was that me or the shock talking?

"Guess the next question is, what the hell were you doing in a closet in Terry Murdoch's place?" His eyes drilled into mine.

"Maybe I should ask you the same question?" I countered. After all, I had come on a mission. Was Neil somehow tied up with Snake?

"I'm moonlighting. I work three nights a week for Ace Alarms. I got a call the security had been breached at this address and I came to check it out. I saw the dog snoring away on the ground and when it didn't wake up and try to rip my arm off, I knew it must be drugged, so I came in."

"But the gate was locked."

"I used bolt cutters. Figured the owner wouldn't mind replacing the chain. Someone had put his dog down for the count so I knew something serious was going on in his house."

I struggled to get up. "Okay, well thanks. I think I'll head home now."

Neil grinned at me and gently pushed me back onto the sofa. "Not before I get a few more answers," he said.

I groaned as I sank back down. My ribs had taken a beating and my butt still ached.

"Who is the dead guy in the closet?" Neil asked.

"His name was Gweek and he lived with Snake. Terry Murdoch, I mean. I knew Gweek because he came in and bought a big stereo system off me the other day. I'm thinking he might have been high on something, maybe drugs," I whispered. "I know Snake because he's trying to kill me."

"Why would anyone want to kill you? You can be pretty annoying at times, but not enough to kill."

"Ha, ha. Actually, I can't figure it out either. He wants to find Bill, but how will killing me help? I'm sure he's responsible for the snake and brick that sailed through my front picture window and for the bombing of my car." I filled Neil in on all the details.

"Wow. This is serious!" He grabbed my hand and helped me stand up.

My legs held. "I was here seeking clues to where Billy might be. Snake seems desperate to find him, but he hasn't said why."

"And did you find anything besides a ten-foot boa constrictor?"

"Its name is Crunch. We've met before, only not on such close terms." I shuddered. "By the way, where is the slimy thing?"

"Back in the closet with Gweek. I wanted to hear your story first before I made any decisions."

"Snake, I mean Terry is in Tessak for the next two days, so I don't know what you want to do, but I know I want to get the hell out of here."

Neil said he would call in to his security dispatch about a break-in as soon as I had left. He would also call the RCMP about Gweek's body.

No one moved. We both stood looking at the ceiling. It was a chess match. My move if I dared.

"So what will Lana think about all this?" I said. It was honestly the best I could come up with under the circumstances. I was badly rattled.

Neil glanced down for a minute then back at me. "What will Riley think?"

"I only saw Riley twice. Nothing is going on."

"Oh sure, and now *you'll* believe I asked Lana out only because you were seeing Riley. Nothing happened between us either."

"At least Riley didn't childishly drape himself like a sweater across my shoulders," I countered.

"I never stuck my tongue in Lana's ear before sliding under a bar stool to do who knows what in front of the entire town."

I gasped. Neil must have seen me the night I barely escaped from Snake's and had too many martinis at Mac's Pub.

Okay. So we were getting to somewhere and it was ugly. But I could explain. And I did. "It was called three-martini . . . floor, only I didn't hit it fast enough, obviously. And nothing happened under there except that I found a quarter and as I recall, I tried to insert it in Riley's boot to make a phone call. Next I remember I was puking out of Ann's car."

Neil seemed to get satisfaction from that. "You hurled from her Audi?"

"I made her stop first. But I did splash my shoes, if that makes you feel better."

I could see that it did. It was his turn. "I phoned Lana to go for dinner because you were making me miserable. She's really interested in Riley but said sure as long as I was buying. And that she wanted lobster. I didn't know you'd be there. Seeing you with that guy really bugged me, for some reason."

I snuggled into him for one quick second. I needed it. "Yes, you with Lana bothered me too."

I felt his arms close around me. The moment lasted forever. But ended in a second.

Feeling a trickle of blood roll down my butt, I squiggled free.

I gathered my remaining strength and turned, hobbling to

the stairs. Neil called after me, "Your butt seems to be bleeding. Did you need me to come over later and help doctor it for you?"

I turned and saw the size of the smile on his face. Every tooth was visible. He was really enjoying this.

"No," I told him, thinking of my sore ribs. "At least not tonight, but one day . . ." and I let that dangle.

I took my sorry self out to the van, stepping over a snoring Prince to do so. I headed straight to my place, driving sideways with the sore half of my butt lifted off the seat, the way my father did when he had gas to get rid of. How demeaning.

Thankfully, my parents were still snoring away. I soaked for an hour in a hot bath with Epsom salts. It helped the wound but not my mental being. I kept feeling Crunch's thick body sliding around mine. Getting rid of that image only left me with Gweek's dead and staring eyes. I put some gauze and taping on my butt and went to bed. I fell asleep dreaming of being in Neil's arms while a gigantic snake wrapped around us.

The next day I was as haggard as a cramming grad student the night before final exams. The alarm clock still lay on the floor from when I had knocked it off yesterday with the pillow. It still managed to get me up early, although I wasn't sure why when there were no kids to bundle or bustle about. With that dreary reminder, I put an extra scoop of coffee grounds in the filter but put in the same amount of water. My parents would be spinning like tops after drinking it, but I was leaving for work in an hour so figured it didn't matter. I needed the extra jolt. I could have just added some whiskey instead, but worried I might fall right into the entire bottle.

I noticed the blinking number on the telephone's call waiting. Claire LeDune. This was getting tiresome. What did she want? She was pretty persistent whoever she was.

It was already eight a.m. but I figured that wasn't considered early these days so I called the number. It rang twice and then was answered by a voice that had to speak quite loudly over the din of what sounded like a lot of children in the background. "Good Morning. Tessak Midland School."

I stuttered, not expecting this number to reach a school. "C . . . Claire LeDune, please," I asked.

"Just a minute."

I heard a click and then more ringing. A new voice said, "Claire here."

"Oh hi," I said. "This is Kathy Sands. We've been playing phone tennis."

A soft chuckle came through. "Yes, I have been trying to reach you," the woman said. "I am Wendy's grade three teacher here in Tessak. We've been wondering how she's been. Will she be returning to class anytime soon?"

My breath sucked in. Wendy! In Tessak! Only three hours away from me.

"I'm sorry, Claire, but you've lost me already. The kids have been traveling with their father, my ex-husband. I had no idea where they had gone to, so I am very relieved that you called. You say Wendy was in your class?"

Now it was Claire's turn to sound surprised. "They're just traveling? I understood they would be staying with us for the remainder of the year, but after the first three days of class, Wendy has not returned. I wondered if she'd fallen ill again. She didn't seem too well while she was with us."

I got Claire to give me as many details as she could over the phone. The number she had for Billy was not in service and the address given was bogus as well. (Some surprise.) My number had been written on a scribbler one of the kids had left in a school desk. Warren had attended classes a few more times than Wendy but now had also stopped coming to school. I could feel both relief and then a rising anger. It threatened to overcome me. If I could only see Billy right now, I'd kick him so hard I'd leave a permanent dent. And what was with poor little Wendy? I resisted the urge to shriek while still on the phone.

I told Claire I would get to the bottom of it and get back to her.

While slightly dazed and trying to compute what I'd learned, I walked into my bedroom and got the pants I was wearing last night out of the dirty clothes hamper. I pulled the crumpled white pamphlet I had found stuffed in the chair out of my front pocket. "Adoption Disclosure Unit of Canada" it said. There was a 1-800 number on the backside. Could this be why Billy was in Tessak? Why he had up and left so suddenly?

I now knew the where of the kids, but I still didn't have the why.

I reached for the phone and entered the written numbers.

"Hi," I told whoever answered. "I'm looking to find someone."

"Isn't everyone," answered a young man. "What can I do ya for?"

"My brother phoned you just the other day," I lied. "Billy Sands. He said for me to call and talk to someone about what he'd found."

"And your name is?"

"Amanda Sands." My heart sped up. Deceit was not my strong suit.

"Mmm hmm." I could hear computer keys clicking. "Your caseworker would be Bob McPhee. Did you want to talk with him?"

No, I wanted to hang up. I was not a phone person. I

needed to see people's faces and their reactions to what I was saying. And I hated the thought of possibly getting caught in a lie by someone that might possibly know my mother. This had helped me keep on the straight and narrow the past 30 years. Even when she lived 5000 miles away. There was always a chance the person knew my mother and I'd get it.

"Sure. Thanks." I swallowed hard. I told myself I could always just hang up before the loud mouth in my head mentioned they probably had caller ID as well. It wouldn't have been hard to figure out from there.

"Bob here, how can I help you?"

I repeated my little fib. "Billy Sands, my brother, said to give you a call."

"Is this Amanda or Tanya?"

"Amanda," I said, feeling my Pinocchio nose grow another inch.

"I'm glad you called," he said. "I was wondering how Billy made out finding his half brother? Did everything go okay? He was supposed to call me after their first meeting but I still haven't heard back. That Perkins can be a slippery guy to catch up to."

"What are you talking about? What half brother?"

"I thought Billy said he'd told you? And that you didn't want to meet Ivan yet, not until Bill had met him and made sure it was all good. Did I get that wrong? Wasn't he at the address I gave him?"

"Well, I'm not sure. I haven't heard from Billy either," I managed. "Maybe I should get that phone number from you and give them a call. To see how they're making out." I crossed my fingers.

"You were all given Ivan's name and address. That much I do know for sure. This isn't Amanda Johnson, is it?" The stern sound in his voice made me have to pee. Ulp. "No, but thank you," I said before hanging up quickly. I hoped my last-minute civility would discourage the man from pursuing who I was. Or from phoning my mother.

I found the number for the Halston sheriff's office and gave it a call. I let the sheriff know everything I had learned. I also told him I was worried my daughter might need medical attention.

The sheriff figured with any luck he could find the address for this Ivan Perkins. He would contact the Tessak sheriff's department and get Billy served a copy of the court papers within the hour.

This was fantastic because our first court date was on Thursday, just two days away. Hot damn! I was sure I'd have my babies back soon.

CHAPTER ELEVEN

I was running late for work so I dressed in a fast outfit of black jeans and a flounced red blouse. It would have to be a deli day for lunch. The thought made my heart lurch for Judy. I wondered if they were making any headway on finding her and I felt a stab of guilt for not having phoned her family the past few days. I knew her mother would be in touch the minute any word evolved, but I still felt horrible for not being the one to keep in contact.

Hopefully this wouldn't be like the past missing women cases where making headway was scarce. Tempers were flaring with the native population's insistence for more police man-power falling on deaf ears. The situation was so sad. Many of these young women lived on reserves, which were miles from the nearest town. Without their own vehicles or daily buses to rely on, many hitchhiked. Their folly was getting into a vehicle by themselves and apparently with the wrong person. Or persons. But Judy hadn't been hitchhiking. She had got into a truck at a busy downtown gas station with someone she had known. Or thought she had.

I left a note on the counter telling my mom to use up the steak and hamburger in the fridge for lunch and dinner. "See you at 6:15."

I pulled on my raincoat and closed the door behind me.

The pouring was relentless today. The rising daffodils might need it, but I wasn't a flower. If the rain kept up, I would need a snorkel!

Once at work, I settled in and got my music order lists done. I unboxed the last of the freight and helped a customer with buying a cell phone. It took a while because of her hearing aid. She kept removing it to hear the operator. I said she should move into a Juneberry model merely because it was large enough to see the numbers on. She didn't care so much about that until I explained the vibrate option. Sold!

While watching Mrs. Haverd quickly hobble from the store with a funny grin on her face, my own phone rang and I picked up.

All I could hear was someone shouting at me from the other end. I pulled the receiver eight inches away from my ear and still heard everything quite clearly.

". . . can't believe you got the sheriff involved . . . embarrassing . . . said I'd pay you . . . you bitch . . . always have to push a point . . ."

I do believe Billy is on the phone, I said to myself. I cheered right up.

"Bill, how are you?" Not caring, I didn't pause for an answer. "How are the kids? How is Wendy?"

"You don't deserve to know how my kids are," he told me. "Not after what you've done."

"Are you talking about being served papers to appear in court on Thursday? Because that is the very least of the straightening out you deserve, you schmuck. If I could have paid extra to have that sheriff shoot you in the ass, I would have." I grinned at the thought.

"I'm talking about that and this sole custody shit. Those will never be just your kids, Kathy. They're half mine too."

I pictured King Solomon and the story about sentencing the kids to be cut in half. "They will always be both of our children, Billy, but someone has to take full responsibility for them for the rest of their lives as children," I said. "My life is way more stable than yours. I have a permanent home. A regular job. The same school they started in. The same friends. And no-one chasing after me!"

He wasn't listening. "I'll fight you for them every step of the way, you know. You better get yourself a good lawyer, with all that money you got." He laughed at me.

I had nothing to throw back for a moment. A lawyer?

"And how am I supposed to make a court date on Thursday, huh? I am working, Kathy. I can't just run off because you decide you want some money. That's not how it works."

"That's how it works when you decide not to pay what you promised for those kids to live on for the past eight months."

"You don't deserve all that money. I've had the kids for months at a time and they don't cost me anything. You're lucky I gave you any money at all. I know how you go through it. You spent that eleven hundred dollars on yourself, don't you lie to me."

I didn't have to itemize where the money he gave us went, but I foolishly thought I could reason with him. I explained where every penny had gone.

"Bullshit!"

This, I reminded myself, was why I was taking him to court. He was as realistic about bills and payments as he had been about marriage.

"Put the kids on, Billy. I want to talk to them."

"Well, they don't want to talk to you. And quit harassing my family," he fired before he hung up.

Damn! I stamped my foot. No caller ID at the store. How could I find out how Wendy was doing? I was worried that she was still sick, and maybe getting sicker. Why else would she have missed so much school?

Then I remembered I hadn't told Bill he was a suspect in Judy Charlie's disappearance. Oops.

Unable to think of anything but the kids, I sat rearranging shopping bags for an hour.

Lana swung by right at noon, licking her gooey glossed lips. She didn't mind watching the shop for a second while I ran next door and grabbed a salad. And I should get a chocolate macadamia nut cookie for both of us because I looked depressed, she said.

I wanted to ask how things were going between her and Neil, but didn't have the nerve. Was it the way he'd said? That he was only a meal ticket for her? Was it over before it had started? I told myself Lana would have bragged if anything were happening.

When I got back to the store with my salad and two cookies, Lana was on the phone. She hung up when I walked in.

"That was your father. He sounded sexy; like a real lover boy," she said.

A lover boy. Wasn't that what she'd called Neil?

I rolled my eyes to the ceiling. It was so Lana. Maybe Neil hadn't been a notch on her stiletto. "What did Dad want? Am I supposed to call him?"

"He said that Billy called about twenty minutes ago. There was a number on the caller ID if you wanted it? I wrote it down."

I grabbed the note she extended and fought the urge to kiss her; she would have thought it a come-on, anyway.

"Want me to work while you use the phone?" she asked, plopping onto a stool and pulling her nail file from her purse.

I didn't answer, simply took the portable and hurried to the back of the store for privacy. The phone rang three times at the other end before I heard my little elf's voice.

"Hello?" said Warren in almost a whisper.

"Oh, Warren," I sighed." Honey, it's Mommy! How are you?"

"Mommy! Hey, Wendy, it's Mommy!" he yelled, the sound going away from the phone as he twisted or turned to deliver the news.

"Are you here, Mom? Are you coming to get us?" he asked.

"I wish I was, baby. But you're with your dad right now. Do you want to come back and live with me?" I thought I knew the answer but still, my heart beat faster all the same. Billy did spoil them rotten and that could sway a child's decision.

"Yeh, I miss you," my boy said. "Dad is away all the time and we're with a really old lady. She keeps her teeth in a cup. And she makes us eat smelly stuff. She took us to her church. We're Jehodas now."

I carefully bit my tongue. There were more important issues right now other than what religious beliefs my kids were being exposed to. "So do you want me to see if I can bring you home?" I asked again.

"I don't want to be a Jehodah, Mom. They make us talk to strangers who are mean to us. I want to come home."

"And what about Wendy? Can Mommy talk to her too?"

"Wendy is sick. And every time Wendy gets sick, Dad gets sick," Warren said. "I feel sick when they're all sicking."

"Okay, big guy. But how does she get sick? Is she throwing up still?"

"She wasn't and then she was a lot of the time. Last night she was roaring in her sleep. Like a lion. I laughed at her but she didn't wake up."

That didn't sound good at all. Had she been high fevered and delirious?

"Warren, I really have to talk to your dad. Is he there?"

"I think so. I'll go look." And he hung up.

I waited five minutes, as long as I could stand it before calling back, hoping Warren would have his dad ready to talk to me by then.

I was surprised when a woman answered the phone.

"Mrs. Sands?" she said.

"Hi, yes, who is this?" I asked.

"I'm the neighbor. Mavis Byron. I've been helping with your children. Are you looking for Bill?"

"I am, Mavis. I need to talk to him about Wendy. Have you seen her, can you tell if she has a fever?"

"I'm looking right at her. She's been sleeping on the couch for three days. I felt her forehead and it did seem pretty hot."

"Where is Bill?"

"Billy? He went to the pub for a minute with his buddies but he's been driving truck for my husband. We got the Prince Squared route. Highway Twenty-six from the coast of Prince Rupin to Prince Grange. It's fourteen hours round trip, so he's on a stopover and heads back out tomorrow."

That meant he drove right through Halston both ways! Thank heavens.

"Mavis, I think Wendy needs to see a doctor. And I know she needs to see her mother. Do you think you can talk some sense into Billy and get him to bring her back? If you ask Warren, he really wants to come home, too." I filled her in on the rest of our sad story. About Billy disappearing with the kids and the joint-custody arrangement not working out. I poured my heart out to this stranger, the one I presumed kept her teeth in a cup.

"I'll see what I can do," was all she said. It was how she said it that gave me hope.

Lana was still filing her nails when I came back to the front of the store.

"Talk to your kids?" she asked.

I couldn't help it. I started to cry.

"Oh, stop that," Lana said, coming over and wrapping her arms around me. I couldn't help but wonder if I would smell Neil on her, but the smell of her cheap perfume was too overpowering. And it was just what I needed to get ahold of myself.

I pushed back a bit. "Thanks, Lana. You can be so nice for a slut." I went wide-eyed when I realized what I'd said.

Lana didn't hesitate and slammed back with, "At least I don't try to have sex in the pub under a table." She quickly covered her mouth with her hands, her eyes huge.

Then we both cracked up. It was one of those side-splitting guffaws that didn't end for quite a few minutes. Every time we looked back at each other we would crack up all over again. Some people moved into the store wondering what all the howling was about. All we could do was point at each other with our legs crossed trying not to pee on ourselves.

My life was a mess.

The smell of Mom's shepherd's pie hit me as I rolled up the driveway. My mother made a mean pie with lots of gravy and mashed potatoes on top. They had used the steak for a lunch stir-fry; Dad said he'd never eaten so well. That was a start to redemption after Ann's night of roasted wonder. I might not have cooked it, but it was being served in my house, which must have counted. Like the Magical Free Milk I used to enjoy when I lived at their place. What goes around . . .

I offered to turn off the broccoli that appeared to have been cooking since breakfast. My father didn't like to chew vegetables. They had to be soft enough to suck through a straw. No complaints; I was happy for any meal I didn't have to cook or pay for at the end.

"If you like this," Dad said, "wait 'til tomorrow. Helen's gone on a meatball rampage. She's made enough to re-sink the *Titanic*. She's a little bored with no grandkids to look after."

The house did look amazingly clean. Even the cupboards were washed inside and out. Mom had been faithfully emptying the drip buckets under the leaks in the ceiling and I hadn't taken the time to notice or to thank her. I did so now. Without the help of my parents I would have been lost. Or at least been locked in my bathroom telling the Rescue Squad I refused to come out ever again.

There hadn't been any calls for anything other than the Rug Specialist. Mother said there was a special on and they were coming Thursday to do the entire house.

I could have advised Mom on better ways to spend her money if she wanted to spend it on us – like the roof, braces or a lawyer to get my kids a normal life. But who was I to tell anyone how to spend their money? Clean carpets would be nice. So would a diamond chandelier.

I was going nuts the next day at work. Head office had sent two city shirts to measure the store for a summer upgrade. There had been a mere one-hour heads-up so I was a whirling dervish battling tumbleweed, piles of dust and static cling.

Once here the head shirt was impressed by the musical instrument display I had set up last month. A dummy rock star filled the front window pointing at a large case of guitar strings and amplifier cords, songbooks, etc. I called in Lana to watch the store while we went for lunch at the Pleasant Valley restaurant, this time getting a table by the fireplace.

I settled in close to the warmth, putting my purse under my chair and hanging my wet jacket over the back. Neil came through the door with two teenagers I presumed to be his children. The freckled-nosed girl looked to be about twelve while the clean-cut young man who closely resembled his dad looked about fourteen. So that would make a difference of six years between Warren and Kelly. Funny as Neil was six years older than me. Plus six versus Riley's minus six. Older and wiser versus younger and bolder. Whether or not anything happened, I had spent a night sleeping beside Riley. Neil and I had yet to do more than hug. I hoped that changed.

They headed straight for the fireplace section as well, probably like us wanting the heat more than ambience. Neil noticed me as he climbed the three steps and we nodded at each other. Just like old times, I thought. Only now Neil had a big secret about me. And I was bursting to tell him about tracking down Billy and the children.

I ate my curried stir-fry, answering questions about our store's common area maintenance increase and the situation with the late janitors' strike, while trying to make a plan on how to talk to Neil later.

By the time we left I was no closer to an idea, but I walked over to their table anyway. Neil introduced me to Kelly and Frances. I commented on Frances' beautiful strawberry blonde hair, but she merely looked at me with a noncommittal curiosity. Neil patted her hand. It was an awkward moment and so, as usual, I let myself blurt out whatever popped into my head. It's called verbal diarrhea. You just open the lips and let the vocal cords take over. No brain involved.

"Why don't you all come to my place tonight for dinner," I said. "My mother has made a mountain of meatballs and we need help to keep them from taking over the place." I grinned like an idiot. It was a wonder I managed to sell anything the way I acted sometimes.

Kelly's nose scrunched up. "What's in the meatballs?"

His dad kicked him under the table and I watched Kelly bend over and make a big show of rubbing his shin.

Frances just kept watching me with those gorgeous brown eyes.

"We'd love to," Neil said. "I should clear it with their mother first. To see what their schedule is like . . ."

"Dad, we're not babies," Kelly said. "We don't have anything going on." He looked up at me. "Do you have Wii?"

"We what?" I asked. I was joking, of course, but they obviously didn't realize that.

A corner of Frances' lip curled up slightly.

"Never mind," Neil said to Kelly, then to me, "What time?"

"I'll be home just after six. Come over any time after that."

The head shirt didn't have any more questions and like the *real* Santa, he disappeared with a wave from the side of his nose. Hopefully like the real Santa he and his entourage would stay away until Christmas!

Lana was working toward owning a bread machine, deciding she wanted to try "this domestication shit," and offered to stay until closing. I didn't mention I had run into Neil or that I had invited him to dinner. Besides, I told myself, it wasn't a date or anything. I had something important to tell the guy who had let me off a very squirmy hook the other night. He could have thrown me, and my injured butt, in jail for breaking and entering. He deserved to know how I had made out with that pamphlet.

I went home and came clean about who was coming for dinner. I then played the "forty-question" game.

"He's divorced. No, we're not having a 'thing.' No, I'm not pregnant, Dad." Christ. Oops. I eyed up the Swear Jar. If I was going to be honest, I owed it most of my next pay cheque.

"That's fine," my mom said. "But I also invited Mini and Kenneth and Ann."

Hoo boy. It was going to be a party all right, especially when my table only sat four people.

While Mom was doing the meal, I spent time working on a new advertising sales campaign for "women in business." I planned to spend Friday afternoon going to shops owned or managed by women. There was quite a healthy list.

I heard a holler and in came Mini, wearing oven mitts and holding a casserole dish. It smelled delicious! No Kenneth followed.

I was right behind her in the kitchen. My mother flew into the dining area with the salt and pepper shakers so I quietly asked Mini what was up. Where was her Galloping Gourmet?

Mini snuffled a bit as she slid the casserole into my oven. Her eyes looked red, like she was going to sneeze, and her top lip trembled.

"Oh no," I said, "trouble in Miniland?"

"I don't believe this," she said, whispering so my mom wouldn't hear, "'e's never 'ome. I'm worried 'e's seeing somebody." The lip absolutely quaked at this statement.

I put my arms around her and all I could think of was my sister. She just couldn't be messing with Mini's husband, could she? Ann loved Mini as much as I did, or so I thought?

My mother whirled back in. "Hel-lo Mini," she sang out, "appies are in the living room."

The doorbell rang and I went over to let Neil and his family in, a bottle of wine and a tetras of juice in his hands. His kids slowly poked their heads through the door.

"Welcome, welcome, come on in," I said, motioning toward the stuffed chairs. Veggies and dip lined the coffee table and Kelly made a beeline. "What's in this dip?" he asked of no one as he scooped a big blob onto a celery stick.

I took the wine bottle and juice from Neil and reached up to give him a hug. He hugged me back. Electricity swirled. An awful good sign. And an awful great feeling in the pit of my stomach. Actually, a little lower.

Then the door opened once more and I heard Warren's voice yell, "Mom, we're back!" as his wet runners flew past the front door mats and he bounded across to reach me.

Oh thank you, thank you. Thank you, everyone, everything, thank you! I opened my arms wide and scooped his little frame up all in one motion. I whirled him around the room. I kissed his hair and his head and his face and I do believe I was crying.

"Where's Wendy?"

"She's asleep in the truck. Dad said you better come out."

I gave my son another long squeeze, but then worried I might be crushing him like Crunch had crushed me so I stopped. I put Warren down and pointed him toward where his grandmother had wandered off down the hallway.

"Grandma and Gramps are visiting! Go give them a kiss," I said and hard as it was, I left him and put on my boots to go outside and face Bill. I told Neil to make himself at home and that I'd be right back. It was good that Neil had an ex as well. He seemed to completely understand.

A big highway truck was parked parallel to my house. It was running noisily and I saw the curtains flutter at Sharon's house before closing again. I opened the cab door and climbed up into the passenger seat. Billy watched me as I closed the door. Wendy was lying all bundled in blankets to her neck in the back sleeper.

"Thank you," I said to Bill. "Thank you for finally coming to your senses."

His hands gripped the steering wheel tighter. "There was no sense in this – I'm just tired of paying Mrs. Byron out of what I make every day. I can't work full time and be with the kids all day too. Besides, I think my little girl isn't feeling too good."

I reached over and gently shook her. "Wendy," I said softly. "You're home." No response. "Wendy?" I shook her harder and then opened up the blankets, feeling the sweat coming from her thin little body.

"Oh my God, Bill. Her fever must be off the map. What were you thinking?" I didn't mean to accuse him of anything. I was panicked. "Get this thing moving," I yelled at him. "We're going to the clinic."

Billy pushed the shifter forward and let the brakes go. He wheeled the rig around, with a trailer full of lumber piled on the back, and began to head down the hill toward town. At the base of the hill he turned right and pulled into the health clinic's parking lot.

I pulled Wendy's burning body to me and started out. She woke up and looked up at me. "Mommy," she said, smiling slowly. It seemed like such an effort for her. She tried to pull her pajama pillow closer, and I helped to lift it. It felt heavier than normal. She held it tight to her body.

"Hi, baby girl," her father said to her over my shoulder, then to me, "I can't come with you. I have to get this load to Prince Grange tonight, if I want to make that court case. I'll be here in the morning. I'll phone you tonight. She'll be okay."

I was glad he was leaving. He couldn't help and would only complicate things if he decided to get in one of his "this is entirely your fault" modes. I climbed down with Wendy in my arms and then reached up, slamming his truck door shut before racing to the emergency entrance.

The nurse inside did immediate triage on Wendy and phoned the doctor on call. Luckily it was my friend Dr. Mandi Keswick who arrived a mere five minutes later.

She checked Wendy's vitals and asked the nurse to hook up an intravenous line to get some fluids into the frail girl. I held my daughter's hand as the tears slid down my face. It is so hard to see your kids sick. At least Wendy was sleeping peacefully again.

"When was the last time she's eaten?" Mandi asked, to which I had no reply. I told her how Wendy had just been dropped off. "I doubt recently," I added, telling her about all the vomiting that had been happening.

"Has she had the flu or chicken pox lately?"

"The flu, off and on for the past two weeks."

Mandi scratched behind her ear for a second, deep in thought. "And do you know if she was given any kind of acetylsalicylic acid?"

I looked blank.

"ASA, aspirin."

I recalled Billy saying he had given her some to help her sleep and told Mandi this.

She shook her head and called the nurse back in. "I want a urine and blood sample stat," she said. She turned to me. "It's a good thing you brought her in."

"What do you think it is?"

"It's a bit early to tell, but I'm thinking its Reye's syndrome. If Wendy was given aspirin while she had the flu it may have caused her brain to swell. If it isn't caught in time, a child can suffer brain damage, even death in rare cases."

My stomach dropped to my feet and my world froze. The words "death in rare cases" reverberated in my head. In my life, rare cases happened all the time. I'd been called that at least a dozen times in my life! I started to sink to the floor and Mandi rushed over to hold me up straight.

She and a nurse settled me in the waiting area and gave me a cup of hot tea.

I begged to use the phone and was given a portable.

My mother's voice could be heard across the street, she was so angry with Billy. I could hear her voice shaking and then she dropped the phone. My dad yelled at her to go find that paper bag and then he grabbed the phone. I repeated the news. He was once again "on my way" to rescue us. Mini came on next and said she would keep the home fires burning with Neil and the three kids. Everyone was settled in playing a card game so there seemed no reason to bust up their evening. Ann called to say she couldn't make it so Mini would help my mother serve the dinner. "No worries, *ma cherie*. Go and look after your *petite fille*."

While I was on the phone, amidst the ongoing tests and frequent pulse and heartbeat checks, Wendy had slipped quietly from her sleep into a coma.

The first tests returned and Mandi told me Wendy would have to be transferred by ambulance to the hospital in Spencer. She insisted three times that I go home and get some rest because this could be a long battle and Wendy would need me if she came to. Mandi would call as soon as that happened. She gave me a big hug and rushed off to call the ambulance. "She's in good hands," she called over her shoulder.

Dad arrived minutes later and we both just stood looking on as my precious baby was strapped to a gurney and rolled into the back of an ambulance. Her closed eyelids looked so pale and I realized it was the first time I'd seen her sleeping without her thumb in her mouth since she had been born. I tucked her pajama pillow in with her and kissed her good-night.

The lights and siren were turned on the ambulance even before they left the parking lot.

I stood crying until my dad came and put his arm around me, steering me into my van. We drove silently up the hill back to the house.

I called Lana straight away and she agreed to work Thursday and Friday for me.

"Not to worry," she said. That was big coming from Lana.

Frances, Kelly and Warren were now playing a board game called Trouble and were hooting and hollering from downstairs. Mom and Mini worked at the dishes and clearing the mess in the kitchen while Neil sat beside me on the couch, rubbing my back. It was very comforting.

I filled him in on having found Billy and the kids through the teacher and the caller ID and finally tracking them right to Ivan's place through the adoption agency pamphlet I had found at Snake's.

Neil said there hadn't been any questions about who had broken in; everyone took for granted the perp left the scene before Neil had arrived to investigate. Gweek's body was in the hands of the police. The most interesting part was that Snake had called the security company and taken a strip off of Neil's boss for the chain on the gate being cut open. He wanted them to pay for it, and told them if they ever went on his property again without first getting his permission, he would have them arrested. Some thanks.

Neil also heard that Crunch had been removed by the police and was being held at an animal sanctuary in Spencer for investigation. I silently applauded. I heard snake was good eating; tasted like chicken. Not that I would ever eat it. Unless, maybe, if Kenneth cooked it. He could disguise the worst, smelliest piece of wild meat as the most succulent dish you ever tasted. He was always trying to convince Mini she should eat more "organic meats," as in wild moose, bear, elk and deer. It was healthier for her. And hunting was a sport they could both enjoy together, walking the acreage of their own property that went far beyond the District's boundary line. Wild game was in abundance in this part of the world.

And so, it seemed, were snakes.

The phone sounded and someone in the kitchen answered it. Mini yelled it was for me, so I grabbed the nearby portable. It was Riley.

"I can't believe the videotape I'm looking at," he told me. "You actually broke in and ransacked Snake's place? What were you thinking?"

I didn't say a thing. I wondered if I could get visiting rights from jail to see the kids when they needed me.

"Kathy, are you there?"

"I have company at the moment, Riley," I said, desperate to change the subject. "But you should know that Billy was back. He dropped off the kids and headed to Prince Grange. He'll be back in the morning."

"At what time? There are a lot of people that want to talk to that badass. I'm included."

"We're meeting at the courthouse in the morning at nine-thirty. It's a long story, but I can meet you and you could return my files. They have information on Billy that I need for the hearing."

He said he'd see me there.

My dodging tactics seemed to have worked.

I poured the last of the merlot into Neil's glass. I had been too busy with everything to get a chance to talk to him as much as I'd wanted. At the moment I really didn't care. All I wanted was some good news. But I'd settle for a big piece of chocolate anything. I would have even eaten chocolate snake.

CHAPTER TWELVE

In the morning, I realized the phone never rang all night, which I wasn't sure how to take. Mandi would have phoned if Wendy woke up, but then no one had phoned to say she was worse. So it was a wash.

My mother was up with me, making a stronger pot of coffee than I had the previous day.

"We're going to need it," she said.

"Meaning what?" I asked.

"I'm going to court with you."

"I'm not going there right away," I told her. "I packed some clean nighties and clothes for Wendy and I'm going to race in to Spencer for a quick visit before driving back for court."

"I'm going with you. Especially when you're all frazzled like this. You had this same look on you the day you lost those boots."

"Mom! I told you, that was Ann! And what about Warren?"

"Grandpa will get him out the door to the bus on time."

"Dad? He can't make toast, never mind get a noncompli-
ant eight-year-old to a bus stop on time."

"Not to worry. I've already packed Warren's lunch, made
them both a breakfast sandwich and have set the kitchen
clocks back ten minutes. They'll make it."

It would have to work. At the very least, Warren would
miss a day of school, but I didn't doubt he would learn plen-
ty from his grandfather. That thought made me fret for a half
second, but I pushed it away.

I dressed carefully in a white blouse with a navy skirt, pulling my hair back neatly into a braid. I put on a light dusting
of make-up, going for the conservative mother versus the
slutty mother that had ended up drunk under the table of a
stranger in public. Would the judge know about it? Would I
lose my kids because of it?

I always seemed to flog myself with everything I could
think of when I was down. Heap it on!

My mother had packed Wendy's clothes into a bigger bag
and added a lunch she made for us, complete with traveling
mugs of steaming coffees. I had to face it, I was glad my parents had come. It was a wonder that they were here for me. I
certainly hadn't deserved this the way I'd acted growing up. I
resolved to try and be nicer to them.

That feeling didn't last long with my mother being a
backseat driver all the way to Spencer. The 40-minute drive
felt like 400 as we careened through the Bulkley Valley.

"Watch out for that truck! Go slower – there's a curve in
the road." And when a rock flew up and chipped the windshield I thought I'd have to have my mother's seat profes-
sionally cleaned.

We arrived at the hospital and managed to find a parking
spot in the crowded area. I checked at the administration
office for Wendy's room number while my mom stopped at
the Seniors Auxiliary gift shop across the hall. She came out

with six red roses assembled in a purple vase. Very cheery.
My little girl's first roses as far as I knew. I slid my mother a
grateful smile for her thoughtfulness. My mind was so busy
between what I was going to say to a judge and how many
pairs of socks and underwear I had packed for Wendy that I
had not considered any presents for my daughter.

We took the elevator up to the third floor and walked
down the gloomy hall to the patients' rooms. The hospital
was very small. Most of the more seriously ill patients were
shipped on to larger centres in Tessak or flown Medevac to
Vancouver. Luckily Mandi figured everything Wendy needed was right in Spencer. An ace pediatrician had already
looked in on my baby and was on call 24 hours if needed.

Room 317 had four beds in it. Three stood empty and
waiting and one held the delicate frame of my sleeping beauty. She looked like a princess with her milky white cheeks
and brown hair curled around her ruby red lips. I told myself
I was not going to cry but within seconds I was a blubbering
basket case. I picked up her warm hand and kissed it while
my mom circled her bed and put the flowers on the bedside
table. She picked up Wendy's other hand and talked softly,
saying she had come all the way from New Brunswick to visit
her. I let Mom's voice drone on, not really listening. I laid
my head down beside Wendy's for a second. I was so tired.
Maybe I should join Wendy in a coma. Would I be able to
talk to her if I did?

I felt someone's arm around my back and looked up to see
a smiling nurse with the nametag *Angie* on a Mickey Mouse–
patterned shirt. She told us Wendy's fever had finally broke
and that we should have a talk with Dr. Keswick, whom she
would page for us. Meanwhile, she must take Wendy downstairs to X-ray.

"What is she getting X-rayed?" I asked.

"Her brain," came the solemn reply.

Mom and I exchanged glances. We watched as Wendy's bed was rolled from the room. We waited for Mandi in the hallway.

When she arrived we exchanged hugs. She had large dark circles beneath both eyes and her blonde hair was hanging half in and half out of her ponytail. It looked like it had been a long night.

"She's doing much better," she told us. "The concern now," and she hesitated for one second, but it was enough to make my heart sink, "is for brain damage. The swelling from such a high, extended fever might have left some lasting injuries. We'll know more after these next tests. Will you be back later today?"

I nodded my head, not able to trust my voice. *Brain damage to the smartest cookie in our crumbled family?*

"But when will she wake up?" asked my mother.

"When she's ready to," was all Mandi could give us. She patted me on the back. "I'll call you at work or at your place as soon as we know more." And she left us, heading to the next room down the hall.

The drive back to Halston was very, very quiet. I felt as fragile as an eggshell and every pothole I hit I worried that I would crack wide open.

We arrived at the courthouse 20 minutes early. I opened the door to the building for my mom and was greeted right away by Neil. He'd been waiting for us. Mom said hello to him, and then turned and gave me a smarmy look I recalled from my first boy/girl birthday party. It was an "I know who you like" thing that was totally uncalled for.

"Mother!" I complained.

"What?"

"Exactly!"

Neil handed me a familiar thick file folder marked "Family." Riley had been around earlier and dropped it off.

"Thanks," I told Neil. "I need this."

"Good luck in there," he said, leaning down to give my cheek an innocent peck. He smelled so good. Then he blazed us a big smile and left to head back to his office.

We checked the court day's roster and saw my name with Billy's listed beneath it. My stomach was upside down, churning and bubbling like a witch's cauldron as I sat in the hall. But I wasn't a witch, I reminded myself. I was here to get what my children deserved from their father. I was here for financial aid for the very roof over their heads. I was here so that they could live a normal life under that roof during an entire school year. I was here to finally put my foot down with someone who had kept me under his thumb for way too long.

I double-checked for all my papers that the court forms had said would be asked for: copies of my last filed income tax statement, our separation agreement and divorce papers and a synopsis of the situation.

The presiding judge was the Honorable Charlotte Wood, supposedly a tough cookie, but a fair one, Neil told us.

The courthouse outside door opened again and in strode Billy, his hand twirling the end of a toothpick that stuck from his mouth. He was dressed in a misbuttoned plaid shirt, scruffy jeans and his weathered old cowboy boots. His hair was mussed and he looked unshaven.

I smoothed down my outfit with my hands.

We never said a word to each other, but went into the courtroom in single file, Billy ahead. He scooted along a bench seat and my mother and I slid into the one right behind as only two long pew-styled benches occupied the small room. Imagine if you were at the fisticuff stage and had to sit in such close proximity to someone. Good thing there was a sheriff wearing a gun at the front of the room. Billy might yet get shot in the ass.

A young native boy, Louie Alix, was getting the riot act read to him for his second offence at driving his motocross bike down the highway.

"And without a helmet on! You, Mr. Alix, are a damn fool, as well as a young man now two hundred seventy-five dollars poorer." The judge banged her gavel on her desk and shuffled papers without giving Louie another glance. Dismissed.

Next.

The sheriff stood and called Billy's name and showed him where to stand. He then called my name and placed me almost beside Billy only further down the railing. I could reach out and hit him, uncomfortable in the knowledge that he could do the same. Maybe we *had* come to the fisticuff stage, I mused. At that moment I sure wanted to kick his butt. Our Wendy was facing possible brain damage and I was finding it impossible not to blame *him* for taking her away from me in the first place. I would have had her in the hospital days before it got as bad as it had. Not that it would have because I would never have given her aspirin for a fever.

Both of us faced the judge.

She kept her silvered head down and appeared to be reading, I presumed about why we were there.

"So," she began, "this is Mr. Billy Sands, and ex-wife Kathy Sands?"

We both nodded.

"And Kathy Sands is filing for Billy Sands to pay the sum owed in arrears of child support of twenty-five hundred dollars, correct?"

I nodded again but Billy cleared his throat and said, "No, *that's* not right, lady."

An eyelid on the judge slid slowly open like a crocodile's, maybe at the word *lady*. She seemed to take another minute and really give Billy the once-over. Her eyes took in the unkempt appearance, the toothpick in the mouth and I assumed the way he kept smacking his rolled-up subpoena in his hand against his other palm.

"So what is right, Mr. Sands?"

"Well, this woman," and he jabbed the rolled paper in his hand toward me, "is not a very good mother. She took money I gave her and spent it on herself. Look at the hairdo, the man-i-cure and the clothes she's wearing. All fancy-dancy. I paid her money that I worked hard for, to help raise them kids. They don't need much, just a bit of food, some clothes and a warm bed, but that's not the way she tells it. I give them lots of love and I treat them real good. Just not with silver spoons. It's not right she's here wanting more. I just gave her eleven hundred dollars."

I could tell it was my mother that was "tsking" somewhere behind me.

Billy turned to give me a resentful glare like he was really giving it to me.

My face was pink and I felt like I was in grade three again, wearing the jumper my mom had made. A pack of girls had swarmed me and poked fun at the way the buttons didn't quite line up straight, how my slip hung below the hem line.

I hadn't been attacked for what I wore for 28 years but it felt the same. I looked down. I'd bought the Calvin Klein blouse at the consignment store in Spencer. The faded leather skirt was from the Salvation Army thrift store in Halston. Total cost $18.75. Would I have to disclose that in public? As for the fingernails, what nails? I had chewed them all off and last time they'd seen a manicurist, I had been nine months pregnant and it was a gift from my mother.

Judge Wood did not acknowledge me or give me any grief. She glommed onto Billy. "I have a copy of your separation agreement before me. Do you also have a copy, Mr. Sands?"

I handed him a copy I'd made.

"Is this your signature at the end of this agreement document, sir?"

Billy looked it over. "Where? What signature?"

I walked over and flipped the document to page two and pointed to where his signature sat just above mine. It was dated five years and three months ago.

"Oh, aha. Yeh," he acknowledged.

"This document you signed says you agreed to pay five hundred dollars a month to Kathy Sands in support for her caring for your children. Is this not correct?"

"Well, yes, ma'am, but we have joint custody, if you'll notice that in there, and I have the kids right now, so I don't need to be paying her anything."

"I also have here a record of all the dates she has had them in her care and when you have had them in yours. Do you have a copy of that?"

Again I handed Billy a copy of the referred paper. I tried to point out what he should be looking at, but he slapped my hand away.

From the look on her face, that didn't sit so well with the judge.

"Mr. Sands, have you a copy of your last filed income tax statement?"

Billy shook his head no.

"You were supposed to bring this paper into the courtroom today. Were you not informed of that?"

Billy glared at her. "No, I was not."

Judge Wood motioned for the bailiff to come forward. She whispered something in his ear and he left the room.

"Did you want to rethink that answer?" she asked Billy.

"I didn't know about bringing in anything," he repeated.

The courtroom door opened and in walked a sheriff I did

not recognize. He looked over at Billy and smiled as he marched up to the judge's podium.

"Yes, Your Honour?" he asked.

"Hi, Graham. Were you the one in Tessak to serve Mr. Sands the summons to appear before me today regarding the matter of funds owed?"

"Yes, Your Honour, I was."

And did you or did you not advise Mr. Sands of all the paperwork he needed to bring with him?"

"I did, Your Honour. I even pointed out the list on the back of the summons of what he would need to bring."

"Thank you, Graham. You can go."

Billy coughed nervously into his hand. He was squirming as he stood. I wished the moment could go on for another few.

Judge Wood looked over at me and asked, "You are applying for sole custody as well?"

"I didn't think I could do it today," I said, "but yes, I am."

"Well, seeing how hard it was for you to get Mr. Sands served and gauging with the attitude, would there be a problem with us doing this right now?"

I tried not to show my surprise. My heart was racing. "No, Your Honour. I have all that I need, I think."

"Mr. Sands, did you want to be brought back into court next month or would you like to resolve this custody issue now?"

Billy looked at me again, a confident look once more on his face. What was the ace he figured he held? Did he know about Riley?

"Yes, ma'am. Let her rip!"

The judge began by asking me about my financial affairs and again I presented her with the papers: my income tax return, my house appraisal, references and bank statements.

Billy was given a 20-minute recess to fill out his financial guesstimate for the court and his statement of why he should obtain custody of Wendy and Warren.

When we adjourned, Judge Wood looked over what we had given her.

It took only three minutes to speak. "I hereby order Billy Sands to pay all monies owed immediately to Kathy Sands. If you fail to do so, I will charge you with contempt of court and have you thrown in jail. On top of this, your wages and any monies coming from the government will be garnish-eed."

"I also order the joint-custody terms to be changed to sole custody in favour of Mrs. Kathy Sands.

"Mrs. Sands, I wish you well with these endeavors and I admire your courage on handling this process by yourself." And she banged her gavel.

I heard rather than saw my mother yell, "Yippee."

I watched the grin on Billy's face as it fell. He looked shocked. I bet I could have pushed him over with his tooth-pick. Whatever he'd tried to tell the judge had fallen on deaf ears.

Me, I felt elated! Judge Wood had done what I could never do with this irresponsible excuse for a father. Maybe now he would listen?

I turned and saw that Riley was standing just inside the door. His eyes were glued onto Billy. He looked for a quick second at me and then stepped forward, taking Billy by the elbow.

"Hey Riley, buddy. How's things?" Billy looked nervously around the room.

"Good for me," Riley told him, "but not for you. I forgot to mention I'm with the Vancouver RCMP and we have a few questions for you. Come this way."

Billy's jaw swung, but he complied.

And Billy Sands once more disappeared from my life. I let go a rattling sigh.

Neil and my mother wanted to celebrate so we left the wrapped sandwiches for tomorrow and went to Brewstirs for foaming lattes and Thai noodle salads. We clinked glasses and recounted every last word that had been said in the courtroom. It had all happened so fast. My kids were going to have a much more solid future.

We finished lunch and said thanks and good-bye to Neil. He promised he would call me tomorrow. Mom and I drove back to Spencer to look in on Wendy. She was plugged into an IV for fluids and had monitors strapped across her forehead. Her cheeks looked less flushed, but she was still deep in her coma. Mandi came by, explaining the results of the X-rays had been inconclusive. They were trying to study the brain activity through the monitors.

I sat by my daughter's bed and talked to her for hours until my throat got sore. I kissed her good night and we headed back to Halston again.

We stopped in at Mini's and she brought us into her warm kitchen before throwing her arms around me. "I think I know that you have some wonderful news!" she said.

I couldn't believe it! Wendy had come out of her coma while we were driving here? Had Sebastian said that? "Is this about Wendy?" I asked.

"About Wendy and Warren," Mini said. She filled the kettle and turned it on. "About the sole custody 'earing. You did win it, didn't you? That's what Sebastian tried to tell me, I think. Well, actually 'e showed me three white doves flying away and a picture of a big foot coming down on top of Billy's 'ead. I actually figured it out myself from there! *C'est vrai?*"

"Right, yes, you were a hundred percent right." And she *was* right. I should be very happy for the three of us. Life was going to change for the better at our house now. If Wendy woke up, that was.

I asked Mom to make the tea and guided Mini around the corner for a minute.

"So has Sebastian told you what's up with Kenneth and all these secret meetings?" I whispered.

Mini's lips pursed and her shoulders slumped.

Guess not.

"But have you asked him?"

"'E won't tell me," Mini whimpered. "'E says I should spend time cleaning the storage out of the shed instead of prying. But then I decided to just follow Kenneth." Mini looked around me for any sign of my mother. "I watched 'im drive into town and then 'e drove up the hill and instead of turning right toward your place, 'e kept going. There is a new subtraction behind called Ruiter Heights. 'E turned into a large driveway. There were four other vehicles around the place as well."

I was puzzled. I thought Mini meant new subdivision, but Ann's area was called Morgan Subdivision. Whose house was he visiting and why?

"I'm pretty sure I saw Ann's silver Audi parked there, too." Mini gave an unconvincing laugh like it was all somehow a joke. Her eyes looked sunken like she wasn't getting any sleep.

I walked over and put my arms around as much of her as I could.

"It's not what you think, Mini. It couldn't be. There has to be a logical explanation."

"Even Sebastian says it is nothing and gets all twisted every time I mention it. 'E won't show me anything about Kenneth. 'Ow can a psychic guide be selective like that? Oh, by the way, Sebastian did show me a vision of your workplace. It was all wrapped up like a present. With yellow ribbon around it and a big bow on the door. But the windows were all dark and clouded and squiggles of some kind streaked down the glass. I think Sebastian means for you to be careful if you go to work today."

I *had* been planning on popping by to check on Lana. Sheesh, what next?

"But what do you think I should do about Kenneth? Should I tell 'im I followed 'im?" Mini asked.

"You just have to take that man of yours by his ear and drag him out of that place," piped a voice from behind me. I jumped out of my shoes and whipped around to see my mother standing there, a saucer and teacup in her hand. She took a sip and smiled at us.

"When it comes to putting your foot down with a man, sometimes you have to use *both* feet. Not just one."

We stared at her, mulling that over. "A baseball bat works wonders too," she added. It was nice to see Mini laugh.

But the upturned mouth quickly went south again. "I just love Kenneth so much. I'm worried that something I won't like is going on behind my rear. And my 'eart has fallen out of 'aving this big party for our anniversary. I mean, there's still crime scene tape around the property, and RCMP and family of Kitty's and Judy's coming by. That investigator, Ted Perdue, 'as practically made it a daily pilgrimace. Did you know they found a toothpick on Kitty's body? The same kind Billy chews? It was still in its wrapper in her pullover pocket."

Mom and I exchanged glances, hers a very angry look.

Did she think Billy was capable of this?

And was he? I was starting to get my own doubts with all this evidence piling against him. But I was not going to sit around and let the police stack up evidence just because it was the most obvious route out. Like Kenneth's disappearances, it was possible there was another explanation.

I took Mom back to the house and we were both relieved
to see Warren charging around the living room in his Batman gear. Regi was at the kitchen table entertaining three of
Halston's homeless drunkards. The stench of their having
slept in garbage bins and filthy blankets hit me from across
the room.

"Dad! What were you thinking?" I started.

These men were nicknamed the Mall Security as they
hung out at the shopping centre every day. The shopping
carts were chained together, costing a dollar coin to use
which you got back when returned. The "Security" waited
inside the warmth of the mall hoping a rushed customer
would leave their cart in the parking lot. It only took two
dollars or loonies to get a beer at the mall's liquor store.

All heads were down, concentrating on their cards. They
were playing poker. Regi had most of the chips and what
looked like a half pack of someone's cigarettes, a shiny button, a food voucher and something wadded in a silver packet.

"Game's over, fellows," I said. "Time to head back to
work." I gave each of Regi's new acquaintances a meaningful
look. They were quick to scuffle out of their chairs and head
to the door.

"Same time tomorrow, fellas," called Regi good-naturedly.

"Nope," I said, cutting him off. "This casino has officially
been busted. Game's up!"

The Rum Rats fled at the word "busted."

"Regi, how could you?" squawked my mother, who
whomped him over the head with her purse. "You're supposed to be spending time with Warren!"

Regi shrugged. "Warren went 'all in' early. He was out of
the game half an hour ago. What was I supposed to do?"

Mom "tsked" again and marched down the hall toward
her bedroom.

I gave Warren a big hug and kisses, made a quick call

about Wendy's condition which hadn't changed and said I'd be back in an hour. I wanted to check on some expected freight at the store and see how Lana was doing.

I hopped into the van and drove back down the hill.

The store was busy when I arrived. Boxes of freight were piled high just inside the back door. People were waiting for help with the bread makers and stereos so I did swing-bys with pamphlets and then took them on one by one as best I could. Even Lana made an effort, getting off her stool and opening an iPod case for a woman trying to buy a grad gift for her teenager.

"Whatever," I heard Lana tell the woman.

After it died down, Lana showed me a credit application she had filled out for someone looking at a "NEW HOME" package. A stereo, microwave, bread maker, 2 iPods, phone set, television and a DVD recorder for a low cost of $3999. Financed at 21% interest, but the company we dealt with was willing to take kids and risky buyers the banks would not normally touch. I knew the client and it looked promising so I started phoning in the application.

Lana approached the slew of boxes in the back. One box stuck out. Not a big one. Only 12" by 12" square. Lana shook it and showed it to me where I stood with the phone cinched between my ear and shoulder. The box was addressed to me and not to Halston Electronics World. I nodded at Lana. "Go ahead," I mouthed.

She shook it again like a kid checking out a Christmas present, then took the box cutter and opened it wide. Before I could register what happened something flew out of the box and hit Lana in her throat. It wasn't big, but it was long and skinny.

She screamed and dropped the box. The thing that had hit her landed on the linoleum and slithered away toward the stack of boxes.

I pulled the phone from my ear. "Lana?"

She just stood there in shock with her hands around her throat. Her eyes gradually swiveled to mine. There was no one home in her gaze. I watched her knees buckle as she collapsed to the floor.

I hung up on the finance agent and dialed the number for the ambulance. I gave the person on the other end the details and quickly disconnected.

I ran to Lana and pried her fingers from her throat. Two identical holes were embedded in the side of her neck, already looking red and swollen. A snake bite!

I looked toward where the snake had slithered, terrified it would return, but knowing the ambulance attendants would need to know exactly what had bitten Lana. I could hear a rattling sound close behind a television box that sat on the floor between the counter and us, and knew instantly it was a rattlesnake. Not hard to come by in British Columbia. This was very serious.

"Don't move," I told Lana. "Help is coming. Just stay still. The less you move, the better, as it could speed the poison through your system."

"Oh my God, my tongue is going nummmb," Lana said, wide-eyed and panicked.

I kept one eye on where the rattle was coming from and one on Lana until the ambulance arrived at the delivery back door. It was attendants T-Bone and Michaella and they were on her in no time. Michaella used her radiophone to call for police backup, and then made a call to the local veterinarian, who came and got the snake. It was put in a cage that was labeled for evidence by Corporal Currie, who looked like he was going to come out of his skin. He was visibly shaking as he made a wide walk around the boxes to talk to me as Lana was loaded into the ambulance.

Currie cleared the store of all the lookie-loos and then

proceeded to place crime-scene tape across the front door of the store. I started to protest, but Currie insisted it was police procedure and heaven forbid he should stray from the book!

So I locked up and went home. I could do nothing more at the store, nothing more at the hospital, nothing more for the case against Bill. It was time for a rest. I could feel the weariness right inside my very bones. It was overwhelming.

No one was there, or so I thought, and the note on the fridge said "We're at Mini's helping to make blintzes. Home at six with dinner."

I didn't have time to figure out what that meant because I heard a crash coming from the kids' room. What now? I grabbed the marble rolling pin from on top of the fridge and tiptoed down the hall. Another crash, lots of rustling noises. I peeked around the doorframe and saw Billy with his back to me on his knees in front of the bunk beds. I lowered the rolling pin. He was firing toys out from under the bed into the middle of the room. The kids' things had been strewn without a care to whether or not they broke. It never looked this bad even on their highest energy days.

"What are you looking for?"

Billy's head whipped around. "Jesus, you startled me. Where's that Barbie camper van I gave Wendy?" He scuttled on his knees over to their large plastic toy box and turned it upside down, dumping the contents to the floor. He sifted through all the small objects, looking for what I couldn't tell. Obviously not the camper van. It would never have fit in the toy box.

"Where is it!" he shouted.

"Sheesh," I said. "Who got you so frazzled? The police? Were you able to clear all this up about Judy? Do they know what happened to her by now?"

Bill's eyes looked crazed. "This is serious, Kathy. I don't have an alibi for when Judy went missing. But that's the least of my worries. Right now I need to find where the hell that camper thing is!"

I started to laugh at him. He looked so ridiculous crawling on his knees around the room. But the laughter died when I watched another man slide silently into the room. He was wearing coveralls that said Rug Specialist Carpet Cleaning and he had a gun in his hand. He sure didn't look like he was here to clean our carpets. He was moving quickly up behind Billy.

I didn't recognize him, but then again I did. He really looked like someone, but I couldn't figure out whom. He definitely was not from town. He put the gun to the base of Bill's skull and said, "You have two minutes to produce it, Billy, or you are going to make one hell of a mess in your kids' room."

The man then pointed the gun at me. "Where is it?"

"Who are y . . . you?" I stuttered.

"Never mind," he said, the gun never wavering from the angle pointed right between my eyes. "Where is the bike?"

I had no idea what he was talking about. What bike? I studied the man now holding Bill around the throat with his one arm. That was it. That was who he looked like. Like Billy! Now that I saw it, it was uncanny how much they looked alike. Same height, same crooked nose, same brown cowboy boots. The man had grey hair, which made him look about ten years older, maybe a little less.

"Hel-loo," came my mother's voice from the kitchen, "dinner is ready. Get it while it's hot!" she called.

I heard my dad say, "It's hot. She's hot. We're hot."

Then Warren's voice. "You're hot. I'm hot. She's hot. Wahoo." The slap of hands in the air. High fives.

"Get rid of them," the carpet man growled at me. "Go!"

I walked to the kitchen, trying to force a fake smile.

"Hi, everyone!" I caught Warren as he leapt up at me. "I

need you to go to the store for something. Right now," I said. "I need paper towels." It was the first thing that popped into my panicked mind.

"Don't be silly," my mother said. "There are four new rolls in the hall closet. I saw them when I was cleaning."

I rolled my eyes at her. "Then I need four more." I glared at her, hoping she would get my meaning that something else was up!

A look of enlightenment came upon her face. "Oh, is someone else here, dear?"

I nodded my head but said, "No" loud enough for the Smiths next door to hear and then shook my head toward the front door. I mouthed the word "go" and closed my eyes. If I couldn't get rid of them, chances were we would all be killed. All five of us instead of just Billy and me.

Her face lit up like a flood light. "Oh my goodness. It's Neil. Is he indisposed? Did we walk in on something? Oh, Regi. This is good. This is so good. Come on, Warren. Reg. We'll take the van, honey, if you don't mind." She chuckled. "Of course you don't. . . . How long will we be, Kathy?"

Thank heavens. Even if she got the reasons wrong, it was working.

"Just need about thirty minutes."

"Oh, you go, girl," my mother said.

I couldn't help myself. "Mother!" My cheeks pinked up.

"I'll just be a second," said Dad as he started down the hallway toward Wendy and Warren's room.

"No, Dad. Stop!"

As usual, Dad listened to no one. "Just going to get my hat . . ." He glanced into Warren and Wendy's room and must have seen the gunman. "Oops. Hello," I heard him say in a high-pitched voice.

A shot rang out and my father fell forward.

"Dad!" I screamed. I forgot everything and ran toward him.

"Shit," I heard the man say and he came out of the kids' room with his arm still around Billy's neck.

"You find it," he yelled at me as he passed my dad and me. "I'll be in touch."

He walked backwards down the hall with Billy, the gun pointed unnecessarily at us – me now kneeling on the floor beside Dad. Blood was pouring out from around his hands that were holding onto his right thigh.

I heard a *whonk*. I looked up and saw the gunman sag a bit after Mom hit him on the back of the head with my largest cast iron frying pan.

"Christ," the man swore. He looked a little cross-eyed but he did not go down. "You people are crazy."

He left out the front door, shoving Billy into a silver extended cab pickup that closely resembled Bill's white pickup. As it sped off I noticed the rear tailgate was also missing. What were the chances?

CHAPTER THIRTEEN

Mom came running with kitchen towels which I pressed on Dad's leg to try and stem the blood flow.

"Phone the ambulance," I said with a sigh.

T-Bone and Michaella arrived 10 minutes later with all four eyebrows raised between them.

"Did you time her?" Michaella asked her partner.

T-Bone grinned before adding to me, "We're starting to think you have a crush on one of us. Either that or you figure we give travel reward miles."

Dad was placed on a gurney and carried out, the attendants saying "Um, hmm" to the jokes that spilled from his lips. Today he seemed stuck on blonde jokes.

"How do you drown a blonde?" he asked no one. "You put a scratch-and-sniff sticker on the bottom of the pool."

Um, hmm.

"See you at the clinic," T-Bone called over his shoulder. "Dr. Tempo will be attending. He's only a few minutes behind."

I wondered if Mandi was still in Spencer working the ER

and if she'd had to deal with Lana's snake bite as well as Wendy.

Mother scrambled into the ambulance and sat beside Regi, who blew kisses at my wide-eyed son. Warren seemed more energized than traumatized.

"Holy cool! Grandpa took a bullet! Just *wait* 'til I tell Kyle. Can I phone him, Mom? Can I?"

"No," I said as I moved toward the kitchen. A large box marked "Pizza" sat on top of the stove. I flipped it open. It was a meat-lover's, Warren's and my favourite. "Why don't you have a quick bite, then we'll go see your 'way cool' Grandpa?"

I took more old towels from the closet and covered the bloodstain on the carpet. I would deal with it later, hoping secretly that my mother would beat me to it.

Dr. Tempo managed to pull the bullet out of Dad's thigh with a pair of forceps, while being asked why blondes can't dial 911.

Dr. Tempo just smiled politely, washing the wound with disinfectant before stitching up the gaping hole with sutures.

"Because they can't find the eleven on the phone," my dad said, slapping his injured knee and frozen or not, howling at what he'd done. Who was the dumb one?

Dr. Tempo called the emergency room at the Spencer hospital for me. He learned there had been difficulty getting the antivenom snake serum but after multiple calls they managed to find some in Tessak. It had been helicoptered in. Lana would recover and be released tomorrow if all went well overnight.

Wendy was still in her coma, but her brain waves looked regular and Mandi figured her body was taking time to recoup. The poor dear had stressed herself to the limit, but she would come out of this. Mandi was sure of it. My relief was palpable.

Sergeant Tart and Corporal Currie hustled in to the clinic and ordered me into an examination room. Tart kept shaking her head.

"We've never had any situations like this in the history of Halston," she told me.

"What is going on with you? A snake attached to a brick thrown through your front window, your car blown up, a poisonous snake delivered to you at work and now your father gets shot?"

She forgot to add I had almost been snake food and had found a dead body in a closet, but of course she didn't know about that and I was going to leave it that way.

I gave an unconvincing "and your point is?" look, but I was shaking inside. She was right. This was scary stuff.

I described the man they were now looking for, making sure they knew how I felt about the resemblance to Billy and how their vehicles were so similar. I told them they might want to ask this mystery man where he'd been when Judy Charlie disappeared. They left still shaking their heads.

Meanwhile, Dr. Tempo applied a gauze pad to Dad's leg before sealing it with surgical tape. He told Dad to keep it elevated for the next few hours. Mom said she had duct tape in her suitcase and would strap him to a chair when they got back to the house. She gave Dad a piercing glare. A glare like that would have caused nightmares for the rest of us, but it flowed off Dad's back like water. "As long as there's a bottle of scotch within my reach . . . and a pretty girl's butt to pinch," he said to my mother, grabbing for her.

The painkiller had obviously kicked in.

Ann showed up, flying into the emergency room all a dither. "Why do I always have to hear things third hand from a dead charades player?" she boomed, stamping her foot. "Why didn't anyone call me?"

She saw our father and rushed over. "Dad! What did you

do this time? What happened to your leg?" she clucked, scowling at him like he was an errant child.

Then to Dr. Tempo, "Will he live? Is he going to be okay?"

Once the doctor filled her in, my sister turned her anger on me.

Why hadn't I phoned her right away? She had been told by Kenneth, who had been told by Mini at breakfast. Sebastian's image showed Mini a bottle of scotch with a hole in the side of it. The bloody booze kept draining out, very slow, which Mini had taken to be a good sign. It took her a while, but Mini figured out something was going to happen to our dad. And possibly one of his bottles of scotch.

"But I never thought he'd end up here! That he'd be shot at! What have you got yourself involved in now, Kathy?"

Like this was all *my* fault? My anger flared. "Where are your snow boots, Ann?" It was all I could think of.

Ann's jaw dropped and her cheeks pinked. She flashed a quick look at Mom's expression to see if it had changed.

"We were eating pizza, Auntie Ann, that's why Mom never phoned you!" Warren answered bravely for me.

But I wasn't the one who needed defending here. "How could I call you when you're never home anymore?" I said, my eyes narrowing slightly. "Where have you been disappearing to all these evenings?"

Ann's eyes popped wider and her mouth totally unhinged. "Wha . . . what?" she sputtered.

I covered Warren's little ears with my two hands. "You heard me. What have you and Kenneth been doing together all these nights? Mini is beside herself with worry and if I find out anything is going on between you and him, I will . . ."

My mother, having seen this version of a showdown

between her three kids countless times, cut in. "Kathy. That will be enough. What Ann does in her . . ."

I ignored her. My sister wasn't getting off this hook that easy. "What about it, Ann? What have you been doing?"

Ann turned her back to me and gave my father a hug. She walked toward the exit sign. "You'll find out soon enough." She stopped and gave me a glare. "What is it with you anyway? Isn't there enough gossip in this town without starting more rumours?" She left still mumbling to herself.

I was herded to help my mother fill out the release papers for my father's ambulance ride before we were finally able to pile back into the van. Well used to crutches, Dad was tossing them around like giant batons, while telling his twentieth blonde joke: She slept with a Brazilian. How many is a Brazilian?

Warren was right on my father's heels like a miniature terrier. "What's a blonde, Grandpa? Do we know any? Is Grandma one?"

I drove them home and reheated the leftover pizza.

The phone rang and I glanced at the caller ID. Number not identified. I didn't want to, but I picked it up. It was Snake.

"Where isss it?" he hissed.

My blood went from normal temperature to boiling. This man had caused so much misery in my life. "What is it you're looking for?" I shouted. My mom poked her head around the door, a question on her face.

"The motorbike with the key. The key and the numbers. Where did Billy put them?"

"I have no idea," I said, "but if you're so hot for me to find something for you, why are you trying to kill me?"

"I figured Billy would come to your funeral. Or at least bring the kids from wherever he was hiding. Turned out, he came back anyway. So you're halfway there. Find that bike and we'll let you live."

"Who is 'we' and who was the guy that came here and shot my dad?"

"Ivan shot your dad?"

"Who is Ivan?"

"You better be careful around that guy, sweetheart. You think I'm bad? He is one deadly dude."

"But who is he? What does he want with us?"

"He wants what I want, that bike, so you'd best get it and get it to me fast! Or your cute little buns will only be good for mounting on a wall."

I huffed and hung up on him. I watched as Mom went to the freezer and took out a fresh emergency tub of ice cream and returned to the dinner table.

Funny, I didn't drool or run after her. Probably because I was so puzzled. They were looking for a motorbike with a key and numbers. What motorbike? What key? And why had Billy been so desperate to find the Barbie camper he'd brought for Wendy?

I walked down to the kids' room and opened their closet. There sat the camper van where I had put it last week when the kids had left town with their father. I pulled it out and sat with it on the floor. *Talk to me,* I told it. It just sat there.

I opened the side door and looked inside. It was empty. If there was supposed to be something in there, that meant Wendy had opened it, seen this motorbike thing they were all looking for and had put it somewhere. "Shit."

"That's money in the Swear Jar," yelled Warren gleefully, as he pounced onto my lap, almost knocking me sideways. "Hey, why are you playing with Wendy's camper?"

"Mom was looking for something," I said. "A little motorbike. Did you see one of those, Warren?"

I stood and my son grabbed onto my knee. I walked in a

circle giving him a ride on my leg. He loved it when I did that.

"Yeh, sure."

"Yeh sure what, big guy?"

"Yeh, Wendy got a motorbike and a camper van."

My heart raced. He had seen it. "So where is it?" I stopped walking him round the room and bent down, looking straight at him. I let him know this was important. To me, to us.

"I dunno."

"I dunno" was the usual culprit for everything missing, broken or wrong in our house.

"Not good enough, Warren." I put my hands on his shoulders. "Mommy and Daddy need to see that bike."

Warren let go of my leg and ran to the toy box. He looked like a miniature Billy as he tossed the toys from it, looking for the bike.

"Not in there, I checked."

Warren put his little hand to his chin and seemed deep in thought. It would have been comical had this not been such a serious situation.

"It's in her pillow maybe. She keeps anything impotent there."

I smiled at his use of the word "impotent" and gave him a huge hug.

"I want you to stay here with Grandma," I told him. "I'm going to Spencer to visit your sister."

Warren gave me an extra-huge hug. "That was from me to Wendy. Tell her to come home now. She can sleep in a comma right here!"

I smiled again at his use of words. "You bet, big guy. I'll let her know."

I went out and told my mom what I was off to do and got in the van with a hot mug of coffee. An endless day.

The hospital was very quiet. All visiting hours were long since over. I didn't see a nurse – they must have been in a coffee room or needed elsewhere for the time being.

I tiptoed into Wendy's room and watched for a minute as her chest rose and fell in sleep. Then I broke down and wept. I couldn't stop it anymore. I cried for my daughter, for Judy Charlie, for Lana and for my father. While I was at it, I cried for me too. I was mid-wail and really starting to wind up when I heard Wendy's sweet voice.

"Don't cry, Mommy," she said.

Oh man. And I thought I had been crying seconds before. There lay my daughter with her eyes open and clear, telling me not to feel bad. I quickly thanked the heavens and promised to floss and do everything right from now on in exchange for this miracle.

I did as I was told and wiped off my face. She asked me for something to drink. I got her a cup of water while I rang for the nurse. Someone should know Wendy had come out of her coma.

The nurse came and took one look at Wendy and sped from the room with a big smile on her face.

Wendy and I talked for a few minutes. I gave her Warren's hug and then she said she was very tired and could she go back to sleep?

"Yes, my darling. But oh, wait. Do you have that motorbike Daddy gave you?"

She reached for her satin pillow and dug into the pajama pocket across the bottom of it. She pulled a toy motorcycle out.

It was much bigger than I had thought it would be, about six inches long and four high.

"You can let Warren play with this."

"Thanks, honey, but I'm afraid Daddy gave this to you when he shouldn't have. This bike belongs to someone else."

She looked sad. "So I have to give it back?"

"Yes, but we will try and get you a new one. Do you mind if I take this with me?"

"No." She gave a big yawn.

"Good." I kissed her forehead, happy to feel it was nice and cool. "I'll see you tomorrow night, but Grandma will be here first thing in the morning when visiting starts. Is that okay, pumpkin?"

She went back to sleep before she could answer.

The doctor on duty came in and checked Wendy's vitals. He opened her eyelids and flashed a light into them before saying everything seemed to be fine. Wendy had come back to us and there didn't appear to be any damage. They would wait until morning and put her through some different tests to assess her further.

I kissed Wendy again and left the hospital. The motorbike was in my purse and that was where it stayed the whole drive back to Halston. I kept looking at my purse across the seat on the passenger side, worried it was going to go somewhere. But it stayed put.

I brought it into the house. The hockey game was still on and Warren was leaping from chair to chair all sugared up. I said hello and told everyone the good news – Wendy was finally awake!

I excused myself for a minute and went into the bathroom and locked the door. I pulled the motorbike out of my shoulder bag and took a closer look at the miniature model that had been causing all the problems.

This was no ordinary toy. It was all black with real chrome pipes and handlebars. It had an orange teardrop gas tank. It was beautiful and must have cost someone a fortune. I flipped it over.

A large key was taped beneath the body of the bike. On both sides of the bike were miniature saddlebags. I snapped them open and found a scroll of paper inside the left one. It unfolded to show me a line of numbers. I returned it to the saddlebag.

With the bike safely hidden in the bread box, I picked up the phone and called the RCMP, asking to talk to Sergeant Tart. I was in way over my head and knew it.

It was late so Central Dispatch in Tessak once again took the call and I sat by the phone waiting.

To her credit, the sergeant was off duty, but she came over right away in full uniform. (Did she sleep in that get-up?)

Tart listened as my story unfolded before making calls from her shoulder radio. Within 10 minutes I had Corporal Currie and the newbie Constable Lyons on my doorstep. They arrived in civilian cars.

Warren bounced into the room, still high on whatever mix Grandpa had been plying his cup with all night. I never gave the kids pop or sugar-added juices – they had enough energy without the added kick.

Warren took one look at the gun on Joe Lyons' utility belt and made a move for it. In a lightning-fast motion, Warren grabbed the rookie's holster and would have had the gun out if he'd known how to undo it. A shocked look showed on the cop's face and before any of us could react, he flipped Warren onto his back. Warren's face clouded and for a minute I thought he was going to cry. The kid would never hurt a fly and he didn't understand the grave line he'd crossed over.

It was scary to see how slowly the new cop had first reacted, though. My confidence in his ability to protect me was shaken. Okay, but he *had* wrestled Warren to the floor. I couldn't do that. Where was Lyons when it was bedtime on a Saturday night?

After a serious look from me, Warren mumbled "I'm sorry" before speeding off toward Grandpa, who was sprawled on the couch with his foot up. The painkillers were enough to keep Regi tied down.

Everyone settled at the kitchen table to hear Tart's plan. A trap could be set for this Rug man we presumed was Ivan, who had Billy. We went over the facts one last time and then they left, Tart to make calls to head office. She took my phone off the hook before leaving.

"Don't answer your door and don't take any calls until I return."

That sounded easy.

We sat in the living room watching a hockey game, Dad shouting obscenities at every whistle. He was half out of it between the painkillers and the scotch and didn't seem to understand the plays called. Sometimes he was talking football: "No damned way! That was a first down!"

Meanwhile, Warren kept yelling "Cha-ching," as he kept track for the Swear Jar. He told his grandpa he accepted credit cards.

I started to drift off as I watched the players move the puck back and forth on the television screen. It was the Vancouver Canucks playing the Montreal Canadiens – my two favourite teams, east and west – but it was a slow game without a lot of scoring. The day's events were finally catching up to me and I snuggled deeper in the overstuffed armchair I was in. So I admit I lost track of a few things for a minute. Like where my son had gone.

I snapped to when the doorbell sounded. It was Sergeant Tart, Corporal Currie and Corporal Lyons, whose jumbo ears had popped out from beneath his police cap. He looked like a teenager.

Tart had a new plan with the help of head office. A three-car backup was coming from Spencer, Graffers and Banner Lake detachments. We didn't usually get murderers in this neck of the woods. Yes, we had suicides and murder/suicides

within families, but Halston had just been through two unexplained murders and now two attempted murders.

Tart put the phone back on the hook and I was told to tell
this Ivan or Snake or whoever called next that I would bring
the toy motorbike to wherever they wanted. The cops would
put a tracer on the bike and follow me and nab Ivan and
Snake at that point.

"But how will you know what the key fits?" I asked. "Or
what the numbers are for?"

Tart hadn't thought of that.

I was putting my life in these people's hands?

Currie piped up with another plan and then Tart countered with her own.

As they bantered back and forth, I realized I hadn't heard
Warren pinging around for quite some time. While the plans
were being hashed out, I thought I should find where he'd
crashed. That kid fell asleep anywhere. If he was standing
when he went, hopefully there was a soft chair around to
catch his head. I once discovered him face-planted on a
kitchen chair, still standing up, snoring away.

Warren wasn't in the living room or kitchen, so I went
down the hall. Not in the office or his room or my room. I
went downstairs – no Warren. I went back to his bedroom
and that's when I noticed the camper van was gone and the
bedroom window was wide open. The toy box had been
pushed to directly beneath the gaping window. It would have
been easy for Warren to climb up and out.

"Warren," I shrieked to no one. Tart and Currie came
running in, guns drawn.

"Cripes," I yelled, terrified from the way they had rushed
in ready to shoot something. "Put those away!"

I leaned my head out the window into the cool, dark air.
An old, rickety ladder I had inherited with the house was
propped below. There was no sign of Warren anywhere.

"Warren. Warren!" I yelled some more.

I pulled my head back inside. "He's gone," I sobbed. "Crap!"

There was a knock at the front door. I heard Mom answer it, chatting away to whoever it was.

I peered down the hall and saw Riley's frame once again gracing my home. I half hoped he had a bottle of Maple's with him. Not that I wanted to get naked in front of him again – well, not at this particular moment – but a drink would sure be all right.

I went out to greet him, frantically explaining that Warren had gone missing. Riley didn't look half as upset as I'd hoped. This man just didn't seem to get the connection with kids.

He motioned for me to take a seat in the living room across from where my dad lay snoring. "I was sent in to take over this plan." He looked directly at Tart, who had taken a seat beside me, but there didn't seem to be any resistance there. I felt a bit relieved at the idea. The Keystone Cops seemed a little clipped for experience.

I quickly filled Riley in on all the details, hoping that things would speed up now that Warren was missing. This reeked of Billy! I bet he'd lured Warren outside and got him to bring the van with him.

So now Ivan and Snake had Billy and my son. I didn't care what they did to Bill, but surely these men wouldn't hurt a boy? A flash of the news and the body of Kitty Tyson came to mind. I was certain it was this Ivan who was responsible for Kitty's death. It couldn't have been Billy, and the resemblance between Bill and Ivan was uncanny. Not as much in their looks as in their height, build, clothes and choice of vehicles. How could it get any closer than that?

Riley's idea was to wait for Snake or Ivan to call, and they would because the camper van no longer held what they were looking for. The motorbike was safely hidden in my bread box.

I was to arrange a meeting place to exchange what they wanted for Warren and Billy, if Bill wasn't dead already. I crossed myself. It really would be horrible if the kids lost their father. He might be irresponsible and not much better than a wayward child sometimes, but he had a big heart and really loved his children. I hoped he didn't die, but I wasn't averse to him getting the stuffing kicked out of him. That wouldn't be too bad.

When the call finally came, we all jumped. My mother had joined the mustering, letting my father sleep with a breathe-aid strip stuck across his nose. As if that would help the industrial-size snores swirling around us.

It was 10 minutes to midnight. I had made a third pot of coffee strong enough to make mud pies with and felt like Warren must have hours before. I wanted to pogo stick around the room. At the sound of the ringing, my mother swore and then darted a guilty look to me.

I pointed toward the Swear Jar on the fridge and then answered the phone. "Hello." Deadpan. No emotion.

"Do you have what I want?"

"I do."

"Are you willing to exchange it for your husband and kid?"

I said a quick mental thank you that they were alive. "He's not my husband. But yes, I want them back."

There was a second of silence. "I want you to bring the bike to Snake's house on Heritage Road. I assume you already know where that is?"

"I do." Then I shivered. At least Crunch had been removed. But there was still that oven-eater Prince and, of course, Snake himself. Ugh.

"Meet us there at one a.m. sharp. And you can tell those

cops with you to stay at your place. If I see one cop's hat or head, this wound-up brat of yours will be missing his tongue. Understand?"

"I do." And I meant it. While I wanted this creep to pay for kidnapping Warren, shooting Dad and possibly terroriz-ing Kitty and Judy, I would do nothing to jeopardize the life or tongue of my son.

Okay, and his miserable father.

I hung up the receiver, catching Dad's loud moan from the other room. Ivan had some serious penance coming.

"One o'clock at Snake's place. No cops or he'll maim Warren. He was quite firm about that!"

My mother gasped before owling around the room. "Is this for real? Is there a hidden camera show taping? Things like this don't happen in Canada, do they?"

I patted her knee. "Hang in there, Mom. You know what? It's late but I've this incredible craving for some of Wendy's favourite cookies. Remember the chocolate sandwiches with the white iced filling you used to make? The recipe is in the pink cookbook folder above the stove. I have a ton of cocoa in the closet. We can take her some tomorrow. I know she'd love that!"

Mom wandered off in a daze toward the kitchen. When troubled, we baked. I wished I could join her.

Riley put a tick-sized tracer in the van and on the mini motorbike before placing a one-way taping wire under my shirt. My stomach fluttered like mad when he did that and his grin told me he was enjoying himself as well. Riley said they could listen and record with the device. He then tried to give me a handgun, but I turned it down. "I would end up shooting myself in the foot," I argued.

"Okay then. I or one of the constables won't be too far behind you," he said.

I was ready. I went to the kitchen and gave my mom a kiss

on her floury cheek. She already had the dough made and was piling blobs of it on cookie sheets. My dad woke up when I kissed his forehead, and although he grimaced when he sat up, he demanded to know what was going on. He seemed semi-rested and clearer headed. I filled him in on the latest then said I really had to be taking off.

I checked my watch. It was ten to one.

As I started to head out, Sergeant Tart's pager went off. I waited another minute while she called in and listened as dispatch said a bomb had gone off in the Halston shopping centre. The drugstore had a huge gaping hole in the side of it and someone was stealing the drugs from the dispensary. All hands on deck!

Tart and Currie bolted for the door, Tart barking at Lyons to stay with Riley. Lyons looked like a forlorn younger brother who was being left behind from the pool party, as the two senior officers peeled off.

Feeling sick from nerves, I used the washroom one last time before stepping out into the brisk spring air. It snapped me to attention pretty quick. I got into my van. The motorcycle once more rode shotgun in the passenger seat.

Thankfully I didn't know at the time that Riley had stuffed Lyons into the back of the van and covered him with a blanket. I would never have taken the chance with my son's tongue like that. I also would have turned around and thrown Lyons out at Riley's feet, telling Riley I never wanted to see him again. Whatever was with him and kids?

As said, it was good that I didn't know.

I drove slowly to Snake's place. "Wouldn't want to get a speeding ticket," I said out loud, hoping it was heard through the wire on my chest.

The gate across the driveway at 3001 Heritage Drive was ajar. I pulled to a stop across the street, afraid to get too close yet. The moon was full and I could see right away Prince was not at his usual post. I picked up the toy bike and got out of the van. I looked carefully around and could see no one. Things were deathly quiet as usual, not only on the street, but in the entire area. Not a single dog barking or a vehicle coming or going. I'd never felt so deserted in my life. Okay, that was a lie. My dad left me at a gas station once. It was over three hours before he returned. His story was that he forgot me even though his breath smelled like beer.

I knew Riley was going to be somewhere in the vicinity but I had no idea where. I would have to trust him, something I was not used to doing with any man these days. I sauntered toward the back door of the house. The smell of fresh doggy doo hit my nose and I looked down. "Shit-ski," I garbled, trying to pull out of a swear word as I saw my sneaker was ankle deep in a pile of Prince's crap.

Snake picked then to step out of the shadows of the gate behind me. I hadn't even seen him when I walked past.

The silver rings on his fingers flashed as he snatched the bike from me. He grabbed my left arm with his other hand and then flipped the bike upside down, noticing the key was still intact.

"Purrfect," he hissed.

He pushed me roughly toward the stairs that led into the house. I gratefully went toward them to try to scrape some of the stink off my foot. The smell was gagging me. What did they feed that thing? Oh, right, I remembered. But what had the salesman eaten to come out smelling that bad?

"You've got what you want," I told him. "Now send Warren and Billy out." I tried to sound brave but my voice was jittery, like I was once more seated at the back of a school bus as it drove across the yellow line rumble strips.

Snake shoved me forward again and motioned up the steep steps. I gulped in cool night air before forcing my poopy foot and then my clean one back up those dreaded stairs. The window that I broke the other night had been boarded up. It made the place look like a crack house. Maybe it was a crack house? What did I know?

I stood before the closed screen door and waited. "Open it. Go in," said Snake.

As I opened the door, Prince's head, which was the size of my entire torso, popped up from where he had been stretched out lying on the kitchen floor. He took a sniff in my direction, licked his lips and in one swift motion was righted on his feet and trying to run. I thanked my lucky stars for linoleum. Once again he was spinning his wheels, not able to get purchase even with his sharp claws on that slick surface.

"Down, boy!" barked Snake. "Not yet," he added.

Not yet? I felt a squeeze of pee run down my leg. I'd mentioned how I felt about mean dogs, right? Any dogs actually. Big ones, small ones. To stand here and be promised to a pony-sized hound from hell as though I were a shrimp appy was terrifying. My entire stomach was churning like I was going to vomit. What a way to go, I figured. Smelling of pee, dog poo and vomit. My mother would be too embarrassed to attend my funeral!

Snake's arm reached out and he opened the door leading to the basement. Last time I was down there I had been lurched at by a dead body and crushed by a giant snake. I shivered, not wanting to return, but again, Snake insisted.

He flicked on the light from the top and we descended, me in front so I couldn't run away, Prince in the rear. Snake walked to the far end of the basement and the dog followed, sniffing me wildly as he passed my leg.

Keeping one eye on me, Snake reached beside the far window and pressed a small hidden button. The entire wall with the mural of the gravel road and fall leaves began to slide away. It was slow, and I could faintly hear a motor's hum as

the wall slid back on tracks into casings I had never noticed
before.

Behind the fake paneling was a solid wall of concrete in-
terrupted by a tall steel door with a pin-code lock above the
doorknob. Snake moved to it and pulled the tiny scrap of
paper from the miniature motorcycle's saddlebag. He put the
bike down on the floor beside him and looked over his
shoulder at me.

He told Prince to "guard." The Doberman sat beside me
and started rolling off a low growl from his throat. A water-
fall of drool cascaded from its mouth. "Make one move and
you're dead," Snake said. I believed him.

I remembered the wire beneath my shirt. "We're going
behind a wall in the basement," I said to the room.

"Shut up!" yelled Snake.

Prince stood, his nose pressing into me while gobs of sali-
va poured down my shaking leg.

Snake returned to his work. He looked from the scrap of
paper that held the combination to the pin-code pad, then
back to the paper again. His finger rings clinked as he
punched in numbers. It took him two tries, but then we
heard a click. Snake grunted as he placed his bulk to the
door, swinging it ajar.

A smell of damp mustiness assaulted my nostrils and I
stepped back in reflex. Prince deepened his warning growl.

Snake bent down and picked the toy motorbike off the
floor, removing the key beneath it. He tossed the motorbike
into the plastic basket of toys on the floor. "If Billy had just
left this where it was hidden with the other toys, life for you
would have ended much sweeter." He flashed me a sick
smile. "You might have just died in a car accident or old age
or something."

It looked like the journey for the police tracking device
was about to end.

Damn.

I couldn't see a thing. It was completely dark in the space before us as Snake walked down a step, motioning for me to follow. He reached behind me to push the entry door closed and I heard another click like a lock had been reset. He pushed somewhere on the wall and the tiny motor started whirring again, assumedly closing the wall paneling on the other side. How were Lyons and Riley going to find me now?

We descended a dozen steep steps before Snake hit what I assumed was a light switch on the next room's wall. The brightness of the exposed bulbs that hung down showed more rooms past this one that stretched as far as I could see. It reminded me of the bomb shelters people had built in the '50s. This one could have fit the entire Halston Electronics Warehouse in it.

Once past the bottom step, we were on hard, uneven ground. The bottom part of the sidewalls looked like it was bedrock. I saw a long grey slug hanging from one of the jutted crags. It was so cool and damp in here, like being under a boulder. If I had to stay too long, I was sure I would start to sprout gills like a mushroom.

Once further inside we came to a wider space. I ran my hand across a beautiful pearl-inlaid teak dining table. Past that was an oval cherry wood conference desk that looked like it would seat twenty people, give or take. But there weren't briefcases piled on its surface. About a dozen digital scales dotted the top with large stacks of different-sized baggies piled around them. Various utensils and large jars of powders were scattered about. A place to prep drugs for the street.

Beside the conference table was a kitchen twice the size of the one in Snake's downstairs family room. It seemed complete with a full-sized fridge, stove, dishwasher and two sinks.

The other half of the room had stacks of long wooden

crates, all marked with the words "AMMO" in black stenciling.

I looked at Snake with a question and he smiled. "Arms. You're looking at the Grand Northern Arms Cache, right here in good old Sleepy-Town Halston."

The number of boxes went on forever.

"What would you ever need an arms cache here for?"

"A little problem we've developed called the Banditos."

I thought I saw something slither in the shadows near Snake's boot.

"Banditos?"

"American bikers trying to muscle into our programs."

He said the word "programs" like he was a schoolteacher trying to sell a kid a reason to stay after school. What a total slime ball.

"Programs?"

He pursed his lips the way my grade three teacher used to do whenever I asked a question she figured was stupid. "Little Miss Naïve. Our member drives, of course." The sarcasm dripped from his voice and then he laughed, deep and long.

I felt something solid slide quickly across the top of my poopy runner. I screamed when I saw it was not one but two three-foot snakes traveling in opposite directions. The larger of the two stopped and coiled, raising its head in my direction.

Holy crap! I quit breathing.

"How convenient," Snake hissed. "If you even sneeze, I won't have to worry about getting you iced anymore."

My skin crawled and I held back a shriek as something rubbery glided across the skin on my ankle. Get it off me, get it off me!

Even the Big Bad Prince was backing up from me. Fear was in his eyes and I did not take that as a good sign. Here, boy, fetch the wriggly, brown-spotted stick.

Snake walked away from me, the skeleton key extended in front, and I could hear his footsteps echoing further down past all the crates. Prince tiptoed past me and my problem and went to join him.

I heard the echo of a key click into a lock and within a few seconds, I felt a breeze of fresh air hit my face. The air seemed to revive the snake holding me hostage and it uncoiled itself and wiggled back and forth into the far shadows.

I took a deep, grateful breath. How many snakes were living down here? The place seemed to be teeming with them. I reminded myself to be careful of where I stepped.

"Get me out of here," I whispered to my chest. The sound carried far down the hall.

"No talking, I said," came a stern reminder.

I slowly picked my way to where Snake had gone. After passing more of the AMMO boxes I got a good glimpse of a set of more steep stairs that ended at an opened set of massive doublewide doors overhead. The key from the bike must have been for these doors. So that was how they got that full-sized pool table into the basement. They could have rolled an entire fleet of pool tables in here. Opened a pool hall. But I could see the place had much grander designs than a lowly rec hall. It was a lowly drug warehouse. Probably a one-stop shop. Get your drugs, your guns and your money and hit the streets of all these small defenseless communities. There was a ton of money in these little mill and mine towns and not much to spend it on. Once you developed a drug habit, you didn't have a lot of choice anymore.

There were 10 large steps leading up to the overhead doors and out of the bomb shelter into the black night air beyond. Snake walked up them. In a few short minutes he returned, hanging on to one of Warren's arms. Billy stumbled down behind them. Both had their hands duct-taped together in front of them and a piece of silver tape over their mouths.

"Warren!" I shouted. I was overjoyed at seeing my son. Other than the tape, he looked unharmed.

Billy threw me a sheepish look. I could have kicked him exactly where it would hurt the most on a guy, but wouldn't in front of our son. How could he have gotten Warren involved in all this?

Warren ran over to where I stood. He pressed himself against my leg hard enough to make me toughen my stance. Prince was a blur as he left his guard post and lunged at my throat. I grabbed Warren and we barely managed to pull ourselves aside enough to miss the attack. The dog circled and Snake yelled, "Prince! NO! Down!" And Prince sat. You could see the heart pounding in the dog's chest. My own heart was doing a Riverdance of its own.

I put my arms around Warren, hugging him into my leg, and told him it would be all right. I never believed a word of it, but what could you do?

An army of scruffy-looking bikers, their ratty long hair either tied back with bandanas or swinging freely, the backs of their jean jackets proudly displaying the Hells Dragons symbol, came down the stairs, marching past us single file. Most of them gave me a lingering ogle that made me feel like I'd been stripped naked and put into some uncompromising positions. One took his fingers and pantomimed a, well, never mind. It was disgusting and my skin puckered up in horror. I hoped with all my might that they would never get a chance to touch me. It was enough to put you off sex for life just thinking about it.

They came back past Billy, Warren and me two at a time carrying one box each. The containers looked very heavy and the big men grunted as they lifted them up the steps. A minute later we heard the sound of what I gathered was a transport truck driven up to the cellar's opened doors. Air brakes hissed and before long the beeping of a backup signal was going and lights were flashing through the hole. When I stood on my toes, I could make out a large white transport truck. I guessed the arms would be loaded into the back of this for transit. I also guessed it would take them a while; there were a lot of boxes.

Snake was busy barking out orders and didn't notice when I pulled back a little more into the shadows. I pulled Warren with me and Billy followed. I gladly ripped the tape from Bill's mouth as fast and as hard as I could. His eyes went as round as Frisbees. Frisbees in a lot of pain. His eye sockets filled with water.

"What did you do that for?" he sniped.

"Do what?" I said before covering the device beneath my shirt with my hand. I whispered to Billy, "A girl has to get her punches in when she can."

I felt bad, but I left Warren's on, knowing the hailstorm of chatter that would ensue if I removed it.

"How did you get here?" I asked Bill.

He rubbed at his sore lips with his taped hands. "We came in a transport truck. They're getting ready to take everything to Tessak. There's going to be a big 'house-cleaning party,' they called it. A turf war of some kind. It sounded like a real hot damn, kickassy kinda time."

"Jesus, Bill," I said in disgust. Warren tried to say something that I knew was a muffled Swear Jar reminder. I talked to my stomach again. "I hope you got that. We're underground close to Snake's house. Big doors in the ground lead down to where we are. Hurry!"

I tried to get the duct tape off of Billy's hands but it wasn't budging.

"Hey!" yelled a voice from up above. No, it wasn't God as I'd hoped. "Watch those people. They're trying to get loose." It must have been Snake because everyone snapped to attention. He apparently was running the entire show.

I looked over my shoulder. A burly, sawed-off man with stumpy legs and a head of grey curls came closer, his gun aimed across the hall at an imaginary bull's-eye on my back. He stood unmoving on the other side of the room but after a few minutes, he was no longer looking at us. He was watching the boxes go by and disappear up the stairs. I guessed he wasn't supposed to kill any of us yet.

I stopped what I was doing to the tape on Bill's hands, but leaned toward him until my lips came just to his ear, and whispered, "Where is Ivan?"

"Who is Ivan?" Bill whispered back.

"The guy who took you from my place."

"His name is Ivan?"

What was with the weird look?

"Yes, don't you know who he is?" I was getting impatient with Bill's denseness. We probably didn't have a lot of time to sit and chat.

"All I know is the guy's a hired hit man. He works for the Hells Dragons."

"The Hells Dragons have a hit guy?"

"So I hear. They don't like to do these jobs themselves. It could come back on the entire organization, so they hire out. The guy that was holding me was one of those guys."

"You mean Ivan Perkins. Did you notice how much he looks like you?"

Bill's head whipped around to give me another wide-eyed look. He mouthed the words, "Ivan Perkins?"

I nodded my head. Guess he hadn't noticed.

"Who were you staying with in Tessak?" I asked.

"You want to know that why?"

"I found out you discovered you have a half brother, and I thought that was who was in Tessak."

Why did Billy look so surprised that I had found that out on my own? He really did think I was that dumb. Sheesh.

And I wasn't even a blonde, as my dad was fond of pointing out whenever I screwed up.

"Yeh, well, I went to find him but he wasn't around. He has a fancy house there. One window wasn't locked so that's where we stayed, but he wasn't home and there were no pictures of him anywhere. Only the mail had his name. It was weird."

"Then who were you driving truck for?"

"The neighbors. Clarence and Mavis Byron."

The babysitter in Tessak. Well, that cleared some of it up for me.

I watched the fifteenth or so box being muscled past us. I had lost count. The pile looked to be more than half finished. And then what would happen? Would they let us go? Not likely when someone named Prince was counting on having us for breakfast. I looked over at the Demon Dog, who was also distracted with the boxes marching past. It was time to do something for ourselves or we might not make it out of there alive!

Chapter Fourteen

Snake came back down the stairs into our sight. He relieved the guy standing over us. "The party is over for you three," he said, shoving us toward the stairs leading outside.

"What?" My mind raced in a panic. Were we going to be let go? Would they actually do that now that we knew what was going on? Right, Kathy, I told myself. And you DO still believe in the tooth fairy. Wake up, girlie!

Now was when a cape and a few super powers would really come in handy. I put out my hands, willing myself to fly. Become invisible. But it never worked.

With no other plan forming in my head, I went on autopilot. I whirled around and kicked Snake as hard as I could in the shin with my poopy runner and then turned to bolt, tripping on my own feet and falling with a sickening thud onto the rock floor at Billy's feet.

Snake had grabbed the apoplectic Prince by the collar and was laughing out loud, as were about three other guys who had seen my big performance.

Even Billy had a grin on his face.

I glared at my ex. "Okay," I said. "You try something."

"Don't bother trying anything," Snake warned. "Just go up the stairs slowly. It's going to be fine."

Yes, just like my roof would be fine if I continued to do nothing about it, I thought. Fat chance.

I put my foot on the first step, wondering what my Plan B autopilot was going to make me do next. Prince wouldn't let me get near Snake twice. Waiting for Peter Placid Pan, who was probably still hoping he'd get to go to the ass-whupping in Tessak, to act on my behalf just wasn't going to happen. What other abilities did I have? My pockets were empty. The only thing I had was myself. And what did that give me? Two skinny arms and legs with quite a few bruises on them.

Wait! I was wearing the good underwear today! Maybe I could take off my outer clothes and distract them. Do a striptease or something? I slumped my shoulders in defeat. No, they would see the police wire and besides, that would probably just get everyone laughing again. Well, not Warren. He would be traumatized for life. As if that wasn't already a possibility, I worried.

I would rather die than add to Warren's woes. And it looked like I might get my wish.

I placed my foot on the next step, stalling, stalling, the wheels in my head flying around, when I heard loud noises above us. First a round of shots being fired. Then the squeal of brakes. Garbled shouting. More shots fired. Prince went ballistic, barking out foam before breaking free, madly roaring past us up the steps and into the night. Snake turned around, walking back down a few steps while bellowing out quick commands to the bikers below.

I reached for Warren's hand and blindly took off in a run, racing up the steps, reaching for the full night air to swallow us. "Come on, Warren," I encouraged, glancing quickly behind me to make sure he was there.

It was my usual fly-by-the-seat-of-my-pants logic, but it was better than getting naked. Warren was right with me. I could feel his other fingers pinching into the skin on my leg through my jeans.

I ran out of the cellar and 30 yards to the first tree in the uncleared part of the forest that I came to and ducked behind it, pulling Warren close. Billy was with us after a few seconds, a grin pasted on his face like this was a game.

I could easily make out the figure of Snake rising out of the hole in the ground, standing at the top of the stairs trying to figure out what was happening. His head cranked back and forth, his hand shading his eyes from all the bright vehicle lights that were pointed toward where he stood. Prince was snarling and jumping around beside him. The dog's jaws snapped at the air around Snake's ears. It was going mental from all the excitement.

"Cut the lights," Snake yelled. No one complied.

"Where did they go?" Snake held a handgun out in front like a flashlight. A few of the Hells Dragons scattered out into the trees, firing shots over their shoulders.

In the clearing about 200 yards away from the cellar opening, I could make out a police car, my eggplant van and Kenneth's blue pickup truck still whirling with a cone of icy dust around them, although they were now at a complete stop. In the back of the pickup box stood Neil and Kenneth. Their unmistakable silhouettes were bathed in moonlight and the metal off the long barrels on their guns glinted in their hands. Ann was in the driver's seat. She also had a long-barreled gun out, hers pointed toward Snake and Prince. My sister really did have a gun. Oh-oh.

Driving my van was my father, his arm out the window with a handgun in it. Where in tarnation had my dad got a handgun from? Please tell me he did not smuggle that all the way from Appleton in his suitcase? Sweet Jesus!

And how was he driving my van? Hadn't I driven it here myself?

Before I could contemplate further, the side door of the van rolled open and three mall security drunkards hopped out. Two were armed with baseball bats and the other had a wine bottle with the tops smashed off them in each outstretched hand. The bottles looked jagged and very menacing. All three drunks stood there unwavering. They resembled warriors from a far-off time waiting for orders of what to do next.

Riley and Constable Joe Lyons exited both sides of the police car they had arrived in. They went into a crouched position and carefully made their way along their respective sides of the front fenders. Riley had his gun out, pointed toward the cellar door and Snake. Then Riley left the protection of the car and scuttled over behind my van. It took him closer to where Snake stood, still looking for the three of us.

Lyons was quite busy merely watching what was going on, his right hand fiddling at his side, probably trying to get his gun out from the secret safety latch on the holster.

Shots continued to pierce the night but not into the air like I'd imagined. First the mall security started to drop. The men wearing the Hells Dragons jackets were aiming guns *at* people! I winced as I saw what looked like blood fly out of the side of one of the men's mouth, and the asinine thought flashed through my mind that he might never be able to drink from a bottle again. He would need to get his drinks intravenously.

The man on his right with the second bat dropped to his knees as well. He was still alive, holding onto his arm, but he had quit the fight. The third man looked at his fallen comrades and released both the broken bottles in his hands, running hell-bent into the woods. Unfortunately for him, Prince closed in behind. The injured man and his partner picked up their baseball bats and ran toward the protection of the forest as well. I hoped they got the opportunity to play ball with Prince or their buddy might soon be missing something valuable. Like his rear end!

My father was left to defend himself with his own weapon – while high on painkillers, no less.

The air was filled with the acrid smell of gunpowder and smoke and it seemed like an arsenal of guns was being shot. From the corner of my eye I saw Neil's outline crumple in the back of the pickup. He must have taken a hit! I shouted and started running toward him. It was a slow-motion thing where my feet were moving, I was going hard, and my head turned to take a fast look at Snake, who had obviously heard me yell. His head swiveled to where I was running. It stopped me cold and we locked eyes. Holy! This man really wanted to see me dead. The depth of the hatred on his face floored me. What was with me and this problem with rejection? My sister called it my "middle child syndrome." I was starting to think maybe she was right. How pathetic if I needed even someone like Snake to like me! Let it go!

Still, I stood rooted to the spot. My legs wouldn't move even though my brain was screaming at me to do so.

Snake closed one eye and aimed the bead of his gun on my head. At the same time, Constable Lyons was running to my right and about to intersect the path between me and Snake.

Was this it? Was it all going to come down to me getting shot in the head? To finally get sole custody of my children just to die standing here?

My body unlocked. "Watch out," I screamed at Lyons and launched all my weight sideways to knock the rookie out of harm's way. We both landed on the ground with a thud. I rolled behind another tree and popped my head up just enough to see all the action.

I watched in relief as Snake fell on his face, his greasy red hair hitting the dirt right before he did. He landed with a thud in front of the cellar doors. I hoped his nose was broken. I turned my head to see where the shot had come from and grinned when I saw Ann in the front of the pickup raise her head from the gun sight. From where I was, it appeared she had been aiming at where Snake had gone down. Wasn't she amazing?

I looked back to where Snake had fallen to watch him raise up on his elbows and start to crawl on his belly across the hard ground. He resembled one of his reptiles as he slithered from my sight back down into his dark hole of a cellar.

More noise as five police cars slid into the clearing, sirens wailing.

Riley left behind my van and with his gun out scurried after Snake. I caught my breath when I saw his head disappear from sight down into the dungeon below. His disappearance was followed by a man screaming. I was certain it wasn't Riley.

Billy and Warren were standing behind trees of their own. Their heads whipped back and forth like they were watching a basketball game.

Lyons helped me to my feet and I scrambled to my van, calling to Billy and Warren to follow. My father was shooting off rounds from his driver's window opening like it was a musical instrument and this was the crescendo. He was straining as hard as he could against the tightness of his seatbelt. Obscenities flowed from his mouth.

The side door was still open so I leaped into the van's backseat. Billy and Warren almost landed on top of me. Bill's hands were still bound in front with tape so I had to reach over him to pull the side door closed. It was almost more than I could do from the angle I was at and on the incline the van had stopped on. As I struggled to close it, my father put the van into reverse and just missed running over someone. The backup sensor was bleating at us, and then the passenger front door opened and Ivan jumped in. The side door slammed shut.

I screamed at the sight of the deadly killer so close to me.

Then I watched Billy as he looked Ivan over, taking in the resemblance for the first time. The corners of his mouth turned upwards.

I could not believe it.

Our heads hit the ceiling as my father careened out of the clearing down the wooded path. He was doing well for someone who had downed as much scotch and painkillers as he had. There was no way he'd pass a breathalyzer, but he was keeping the van going, even if it was out of the frying pan and into the fire with the killer inside with us.

I clicked on my seatbelt and gave Warren a look he knew well. He merely shrugged his little shoulders. Oops. In all the excitement I had forgotten he was still handcuffed. I used my teeth this time to get rid of the duct tape still binding his wrists and then he snapped his own seat buckle in place.

I carefully pulled the tape off his mouth the best I could with the van bucking and hurtling like a bronco trying to ditch all of us. It still came off like a waxing strip. Warren wouldn't be seeing any hair growing around his lips for many years to come.

Dad's foot seemed stuck to the floor. Then finally it was like we were on glass as he shot onto the highway. Head-lights were coming around the corner and my father was still fishtailing us on the road.

"Look out," Ivan yelled. My entire body braced for the crash that never happened. We heard the other car's horn trailing away behind us.

Bill leaned around to the front seat to talk to Ivan. "Who was your father?" he asked.

Ivan looked at him like he had grown a third head.

"Your father," Bill repeated. "Was he Louis Sands?"

Ivan twisted in his seat and glared at Bill. "What do you know about it?"

Billy did a half grin. "Louis was my father too." And he let that hang in the air.

My dad barreled around a curve on two wheels, not having slowed down for a second. No one had any idea where he was headed. I doubted he knew himself.

"Slow down, old man. You trying to kill us?" said Ivan.

"Isn't that what you plan on doing?" I asked.

Ivan grinned, which looked eerily just like Billy's grin only with an evil edge to it. "Oh yeh, I almost forgot."

Like it was some kind of a private joke for him.

"I don't leave loose ends around. You've seen my face." He seemed to drift away in thought before adding, "And your mother has seen my face."

I shivered. It didn't appear this nightmare would ever end.

"And you've seen mine," Bill told him. "Can you believe how much we look alike? I bet you like racing cars, right? And hockey. Do you play hockey? I can't believe you lived so close to me and I never knew about you all this time."

"What the hell are you talking about?"

"Me. I'm your half brother." Bill almost came off his seat trying to get closer to the killer in the front. He poked Warren. "This is your uncle, kid. Unca Ivan."

"You people *are* crazy."

"Yeh, sure," Billy babbled, "our dad, Louis, was a trucker that made rounds from Prince Grange to Prince Ruden. He went through Tessak every month and he met your mother. Penny Perkins. She was waitressing at the William Tell restaurant on the highway. They met and next thing she was having his kid. My mom never knew. No one did. Well, Tanya my sister knew because she'd went with Dad a few times on his route and she was given a quarter to go sit in the truck and wait for him sometimes."

"You just pulled that out of your ass!" Ivan accused. But he looked doubtful, and I knew he was wondering how Billy knew *his* father's name if there wasn't some truth to it.

Billy had Ivan's full attention. The van continued to warp down the highway. If there were any cops around between us and Spencer, we were bound to get nailed by one. I crossed myself for good luck.

"I'm your half brother," Billy repeated, sounding not so sure anymore this was good timing. "You can't kill us." He turned and looked at me. "At least not me." After a second thought, "Or my boy, here."

"I don't have any family," Ivan spit at him, like having any was poisonous.

"Why don't you just shut up about it," my father told Bill. "You're upsetting the man."

"Oh, go piss up a rope, you old fart," Bill said to my dad. There had never been any love lost there either.

"Don't you tell my dad to piss up a rope," I said, kicking at Billy, whose hands were still tied.

"And you, you old cow crunt, you're the one that got us into all this mess."

I gasped and grabbed for Warren's ears. "I never got you into any mess you didn't get into on your own first!" I yelled. Okay, did that make sense? Nobody was really thinking straight anymore.

"I wasn't the one that gave my daughter a stolen present! I'm not the one running from my bills, the police and a sheriff. When are you ever going to accept responsibility for yourself?" I hollered.

"Shut up," yelled Ivan. But it was too late.

"As if you're doing such a great job with anything," Billy fired back. "Wendy is always sick and Warren is a whiny little mama's boy. You can't even look after your own kids like a real mother. Your work is always more important. That and your new boy toys. Well, your house sucks, your van sucks, you suck!"

"You wish!" I hollered. The shouting was reaching a deafening level; even my father started interjecting when he could. It was a full-blown battle.

Ivan turned and pointed his gun at Warren's face.

"I had wanted to have a little fun with you first," he said, looking straight at me, "but I've changed my mind. Either you shut up or I am going to kill you all right now, right inside this van!"

My father swerved the van so hard, Ivan lurched sideways almost on top of him.

Ivan pushed himself upright then held the gun up to my dad's head. "Try that again, you old bastard, and you'll be missing more than an ear lobe when they find your ugly body."

Missing an ear lobe? Hadn't there been a delicate part missing from Kitty, the body found at the Merkleys'? Ugh. That cinched it for me. Ivan really was the highway murderer. At the very least, the one who was disfiguring his victims. I hoped they caught what Ivan had said on tape.

"What have you done with Judy?" I screamed at him as we hit a pothole in the road and got air, landing with a van full of groans from rusted springs and undercarriage.

Ivan reached across Bill and stroked under my chin with the end of the gun's barrel. "The same things I am going to do with you. Enjoy you until I find something better. I haven't had an *experienced* crunt in quite a few years."

Then my father hit the tree.

CHAPTER FIFTEEN

It happened fast. Ivan's gun in my face before Ivan toppling sideways, the crashing noises and screams, and then nothing. We were stopped. Dead.

I frantically looked to my left and thankfully saw Warren looking back. He was still buckled in and his mouth was a big ringed "O" but he was breathing. Dad was sitting in the driver's seat with the airbag trapping him back against his chair. Swear words streamed from his mouth.

The entire right half of the windshield was missing. Ivan and Bill were not in the vehicle.

The missing passenger-side airbag had not been there to contain Ivan and without seatbelts on, the two men had flown out of the vehicle.

I was scared to peer outside.

I heard scrambling before the van's side door was thrust open. I braced myself but it was Riley and behind him was Ann. I was never so happy to see anyone ever.

I unclicked Warren's seatbelt and he crawled up on my lap, his arms strangling me around my neck. "It's okay, buddy," I told him. He wasn't letting go, so I scuttled across the seat and went out, holding him tight to me as I exited. My dad had already been helped out by Riley and was standing beside the driver's door on his one good leg.

I passed Warren to Ann, explaining it was only for a second, and he went willingly, clinging to her as hard as he had to me. I went over and gave my dad a big hug.

He whispered in my ear, "That'll teach those boys to call my daughter the 'C' word."

Now that was putting both feet down!

I kissed Dad on his stubbly cheek. He might have been getting on in years, but he could still take a round out of someone who had pissed him off. He was and always would be my number one hero. I couldn't have taught those guys a better lesson myself. No woman ever deserved to be called that word.

Riley helped Dad into his police unit and told him to put his leg up. It was bleeding again. He must have blown his sutures.

A body lay next to the big tree we had smashed into. It wasn't moving and I was scared for a minute that I had actually been thinking ill of the dead. Was that Billy lying there?

I looked at the cowboy boots at the end of the legs but even in the moonlight, it was too dark to tell. Was that Billy or Ivan? I stumbled closer to where the body lay and bent down. Oh, crap. It *was* Billy. Guided by movies, I felt for a pulse at the upper left of his neck. Nothing . . . nothing . . . wait! It was there. He was alive. A siren's wail came toward us, getting louder by the second. Help was on its way. I felt relief yet still felt an urge to kick the man.

"Where is Ivan?" Riley shouted.

"He must have run off," I shouted back, watching Riley pull a gun out from the back of his pants as he tore into the woods.

A second police truck pulled into the clearing. Constable

Currie and Sergeant Tart popped out. I pointed wildly toward the woods and explained about Riley and Ivan. Tart told us to take Riley's police car and head home. She would be in touch.

You didn't have to tell me twice!

Ann handed me Warren, whose face I shielded from his father's still form as we squeaked into the back of Riley's car beside Dad. Just in time as the ambulance had arrived and I couldn't bear to see T-Bone and Michaella's expressions again.

As Ann drove us back to my place, I asked about Neil and she said he was being sent to the Spencer hospital. There was no other news. Then I asked Dad how the hell he had the van. I'd left it at Snake's place.

"That young cop with the ears sticking out, he brought it back from Snake's. Seems he'd been hiding in the back of it when you left. I heard him tell Riley about the fake wall closing behind you in the basement of Snake's house. Then Neil showed up at your place with maps and they all left. But I also heard the address of where they were headed. Right up the road from the peeler bar! Off in a back field behind a place fenced in like a fortress."

"Yeh," Ann added from the front seat. "Dad was amazing, screeching in like a race car driver. His gun was blazing before any of ours."

"And how did you know about it?" I asked.

"Neil had phoned Kenneth and asked him to bring me and our guns and meet him at Snake's back field. The District of Halston had taken the registration for the firearm safety and hunting program Kenneth and I have been taking all month so Neil knew we were licensed to kill as of yesterday."

Ann wasn't finished. "Kenneth didn't want Mini to know about the hunting course because she cried whenever she saw a dead animal in the box of a pickup. But he figured if he got her out in the field she would feel different, especially after tasting the recipes he had lined up for their wedding anniversary spread. So he surprised Mini with her own camouflage outfit.

She continued, "Kenneth told me Mini squealed when she saw the clothes. Seemed she liked the fact that her large butt disappeared under cover of the green leaf design. Kenneth kept saying to her, 'Where are you? You're invisible, my love.'"

I wondered how Kenneth was going to get Mini to be quiet long enough to stalk something. Maybe they wouldn't be eating as much wild game as Kenneth was hoping to.

Dad leaned forward and patted Ann's shoulder. "You are one hell of a shot, young lady. A secret agent, a chef and now a sharpshooter." He sat back again with a smarmy smile on his face.

Normally I would have found his admiration of my sister annoying, but at the moment I was stuck on the fact that Ann owned a gun. Maybe I shouldn't have brought up the snow boots in front of Mom.

We were all met at the door of my home by a very mellow mother. The smell of cookies filled the house and I noticed the stacks of probably a dozen batches of homemade chocolate sandwiches. They covered the entire kitchen counter and table two deep.

A wine glass and an empty bottle of white wine stood beside the stove. A brown liquor-store bag still partially inflated and scrunched around the top sat discarded beside it. Mom must have switched to Plan B (Plan Booze). She teetered over to the closet to get empty plastic bags to fill for Sergeant Tart, who would be by in the morning for statements from all of us.

Lyons arrived shortly after with Kenneth and told us the rest of the police were at Snake's shelter wrapping up the area. They had ambulances from Spencer come down and take the mall security in. Pieter, the man who had been shot in the mouth, was in stable condition but would have a nasty scar on his face to add to his current collection. His buddy, Victor, was shot in the arm and would survive. The third character, Izzy, had a nasty rip in his butt from Prince. He had to suffer through a tetanus shot and ten stitches.

Since they were all on welfare, the Province of British Columbia took care of their medical bills. I knew this because I asked Lyons. I would have paid it for them in gratitude. They had risked their lives to help save my son and me. After apologizing for having kicked them out of my house in the first place, I would inform them they were welcome back at my house to play cards with my dad or for a hot meal anytime they wanted! After they had showers and I washed their clothes for them first, of course.

"How did you know where in the house to find me?" I asked the rookie.

Lyons puffed out his chest. "I was hidden in the back of your van and managed to follow you into the house and down the stairs just as the wall was sliding back into place. It didn't take long to figure out where that room came out at. You left your keys in the van so I took it back to your place where Riley was waiting. Riley had phoned Neil after hearing you were underground. His chest deflated a bit. "Your dad probably overheard us talking and left shortly after the rest of us. I must have left the keys in the van, too."

I was still reeling from the first fact that Riley had taken a chance with my son's life and sent a cop with me in the van. How could he?

"Tart says we should throw the book at your dad and sister and Neil and Kenneth, showing up blazing guns the way they did, but after Riley calmed her down, I think they'll get off with a warning." He smiled encouragingly.

Mother loaded up more bags of her homemade cookies for the clinic staff, the ambulance attendants and Dr. Keswick. She hobbled alongside my father into Kenneth's pickup to head back to the clinic to get Dad's leg re-stitched. Lyons left in Riley's cruiser.

After gobbling down three of his grandma's cookies, Warren seemed to come back around to his old self.

"Is Dad going to die?" he asked, his bottom lip drawn down almost to his chin.

He looked like he had aged overnight. I felt sad about that.

"No, Warren. Dad's not going to die."

"But how do you know that?"

I swore. It fell out of my mouth before I could stop it. Guess we were all still in a state of trauma. "I know because there's a saying the adults have, that only the good die young, so your dad can't die yet. Not for a long time, anyway." Despite how crazy it seemed, I hoped it to be true.

Warren smiled back at me. "You're only jokin' on me, right, Mom?"

"Yeh, big guy. I'm only jokin'. But he really should be okay. I'll try to find out more tomorrow at the hospital, when we go and get Wendy. Okay?"

He seemed okay with that. His yawn reminded me it was nearly five o'clock in the morning. He must be exhausted. Come to think of it, I was worn out myself.

I carried Warren down the hall and tucked him into his bed. He was out before I could wish him sweet dreams.

With Ivan still on the loose the RCMP were going to get someone from the Spencer detachment to sit in an unmarked car out front of the house. This made me feel a lot better. I was sure Ivan wouldn't bother with us anymore, though. Snake had finally got from me what he wanted – the key and the code numbers. There was no reason to kill me anymore.

Only Ann and I were left. I found her in the kitchen still stuffing bags with Mom's hard work.

Ann assembled two cups, teapot, honey and spoons on a tray. We sat in the living room to diffuse. While pouring tea, she told me more about her hunting course and how handsome the instructor was.

"If he had been teaching nail biting, I would have signed up."

She spilled around mouthfuls of cookie crumbs. "Getting shot at can make you ravenous," she exclaimed. I grinned. Better on her skinny ankles than on mine! Maybe for once that scale difference between us would tip the other way. Yes, I was incorrigible.

Ann hinted that she and the instructor might become an item in the near future. See, I knew she wasn't having a thing with my best friend's husband.

She passed me a steaming mug.

We talked for another 10 minutes before Ann said she felt a bit dizzy.

"Mind if I crash in Wendy's bed?"

"No problem," I told her. "We'll get a taxi in the morning and go vehicle shopping together."

"That works for me. I can spare a little time tomorrow. Besides, Miss Puss is already going to give me the cold shoulder for missing her bedtime snack. What's another few hours?"

I thought Ann just wanted to make sure I didn't get another vehicle in an eggplant shade. I was happy she wanted to come.

I threw back the rest of my tea and gave her a hug. We both headed down the hallway to our rooms.

I never undressed, heading under the covers fully clothed. I dropped off at the count of two.

Right away I had the most bizarre dream. In it I was sleeping peacefully in my bed. I could see the alarm clock beside me blinking back 5:42. I should get up in an hour. Then I reminded myself, for what? The mall wouldn't be open so soon after the bombing. I could get some sleep and check on it after lunch.

I was thinking all this with my eyes closed and then suddenly I was moving. My body was floating through space. It felt warm and cozy and I could hear snoring from Warren's room and soft snuffling noises from what must have been Ann, and then I was cold and still moving. I tried lifting my eyelids to wake myself up but they were like iron curtains. This was turning into a bad dream.

CHAPTER SIXTEEN

With severe difficulty I forced one eye open to a slit. This was not a dream, bad or otherwise. This was real! Ivan was tightly carrying me in his arms. He still wore his Rug Specialist disguise and was hurrying to reach the black van with the grey stripe parked in front of my house.

In front of my house! My eye glanced over his shoulder for the unmarked police car but there wasn't one. It hadn't arrived yet. Possibly they weren't able to find anyone not up all night with the rest of us. It wasn't a big workforce.

I tried moving my arms and legs but my body wouldn't respond. I felt encased in cement.

Ivan opened the van's side door and tossed me inside. I heard the click of a remote lock as he scurried around to the driver's side. I was locked in. I was also trussed up the way Warren and Billy had been. My hands were taped together in front of me.

Ivan used a key in the driver's side door to open it and hop in.

Why was I so groggy? I thought back. The tea? But how? Why? Damn: Ivan, the carpet cleaner, probably targeting my mother! She had seen his face when he shot Dad. Obviously she hadn't used the teapot all night. No one had until Ann made us tea earlier.

Ivan started the vehicle and blasted along my street, turning to head down the hillside.

My garbled, "Where are you taking me," got no reply from him.

We stopped at the only red-light intersection in Halston before turning left onto Highway 26. Ivan roared past Franklin's Motor Products as he hit the open highway.

My tongue was thick and I was desperately thirsty. I tried to pay attention to where we were headed but I kept falling asleep. My head refused to stay upright. When he stopped for a light in Spencer I came to, but once we passed that town I conked out again.

Cool air hit my face. The van had stopped and the side door was being opened. Ivan pulled me upright and slid his arm beneath my butt, lifting me uncomfortably into both arms again. He smelled of dandruff and cheap dollar-store cologne. It was sickening.

Half-revived from the fresh air and adrenaline, I managed to keep my eyes open. We were in a large graveled parking area. An old fire pit sat beside a spray-painted board declaring this was site number 14. The place was vacant save a small truck camper and an array of tall trees. Must be one of the old forestry campgrounds. Funding cutbacks had left them deserted and fallen. People quit coming. Well, most people.

This was what Sebastian had foreseen. But we were nowhere near where everyone had been searching. I guessed we were somewhere around Tessak, three hours from Halston.

The sun was blinding. Ivan used the set of keys in his hand to unlock the camper door. He pulled it open and stepped up, using a wooden box to enter the oversized tin can.

I must have blacked out again for a minute because the

next thing I knew I was lying on a small bed beside Judy Charlie!

"Judy," I squawked, my voice hoarse from extreme thirst.

She never moved. Streams of mucous had dried on her upper lip, which was fat and bloodied. Her left eye was swollen closed and her hands were taped like mine. Her shirt was ripped and she was naked from the waist down. But I could feel her breath on my cheek as she slept. She was still alive and right here beside me.

Then I realized where that was. The joy left and the horror descended again.

This was not good!

Ivan was rifling through a top cupboard over the curtained windows. He gave up searching there and placed his sights on a faded green knapsack lying on the bench just inside the door. He pulled out a six-inch square, dark leather kit and slowly unzipped the middle. It opened flat. From where I was on the bed, I could see four shiny, silver tools held in by elastic ties. They looked sharp and painful.

Kitty's body had been sexually assaulted and disfigured. The ear lobe. He must collect them as ghoulish souvenirs.

The floating heavy blanket of fog quickly evaporated with the flash of a scalpel. I wasn't going to be anybody's sex slave, not even for a minute, and I sure as hell wasn't going to let anyone disfigure either me or this sweet young woman that I loved like a daughter.

My feet were slow-moving propellers from the effects of the drug. Still, I managed to pull them up, clumsily kicking the kit from Ivan's hands while the other foot caught him by surprise on his chin. He raised the back of his hand and smashed me across the mouth. I had been expecting that after seeing Judy's face, so I took the blow but twisted and turned with the momentum of his hand before pushing myself backward as hard as I could, shoving Ivan into the open cupboard door behind. Contact! His head smacked into the corner of the door hard enough to tear it from its hinges. I scrambled to make it to the exterior door and get myself out of there, but Ivan grabbed my shirt and held fast. I slipped into a basic tae kwon do block and using both of my bound hands struck his hand with a side chop. He let go as his other hand rose up to nail me, but I was gaining my strength back and kicked it away. I didn't try for another move, opting to twist the door handle and burst forth onto the ground. I figured I'd have a better chance at battle if I had distance from my attacker.

I dropped and rolled and as I came up, someone grabbed me from behind. I whirled again, bringing my hands around to chop at a windpipe before noticing Corporal Lyons had me. His eyes were globes and I saw fear. Of me! He had a gun in his left hand and me in his right. He let me go and we just stood there.

The camper door banged open again and a shot rang out. Lyons yelled, "Look out!" and then fell backward. I grabbed the gun from Lyons' hand, balancing it between both of mine, and without even sighting, fired off three shots. I was so close that Ivan's head whipped backward and he crashed onto the step before slumping to the ground.

Another rush of energy picked me up and sent me over to where Ivan lay. I punted the gun from his hand. I ran after it and booted it again into a bramble bush. I didn't want Ivan getting up and shooting at us again, like in the scary shows.

The squad car microphone was squawking away, calling for Lyons and informing him backup was on its way. I returned to Lyons. I was sure the kid was dead and I could feel the tears welling. He was so young! His eyes opened and he smiled.

"Lady, could we just call this even?"

I grinned, but said, "No. That's two you owe me now."

"Damn." He sat up and thumped his chest. When he took his fist away I saw a hole where a bullet had gone into his Kevlar vest. "Ow." He winced.

I knew Lyons wasn't the only one that was going to be black and blue for a bit.

I helped him to his feet and watched him sally over to slap handcuffs on Ivan's wrists. Chances were good that he was dead, but I agreed with Lyons. Who wanted to take chances out here in the middle of nowhere?

Lyons cut the tape off my hands and then went into the camper, returning with Judy wrapped in a blanket in his arms. She was trying to open her eyes but looked as groggy or more than I had earlier. Ivan must have doped her while he was gone.

A second squad car containing two officers, Carl and Anand from Spencer, rolled in, sirens off just in case. They felt for Ivan's pulse and couldn't find one. They called for an ambulance just in case. I was glad we were far enough away from Halston that T-Bone and Michaella wouldn't have to take the call.

Lyons waited with Anand for the ambulance, while Carl put a sleepy but smiling Judy and me in the back of his squad car and drove us to the Spencer hospital. He had called ahead and Dr. Keswick was in the emergency room waiting. She checked us over as soon as we arrived.

I had a puffy bottom lip, which made me an Angelina Jolie look-alike (if you only looked at my bottom lip). I was down on my fluids but opted to drink juice over an IV with saline. I felt fine and wanted nothing more than to run upstairs and nuzzle myself into Wendy's arms. Mandi told me Lana had recuperated and gone home but Neil was still in for the night for observation. Maybe I would save some nuzzling for him.

Judy needed more extensive tests. She begged to call her

mother and grandparents first and was given a phone. Her family was on their way and you could bet if they were stopped, no one would have handed them a speeding ticket!

CHAPTER SEVENTEEN

S nake hadn't fared so well. In critical condition, he was flown out to Vancouver under heavily guarded protection.

He died the following day. The coroner couldn't tell if it was from the multiple snake bites on his neck and head or from a single gunshot wound to the chest. My sister Ann, who it was ruled had acted in self-defense, had fired the bullet. Mandi wondered if the venom wasn't sped to the heart by the bullet wound. I preferred that scenario best.

Ann told the RCMP she had taken the hunter's course with Kenneth because she was told by Ottawa to learn how to properly handle a firearm. The RCMP didn't have the security clearance to be told why.

But why hadn't she told me that? I was her sister! Who would I tell? I countered. Or could the real reason she had taken the hunting course be because the instructor was cute? Whom had she told the truth to? Or maybe it all was the truth?

The RCMP obviously knew more about her job than I did, because they promptly ended the questioning.

Wendy was awake when I got to her room, news having traveled before me that I was on my way up. She was dressed and sitting on top of her bed, pillow in hand and ready to go home. Her temperature was normal as was everything else, the specialists figured.

"Is there still all that new food in the fridge?" she asked. "Or did Warren get all the cheese slices already?"

"How about we do a little grocery shop before we head home?"

Wendy bounced off the bed. A very good sign she was better.

"Can we get cake?"

"Sure, okay." I collected Wendy's flowers and grabbed her bag of clothes.

"And ice cream and pie?"

"Probably." I ushered her down the hall.

"And pizza and hot dogs. And those extra-big pickles. "

"We'll see."

And some . . ." She thought for a moment. "I'm hungry."

"No kidding." We both laughed. It sounded like Wendy *was* good to go.

We stopped to thank the nurses before traipsing down to visit Neil.

We walked into the room to catch him surrounded by four nurses, their eyelashes batting shamelessly. Even the male nurse was flirting with him. Sheesh.

Neil's shoulder and chest were strapped in heavy gauze. He was seated in a wheelchair, but could walk. He appeared tremendously drained, they said from the blood loss, and was told to rest in hospital one more day. I guessed the nurses had recommended this to the doctor on duty.

My hero looked genuinely pleased and even relieved to see

us and drew me in very close to kiss me hard on my cheek. My breasts rubbed up against his hospital gown and he groaned.

"Sorry," I stammered. "You pulled me in so fast. I didn't mean to hurt you."

His smile was devilish. "That's not why I groaned." I got a wink. The disappointed nurses got the hint and the room quickly cleared. Wendy pulled at my hand to leave.

"Okay, okay," I said, chuckling at her. "We'll go shopping." I turned to Neil. "If you need a nurse to help you with those bandages when you get home, give me a ring."

He thought about that for a minute. Then the smile again. "Asking for a ring even before we make a date for dinner?"

My face colored. "Call me."

"I'm calling you right here and now. How about Friday night dinner at Lee's Garden's Chinese smorgasbord and then to my place for movies? I'll have Frances and Kelly again, so it will be like one big happy family."

It was a date, and one I was looking forward to. Mental note to self: pack chocolate sandwich cookies and rent the latest hot Wii game.

We stopped downstairs at administration to check Wendy out of the hospital. I asked about Wendy's father, but he had been sent on to a Vancouver head trauma unit. I could call them through a number I was given. I thanked the secretary and we headed home after a quick shop and then a stop at the Sev for a mini pizza and a soda to go for Wendy. She was anxious to get back to her friends and her routine at school. Would she be able to make it to the kids' golf night on Friday?

Golf? Good grief, another club! How many raffle tickets would we have to sell to our neighbors for that?

Here we went again.

While vacuuming cookie crumbs from around the living room carpet, I looked out my window and watched Lyons try to parallel park his police unit between two cars in front of my house. He was as quick with the gas pedal as he was withdrawing his gun from its holster. Cold molasses moved faster.

After I'd saved his life twice, the rookie seemed determined to be my new best friend. Over coffee, Lyons filled me in on a few things.

"It came across the Chief's desk that this Ivan Perkins has been – posthumously – positively linked to four cases of women's bodies discovered along Highway 26. All from the past eight years. Before that, they can't say. It'll remain a mystery for the Inspector to solve for the families."

"Was Judy able to remember any details, like why she got into Ivan's truck in the first place?" I asked.

Lyons put down the muffin he was about to bite into. "She said she was asking people she knew for a lift. She was afraid she would be late for work and needed to get home to change first. Ivan told her he was a friend of her family. He maybe overheard the other kids saying her name. She said he looked familiar and figured they'd met before. She was desperate and hopped in."

We backed up the conversation to better understand what had happened yesterday. The bomb at the mall had been a small one. The side of the drugstore was quickly contained and temporarily repaired while I was on my little adventure with the toy motorcycle. After securing the building with rent-a-cops, which included the security outfit Neil worked for, Tart had then ordered every cop available in the area to Snake's place.

After Riley called, Neil, having worked at the District

office for a few years, knew Snake's property went much further back than it looked. He'd heard the rumours of the bomb shelter being built, but had never witnessed it. Using his keys, he went to the District and got maps of the property and surrounding area. There were aerial shots showing the big field behind and the forest that embodied it. It didn't take much to put two and two together. He wasn't just a handsome face, you know! Mind you, he had yet to show up with a bottle of you-know-what tucked under his arm like Riley had. Some guys got it faster than others. On all counts.

Neil had called his friend Kenneth Merkley, whom he knew owned guns, and asked him to get Ann and then swing by and pick him up. Kenneth had showed up with Ann, her own rifle in tow.

"What happened to Riley when all the shots were being fired? I watched him walk down the stairs after Snake was shot. There was a scream. Was it Snake's?"

Riley made an ugly face. "You would scream too if a lair of deadly snakes waited for you at the bottom of steps you were crawling down on your elbows. In the face, ugh. The scream you heard was Snake's before he went unconscious. Riley backed out and called for the ambulance. The paramedics refused to head down the stairs until animal control could be brought up. Snake was in a coma by that time and was raced to Spencer, all for naught, it turned out."

Lyons also told me Riley had taken a new position in town. He didn't elaborate so I figured it was undercover again. Not many people knew about Riley yet.

The local cops took over with the clean-up at Snake's place. The arms cache had been halted before it left the property. The guns were being catalogued and readied for shipment to the RCMP Vancouver headquarters.

◆ ❖ ◆

I had a wonderful surprise the day following Judy's release from the hospital.

"Yes, this is Kathy Sands. Who's calling?"

"Hello, Kathy. This is Winona and Fred Charlie calling to thank you for bringing our granddaughter back to us."

"You are very welcome," I told them. "Judy is like family in our house."

"Yes, we know that, dear, and that's why we want you to have this cheque made out to you for five thousand dollars. The reward money for finding Judy."

"What?"

After the shock settled in, I tried to turn it down, but it came out more like "No! Re . . . ally? No. Five . . . *thou-sand?*"

Winona's voice seemed to find my reaction funny and she almost sang out the words, "We insist."

"But I didn't do it myself. I . . . there were others, Constable Lyons and . . ."

A soft chuckle this time. "No, this is for you. And your roof that our granddaughter says leaks. She hates the constant drip noise. I think the word she used was torture? It's the least we can do with gratitude."

I ran out of argument and thanked her profusely. I would have to thank Judy as well. A new roof! We would host a backyard party when it was finished to celebrate, I told her. Hot dogs and pizza. Everyone was welcome.

Riley called once to see if we were okay and when I mentioned how dare he mess with Warren's well-being by sending Lyons with me to Snake's, he said he had to go and then never called again. Maybe that was for the best. I felt lucky Warren still had his tongue, although at some moments . . . that's another joke.

Billy called Wendy and Warren out of the blue one day. He was home from Vancouver with a permanent dent in his head. A metal plate had been used to reconnect the fracture in his skull, which meant he would set off metal detectors in airports for the rest of his life.

"Mom, it is so hard Dad let me hit it with a hammer!" Warren gushed.

"Great." I mean, what could you say?

Knowing Billy, his attitude and his inability to hang onto cards, especially one explaining metal in his head, chances were he'd be strip-searched when travelling by air. And you know, it's men that strip-search other men.

Billy returned to the gravel biz for Hardy Crushing, remaining close to Halston for months. His pay cheques were regularly garnisheed until he was caught up. The new roof was nice and dry and Warren got his silver train tracks in his mouth. Wendy got her first manicure because she quit sucking her thumb. It was her one-month present for being free from the tattered satin pajama pillow.

"Everyone give her some room. She'll be fine." Kenneth pulled Mini's face from her salad bowl where it had dropped mere seconds previously. Flecked with green pumpkin seeds and red vinaigrette dressing, Mini's lips moved and twitched as she carried on a conversation none of us could hear.

"What does she do next?" asked my mother. "Does she tell you things while she's asleep or awake?"

"Probably awake," Dad said, "because she's coming to." He slipped his last bite of lemon mascarpone cake into his mouth and "mmmed" as he chewed.

Kenneth gently shook Mini's shoulder, while wiping her face. "Darling, are you back?"

Mimi's hand smacked at the napkin. "'E did it to me again, *non*? Put my face in dah plate?"

"Your salad bowl this time. So correctly speaking, he didn't 'do it again,' as he would say." Kenneth made a face knowing how that sounded.

"Ooh, that man!" Mini shook her fist skyward. "*Absolutement non Days of Our Lives* for Sebastian this week. Ha!"

Mom couldn't stand it a minute longer. "What did he show you? What? Another snake? More money for Kathy?"

"*Non.* I saw a big box of cereal." She thought, trying to remember. "And you two," she pointed to Mom and Dad, "were living in it. But the box habited my backyard?"

Kenneth looked puzzled before saying, "The Drapers' place next door is for sale. Would that be what you saw?"

"You know, I tink maybe!" Mimi stood up to shake my dad's hand. "Welcome, neighbor. I see you will be moving 'ere!"

My mouthful of cake was coughed into my napkin. Surely that was a mistake?

Oh, one could wish.

Within a week, my parents purchased the sizable rancher right beside Mini and Kenneth's. It had 50 acres of land for Dad to ride a lawn tractor around and not get lost. Mom could see him wherever he went (until he figured out he could ride the mower down the power line straight to the local pub). It had three bedrooms and three bathrooms. Selling the spread in New Brunswick got them this rancher plus enough cash to take a two-week holiday in Mexico. So after they'd had their fill of margaritas and fish tacos, my parents were moving to Halston. Sigh.

Oh well, that meant more money for the Swear Jar. Dad had single-handedly paid enough for the kids' first year of college education. Okay, maybe that's a tiny exaggeration.

Sebastian wasn't finished, though. He showed Mini a vision of me sitting at a desk holding a business card in my hand with the letters AID on it. It took us awhile of working on the acronym, but we figured it was Amateur Investigative Detective (or maybe Diva?). It was a very interesting idea. I knew where I could start. Sharon was telling me about a neighbor whose Internet bride had emptied his bank account before grabbing their son and disappearing. Someone would have to look for her.

Now that Judy was back to being my second right arm again, life was settling back into some sort of normalcy.

Some days I still felt like that hamster on a wheel, but at least the scenery was changing.

Author's Note

There are two key points I feel a strong need to explain. First is the seemingly open "gay bashing" that the heroine Kathy and friends do toward the spirit guide named Sebastian. Many of my dear friends are gay and the last thing I intended was to mock or make fun of their life choice. This book *Not Just One* is merely the foundation to other books already written in the series Running From Mystery. The characters will evolve over the next two books and Sebastian's circumstance will change. For now he is portrayed as a snooty, impatient know-it-all who makes no airs about being an old pouf. In his biography, that term was self-descriptive.

The second point I need to clarify is the book's reference to the disappearances, followed by the deaths, of young women last seen on or near a highway. This is largely based on the fact that many young women, predominantly native, have disappeared along Highway 16 between Prince George and Prince Rupert, B.C. (None that I know of were ever disfigured.)I hope by doing so to raise more awareness that it is happening and the first killers are only starting to be brought to justice. To date, two different murderers have been identified. It is horrific and devastating and the more people are aware that it won't be tolerated, the better chance we have of stopping it.

All other references to people, places and events are from the author's imagination, with help from life experiences that may have sparked an idea. Nothing, absolutely nothing, is real in this book.

To My Readers:

I am still in awe of the response to my first book Running From Cancer: a tilted memoir. I hope you found Not Just One even more entertaining and humorous; flying snakes and all. A review when you're finished would be helpful and can be left at my website www.debilynsmith.com. You can also find healthy recipes, the alphabetical anti-cancer prevention tips and more writing previews there.

The next Running From Mystery book is written and in editing as we speak. The fourth book Running From ADD is on Chapter Three. I'm finding it hard to focus with everything else going on (that's a joke). Expect them in 2014.

Until then, thank you for your encouragement. If it wasn't for your validation, an author might take up reading instead of Running all the time.

And the final word goes out to my quietly supportive husband Barry. My heartfelt thanks and love for your patience. I *will* find someone to deal with those dust buggies one of these days. For now, I'll race you to the hot tub.